SUICIDE TOWN

HORROR IN SMALL TOWNS

Boris Bacic

Copyright © 2022 Boris Bacic
All rights reserved.

"Did you really want to die?"
"No one commits suicide because they want to die."
"Then why do they do it?"
"Because they want to stop the pain."

— Tiffanie DeBartolo, *How to Kill a Rock Star*

Dedicated to everyone who has ever struggled with depression or thoughts of suicide, and to anyone who has ever lost a loved one to suicide. If you or anyone you know is struggling, know that you are not alone and you'll always have someone to reach out to, whether it's a loved one or a stranger on the street.

Contents

Prologue 9
Chapter 1 21
Chapter 2 29
Chapter 3 37
Chapter 4 47
Chapter 5 57
Chapter 6 63
Chapter 7 71
Chapter 8 79
Chapter 9 87
Chapter 10 97
Chapter 11 105
Chapter 12 115
Chapter 13 127
Chapter 14 141
Chapter 15 149
Chapter 16 157
Chapter 17 167
Chapter 18 173
Chapter 19 183
Chapter 20 191
Chapter 21 197
Chapter 22 205
Chapter 23 217
Chapter 24 225

Chapter 25	233
Chapter 26	243
Chapter 27	253
Chapter 28	267
Chapter 29	271
Chapter 30	277
Chapter 31	287
Chapter 32	293
Chapter 33	299
Chapter 34	305
Chapter 35	313
Chapter 36	317
Chapter 37	325
Epilogue	333
Notes From The Author	339
More From The Author	341

Prologue

Lawrence laced his boots and straightened his back. He patted his jacket's pockets to make sure he had his lighter and cigarettes, which was all he needed. He looked back at the house to make sure all the lights were off. Lawrence hated when people left their lights on when they weren't using the rooms. What a waste of electricity.

He pulled the key out of the keyhole and opened the door. It was early, and the static outside revealed it was raining again. Big fucking surprise. It always rained here. Probably one of the many reasons why everybody was so negative all the fucking time.

Pulling the hoodie over his head, Lawrence stepped onto the porch, closed the door, then locked it. He rattled the knob to double-check. The piece-of-shit lock seemed finnicky, and he often needed to wriggle the key to lock it.

He walked down the porch steps and stepped onto the wet street. Loud pattering of the rain drummed on top of his hoodie, with occasional droplets grazing his face. It rained just enough to form slippery, muddy streets.

It was the same during winter. It rarely snowed, but when it did, the snowmelt made everyone's life a living hell with the mud on the roads.

Lawrence looked left and right down the street. A group of three people in raincoats stood in front of Phil's house, their figures sorrowfully clustered and facing each other while the rain battered them. Three figures. Someone was late, and Lawrence suspected that it was Clive again, the son of a bitch. If this continued, Lawrence would need to suggest voting him out of the group.

With a shake of his head, Lawrence broke into a stride. The icy droplets felt unpleasant on his face, especially after spending the night in the warmth of his bed. He hated having to get up earlier during the weekends, but this was an emergency, and as a member of the Escorters, he needed to make sure everything went fine.

It gave him solace, knowing that he would be allowed to go back home after the initial ceremony. He would then need to return to the church in the afternoon and then again in the evening for Father Walter's speeches.

"Morning, Lawrence," Steve said when Lawrence approached the figures in front of Phil's house.

Lawrence didn't say anything but rather just stopped to join them. At a distance, they were talking, accompanied by hand and head gestures, but they went silent as he approached, convincing Lawrence that they might have been talking about him.

He didn't give a shit. He knew that they didn't like him too much because of his harshness, but they were all young and didn't understand. This had to be done to keep the town safe.

Someday, they would understand why it had to be done.

He didn't need to look under the hoodies to recognize the three figures. As expected, Clive wasn't there.

"Anyone try calling Clive?" Lawrence asked.

The group exchanged looks as if to silently check with each other if anyone had the bright idea of doing that. "I'll do it," Gary, the youngest Escorter, said as he whipped out his mobile phone. Gary was only twenty-one, but his baby-smooth face and inability to properly grow a beard made him look even younger. The best he could do was a few needly hairs for a mustache, so he, instead, kept his face clean-shaven.

Lawrence pulled out his cigarette pack and put one cigarette in his mouth. He leaned forward to prevent drenching it in the rain and took out his lighter. After a few unsuccessful flicks, the flame came to life, and he managed to light the tip of the cigarette.

He expected Clive to be late at least a few more minutes, so he lit the cigarette. As luck would always have it, he also expected Clive to magically appear next to them when Lawrence lit a cigarette. That always happened, no matter where he was or what he was doing. He would wait for a while, not wanting to smoke because people could need him at any moment. After losing his patience, he would light one up, and sure enough, someone would call him before he managed to take two whiffs.

"You coming?" Gary asked with the phone against his ear. "Yeah, we're in front. Okay, see you." He lowered the phone, pressed a button, and put it in his pocket. "He'll be here in two minutes."

Lawrence inhaled the smoke and then blew it out. The smoke dispersed in the air and disappeared under the rain almost as soon as it left his mouth. "Have you two gone out to Replay yesterday?" He frowned.

Gary looked uncomfortable. "Yes. But we didn't drink a lot."

"Don't bullshit me, Gary. The entire town knows that Clive doesn't go out unless he wants to get comatose drunk."

"No, he was okay last night. Really. He got drunk, but not as much as we're used to seeing him."

"The stupid fuck still hasn't learned his lesson," Robert, the town's butcher, said with a scoff. Lawrence could recognize Robert under the coat from a distance due to his big, round belly. "You'd think that crashing his daddy's car, losing his driver's license, and having cleanup duty for six months would teach him, but no. We should have sent him to Raintown."

"No. Too harsh," Lawrence disagreed. "Clive is stupid, but he's not a bad person."

"Bad person or not, if he messes up one more time, it'll be Raintown for him. That's what Father Walter said."

As much as Lawrence knew Clive needed a slap on the wrist that would teach him not to put himself in such danger, he already had too many chances, and none of them taught him. Raintown would be bad for him, and he would probably never recover fully from it, but it was better than having him put others in the town in danger.

A few minutes had gone by in silence. Lawrence looked at the window of Phil's house. It was dark, and he couldn't see anything past the rain-stricken glass pane. Phil was the town's mail carrier, and everybody loved him. He always brought milk bones with him to feed the neighborhood dogs. He also made fake letters to give to the Hodgson family's daughter, who always asked if there was any mail for her.

Even after his son died—after having wandered too far out of the town—and when his wife threw herself into the canal, Phil continued flashing the same smile and making the same small talk with everyone. In a bigger town, people wouldn't notice it, but Lawrence saw the sadness behind the mail carrier's friendly face and buoyant voice. Ever since his family died, a spark in his eye disappeared, and sadness obscured his smiles.

Lawrence scanned the faces of his fellow Escorters. Gary was the only one who looked relatively nervous, shifting his weight from one foot to the other, his eyes flittering down the street. The others were seemingly composed, but Lawrence knew that everyone was on edge.

All of them have interacted with Phil almost every day; escorting him would be no easy task. Whenever they had the ceremony, they told the Protector that they were here to escort them safely to the church, but really, they were just making sure that the person chosen didn't do anything stupid.

"Hey, guys," said a deep voice from behind Lawrence.

Lawrence turned around. Clive stood with a thin blue jacket and a baseball cap to shield his head from the rain. The visor was blocking his eyes, and Lawrence was tempted to flip the cap off of him to see how drunk he looked.

No time for that sort of drama, though. Lawrence dropped the cigarette on the ground and stubbed it with his boot. "About fucking time, Clive," he said as he turned to face the rest of the group. "Okay, everybody's here. Let's go." He jutted his head toward the house.

As he expected, nobody took the initiative to approach the porch. Instead, they stepped aside, letting Lawrence take the lead. He lightly shook his head at that. As much as he loved being the Escorters' unofficial leader, it also came with a lot of responsibility.

Lawrence climbed the stairs and stopped in front of the door. He pressed the doorbell, triggering a muffled buzz throughout the house. He took a step back and dug his hands into his pockets. The pitter-patter of the rain drowned out any potential commotion inside the house, but Lawrence imagined Phil sitting on his living room couch since the crack of dawn, waiting for the Escorters to arrive, his heart plummeting to his stomach at the doorbell's ding.

Nothing happened.

The door didn't open. The lock didn't click. The curtain didn't move to reveal Phil's peering face. Lawrence buzzed again. The house wasn't that big, so he found it hard to believe that Phil needed too long to open the door. Maybe Phil just got drunk yesterday and fell asleep.

Lawrence gave the door a loud rap with his knuckles. The door was sturdy, and the knocking barely seemed to resound against the rain. Now, growing a little impatient and worried, Lawrence rang the doorbell once more.

Just as he did so, the lock clicked, and the door cracked open, revealing the dark interior. Out peeked the head of the mail carrier, darting his eyes at the Escorters. His hair was disheveled, his eyes bloodshot and adorned with bags. All of it alluded to either him getting drunk, crying, or not sleeping all night long—or all three.

"Hi, Phil," Lawrence said with as much solicitousness as he could. "Are you ready?" He wanted to be gentle with Phil, but also let him know that he didn't really have a choice.

"Yeah, just give me two minutes, please," Phil said with a hoarse voice. Lawrence nodded. Phil retreated into the darkness of the house and closed the door.

Poor son of a bitch.

They were already late, but Lawrence didn't want to rush Phil. He turned to face the Escorters, who looked even more uncomfortable than before. Lawrence detected sadness in Robert's eyes. Clive and Gary displayed fear. Steve looked bored, but knowing him, Lawrence could tell that he was nervous.

Lawrence averted his gaze from his companions and looked at the house across the street. The roof tiles glistened in the rain, tempting Lawrence. He could suddenly see himself glissading down that rooftop uncontrollably.

He imagined smashing his face against the ground and caving in his skull and breaking his neck. The urge to climb up on that house was so strong that he could almost feel his heel slipping on the wet tiles. He squeezed his eyes shut to shake those thoughts away. Those weren't his thoughts.

They needed to hurry.

As he turned around and grabbed the doorknob, he almost slammed into the door face-first. The door was locked.

"What the hell?" he asked, rattling the doorknob. The door opened as much as the chainlock allowed. Phil must have bolted the door quietly. "Shit! Steve, Robert, go around the house! Don't let him get away!" Lawrence commanded.

On a whim, Lawrence rammed the door with his shoulder. The door rattled but remained stuck to the chain. His shoulder hurt, but Lawrence tried again and again. The door did not budge.

"Let me!" Clive said.

Lawrence stepped aside and allowed Clive to kick the door down. A crunch came with each kick, splintering the door, giving way to the impact. Anger swirled inside Lawrence. Why the hell would Phil try to do something like this?

What do you mean, why? It's obvious why he did it.

Clive kicked the door down. It gave in, surrendering to the floor. Rushing past Clive, he made his way inside the dark corridor. The foyer was too dark, and it wasn't just from the gloomy weather. Phil must have pulled the blinds on all the windows to create such an unnatural darkness.

"Phil?" Lawrence called out as he took a step farther into the house.

With the pattering of the rain muffled, the silence in the house seemed oppressive. Lawrence's fists clenched and unclenched, desperate for a defensive object to clutch. He had known Phil for years—yes, and Phil was not a violent man, but who knew? People did all sorts of crazy shit once they were chosen as the Protector.

No, not Phil.

Loud footsteps thudded from somewhere in front. A moment later, a bulky figure ran into the foyer and stopped in front of Lawrence. "Not here," Robert said through heavy panting.

As if on cue, a muffled crash came from upstairs. Robert and Lawrence looked upstairs at the ceiling instinctively. *Oh shit,* Lawrence thought to himself. He didn't wait for the others. He jackknifed toward the stairs. It was dark enough to obscure the top of the staircase, and he expected Phil to jump out from somewhere and attack him. Did Phil even have a gun?

Quiet thuds of his fellow Escorters' boots behind him gave him some assurance. It also reminded him that, as being the unofficial leader of the group, he couldn't show that he was afraid. He had to be an example for them, especially for the young ones like Gary.

"Phil!" Lawrence shouted, expecting no response.

As much as he wanted to rush, Lawrence took a tentative step forward, then another. His eyes had adjusted to the dark, but he still had to be careful where he stepped. It was too quiet, and that made Lawrence uneasy.

"Are you sure he didn't slip through the backdoor?" he asked in a whisper.

"Yes. I'm sure," Robert said from behind, sounding like he was offended.

Lawrence had half-hoped that Robert was wrong. He would rather face the council's wrath for letting a Protector run away than having to haul a person—who he had known all his life—to the church against his will. He didn't bother keeping quiet. He let his boots clomp against the steps to let Phil know they were coming for him—whether he liked it or not.

"Phil! Are you up here?" Lawrence asked, mostly just to kill the annoying silence.

Still no answer. Lawrence reached the top of the stairs and peered toward the corridor. It was less dark here. The bedroom door was ajar. Lawrence strode toward the door, more courageous, with the presence of the meager light in the hallway. He stopped in front of the bedroom. Phil was in here; he was sure of it.

"Phil?" Lawrence tapped on the bedroom door.

Of course, no one answered. The Escorters were already late, thanks to Clive—and now, thanks to Phil. If they didn't manage to capture him, the council would be pissed. Lawrence didn't plan on wasting any more time trying to be gentle. He pushed the door open and stepped inside.

"All right, Phil. Time to g—"

The sentence died in his throat when he beheld the sight in front of him. He froze in his steps, causing Robert to bump into him from behind.

"Jesus fucking Christ," Robert muttered from behind.

Phil gurgled and choked as he swayed, the rope hanging from the ceiling's beam. He was facing away from them, clawing at his neck, flailing his dangling legs. Lawrence was grateful that he couldn't see his face.

"Fuck," he muttered to himself.

Robert tried to walk past Lawrence to assist Phil, but Lawrence put a hand on his chest. "No," he commanded.

"The fuck you mean, no? He's fucking dying!" Robert interjected.

"Let him die, Robert."

"Are you out of your mind? If the council hears about this—"

"Then what?!" Lawrence got in Robert's face, aware that his spittle flew onto the butcher's face. Robert shrunk under Lawrence's threat. "Let him die, Robert," Lawrence said. "He's suffered enough. It's what he wants and deserves."

He thought he detected defiance in Robert's face, but if any existed, then he was too scared to object. Lawrence looked at the other Escorters in the room, their wide eyes darting from Phil to Lawrence.

Lawrence turned to face Phil. The gurgling was barely discernible now. His face had turned to the color of a plum. It was a shame his neck didn't snap to make it painless, but it would be over in a minute, anyway.

They watched as Phil's swaying and flailing weakened. He stopped struggling, his hands limp at his sides, his lead legs flaccid. Lawrence wondered what went through his mind in those final moments as his brain ran out of oxygen, his vision growing dark.

It was difficult to understand that the person hanging by the rope in front of Lawrence was the same person who played poker with him and the other guys every Friday night for the past five years. It was difficult to process that he would no longer be with them.

At least you're finally with your wife and kid, Phil, Lawrence thought, choosing not to utter the words aloud. As the rope stopped swaying, silence draped the air. Even the Escorters' breathing went mute.

Phil was dead.

Chapter 1

Dean's phone woke him. He had turned off the sound, but the strong vibrations on the wooden surface of the nightstand negated the silent mode. He reached toward his nightstand, his face still buried in the pillow, his eyes unwilling to open.

His hand accidentally shoved a brick-like object onto the floor. *Shit,* Dean thought to himself. He forced himself to open his eyes, and through a blurry vision, he scooted to the edge of the bed to look for his phone.

The incessant ringing grew more annoying, with the caller refusing to give up. His phone was nowhere in sight, and he was sure that it had fallen under the bed. He blinked to clear up his vision and reached under the bed, patting the floor.

His fingers brushed against the blocky outline, and he was finally able to grasp and pull it out. Dean rolled over on his back and looked at the phone's screen. It had stopped ringing by then and showed one missed call. He also couldn't help but notice that it was past eleven a.m.

"Fuck," he muttered with a croaky voice. He hated waking up so late. It wasn't like he had any work to do; he just hated the feeling of the day slipping too fast.

Dean unlocked his phone and looked at the number that had called him. It was his literary agent, Alex. It had been a while since he and Dean spoke. Maybe he was just calling to see how Dean was doing. Dean would call him later. He needed some breakfast and coffee first.

He threw the blanket off and willed himself to get out of bed with a groan. He dragged himself to the bathroom to relieve his screaming bladder, then to the kitchen. His apartment was small: one bedroom and one living room connected with the tiny kitchen. Dean rarely cooked, so he didn't care about getting an apartment with an ostentatious kitchen.

Dean opened the cupboard and pulled out the tiny jar where he kept the coffee. It was almost entirely empty. "Shit," he said to himself. His need for a morning cup of joe suddenly grew tenfold when he knew he had none in the apartment. He, instead, would make some breakfast. It had been a while since he actually cooked for himself, so he wanted to start for a change of pace.

He opened the old, rusty fridge and glanced inside. Not much food remained, but he did have eggs. Dean tried to remember how long they had been sitting in there and if they were safe to eat. It couldn't have been more than a month, right?

"Just three eggs. That can't possibly kill me," Dean said as he grabbed the carton of eggs.

It felt light in his hand, and for a moment, he wondered if there even were any eggs in there. He flipped open the carton. Three eggs stared back at him. Just the right amount. He couldn't be sure if that would be enough for him, but it should hold until lunch, whenever lunchtime would be.

The frying pan was still on the stove, but it looked like it contained the fossilized remains of whatever he cooked in it months ago. He decided to give it a scrub just enough to kill the taste of the old food.

It was a lot harder to clean the pan than Dean expected, and he needed to put his shoulder into it. By the time he had scrubbed off the layers of grease and stuck food, the pan had changed its color. By then, Dean didn't want to stop until it was spotless. This minor chore suddenly made him feel productive after months of living like a slob. It pushed him into action to clean the dirty dishes that had been sitting in the sink for God knows how long. It felt good to see the plates gleaming white and drying in the dish rack. He might even do the laundry later or vacuum the apartment.

Now that the frying pan was clean, Dean didn't feel like cooking in it. He reluctantly took out the stick of butter from the fridge and smeared it on the pan. He turned on the stove and waited for it to heat up. While waiting, he went around the apartment, picking up the dirty clothes and stray socks. He put them inside the overflowing basket in the bathroom. Dean would need to take the clothes to the laundromat later.

The crackling pan beckoned him to rush back to it. As he cracked the eggs, he expected half or whole baby chick fetuses to fall into the pan due to how long he had the eggs, but they were just regular egg whites and yolks, much to his relief. The thought of dropping a chicken fetus into the sizzling pan twisted his stomach. Not enough to chase away the hunger, but still.

While waiting for the eggs to cook, Dean went back to the bedroom and got dressed. He returned to the kitchen with his phone and browsed the news articles. Nothing of interest caught his attention: news about Biden and his new tax plans, news about Trump—those have been resurfacing lately—an article about growing a healthy avocado, and an article about global warming, but one caught Dean's eye.

The article had a picture of him wearing a tuxedo, flashing a PR smile. The picture was taken at his book signing in New York two years ago. He read the article's headline. "Will Dean Watson Ever Write Another Good Book?" Dean rolled his eyes. In the past two years, he had seen a myriad of news articles about him—most prominently after the accident—but then they slowed to a halt. News about him still popped up from time to time, but the public had mostly forgotten. Even the fan mail barely arrived anymore, and when it did, Dean didn't write back.

He liked it better that way. He didn't miss the fame at all, especially since he never knew these days if he should expect fan mail or death threats. A pop from the pan pricked his ears, reminding Dean that his eggs needed attention. He hadn't even decided how he would like his eggs, but one look at the pan was enough to tell him that it was too late to have them scrambled.

"Sunnyside up it is, then," he said to himself.

He grabbed a spatula that he had finished scrubbing earlier—it took him a lot of effort—and stuck it under the eggs. To his dismay, the eggs were stuck to the pan. As soon as he flipped the mangled remains of his breakfast onto the plate, Dean put the pan under cold water in the sink and then washed it. If he left it for later, he would probably be too lazy to wash it again.

His phone rang again.

Dean dropped what he was doing, wiped his wet hands on his T-shirt, and picked up the phone from the kitchen table. It was Alex. Dean accepted the call and turned on his speaker.

"Hello?" he said as he placed the phone on the table and turned around to get his breakfast and a fork.

"About time you answered your phone, Dean." Alex's stern voice came from the speaker. "Where have you been?"

"Sleeping. Where's the fire?" Dean asked as he pulled out a chair and sat at the table.

"Well, you better get used to waking up early because I have news."

"I'm listening," Dean said.

A moment of a pause ensued. Dean was compelled to look at the phone just to make sure the call was still on.

"Okay, listen very carefully to me now, Dean," Alex exclaimed theatrically. "You're not drunk, are you?"

"No, darn it. Just get to the point," Dean said, impatient and frustrated.

"Okay, listen. I managed to convince a publisher to sign a deal."

"You what?" Dean asked, unsure if he heard Alex correctly. He had a piece of overcooked eggs on his fork, hovering in front of his mouth.

"Yeah, listen," Alex continued, "we didn't sign anything just yet, but this publisher wants to work with you. We can't miss out on this opportunity."

"Who's the publisher?"

"Dark Curtains."

"Dark Curtains? Alex, they're tiny. Their books are horrible in quality. Their editing sucks. Their marketing sucks. Their—"

"Dean, listen to me," Alex demanded. "I went through a lot of trouble to secure this deal. None of the bigger publishers want to work with you. You understand? None of them. After what happened, they're afraid of staining their reputation by publishing someone like you."

Dean dropped the fork onto the plate and gritted his teeth. A piece of egg white flew off the plate and onto the table.

"Are you seriously going to lecture me about it again?" he asked.

"I'm not lecturing you. Listen, my point is, I went through all the major publishers. No dice. We have to start with this small one, and when the public welcomes you back with open arms, the big ones will want to work with you again. All right?"

Dean pinched his nose's bridge. He should have been ecstatic about this, but all he felt was dread. Not just dread. Fear. He remembered how the public reacted after hearing about the accident, and he was afraid that exposing himself would only reopen old wounds.

"How did you even manage to get the publisher to sign the deal?" Dean asked.

"You know me. I have really good persuasive skills. I told them that you'd come up with something within thirty days."

"Thirty days?! Are you out of your mind, Alex?"

"No, just—"

"I haven't written anything in almost two years, and now, you want an entire manuscript?"

"Dean, you—"

"I don't even know what I need to write ab—"

"Dean, shut the hell up for a second and let me finish!" Alex rarely raised his voice, but when he did, Dean went quiet. "You don't need an entire manuscript. All right? You just need something to show the publisher that we mean business. A prologue, a chapter—hell, even just a couple of thousand words. We just need *something* to sign the deal, and then you'll have more time to write the entire manuscript."

Dean leaned back in the chair and tapped his fingers on the table. One chapter. That made it easier for Dean, but it still didn't help because he suffered from writer's block.

"Thirty days is still not enough for me. Alex, I have exhausted all my ideas and don't know what I could possibly write about. And this can't be just some spin-off of my main books. It needs to be a hit; otherwise,

26

people will know that I lost my talent, and they'll never buy my books again."

"You're right. The book *has* to be a hit. Look. I know thirty days is tight, but you've pulled off worse. You can do this. Just one chapter, man. That's all we need."

Dean stood and paced the kitchen. His eyes fell on the clean dishes, but he didn't even register looking at them. He needed more time, but he didn't have it. Thirty days would be enough for any normal writer, but Dean had quality to worry about. He had to do a ton of research first, write the first draft, then revise that draft. Right now, he had no idea where to even begin.

"I need more time, Alex," Dean said.

Alex sighed, meaning that he was about to say something that didn't go in Dean's favor. "Dean, look. I went through hell and high water to sign this deal. This is the best I could do. If we screw this up, it's over. Nobody will ever publish your work again. That means your career as a writer will be over. The royalties for the books you published are still relatively good, even with the public backlash, but how long do you think it's going to keep you afloat without new releases? You have no other choice, Dean."

Alex was right. The salary Dean received every month was enough to let him live somewhat comfortably, but the royalties were dwindling. It wouldn't be long until his books fell into oblivion, and he had to find a regular nine-to-five job. He dreaded that. After almost two years of not lifting anything heavier than a spoon, he couldn't imagine working as a blue-collar worker—if anyone would even hire him.

"Does the publisher have any idea what they want me to write about?" Dean finally asked.

"No. You have the freedom to write whatever you want, but I need the manuscript submitted by November fifteenth at the latest."

"Great. So, I have twenty-five days to pull something out of my ass."

"As I said, you have full creative freedom. You can write about whatever you want. I know you've exhausted your ideas for crime fiction, so why not focus on something else? Write a horror story. Horror is everywhere these days. You can write a story about toys coming to life and murdering people. Or a story about a haunted house."

"All those stories are overused, Alex. I need something different. Something original."

"Whatever you want to write about, I don't care. I just want to have something by November fifteenth. Can you do that?"

Dean sucked in a sharp breath. He looked toward the small, cluttered living room. He couldn't live like this forever: renting a small place in Gresham, with nothing nearby. He wanted to go back to his old glory days, when he was renting a penthouse in the center of Portland. He wished that he was smarter with his finances then and bought his own place.

But just like his parents, when they opened their own restaurant in Hawthorne twenty years ago, he thought that the money would continuously trickle in, so he hadn't bothered saving. He thought he was always going to be a bestselling author, but ten seconds of carelessness, along with his fame and cash, were gone in an instant.

"Okay, Alex. I'll do it," Dean said.

Chapter 2

Dean was no longer hungry after his phone call with Alex, but he forced himself to take a few bites for the strength. The eggs were terrible. Not only were they too burned at the bottom, but he forgot to add salt, which made them bland. He had nothing else in his fridge to add to the taste.

While struggling to chew the egg whites, he replayed the conversation with Alex. He had only twenty-five days. Dean felt like he was losing precious time, even while eating his breakfast. He had to get to work as soon as possible. But what could he possibly write about?

He had it in his mind to write crime fiction—since it was his forte, but just the thought of it made him sick. He had written too many crime fiction books, and they were a hit, but he no longer had any fresh ideas for that genre. Anything he wrote in crime fiction would be derivative and unoriginal. He had to go for something else.

As he sat in the living room, he went through the list of genres that sold well. Historical fiction was a no-go for him: it would be entirely new to him, and the inaccuracies could render bad reviews. Science fiction could work, but there was no way Dean's sci-fi book could compete with all the big fish out there. Romantic fiction was always awkward for him, so that was out of the question, as was erotica. Besides, he didn't want people to label him as a cheap erotica writer, trying to make a comeback. What about humor? No. He tried passing off humor in some of his books, and it went over the audience's heads.

After going through the possible genres, Dean deduced that only two genres remained as options for him: thriller and horror. He had written both before, and they were well received. Not as well as crime fiction, but then again, the audience for horror and thriller was much smaller than crime books. Thriller and horror were often closely related, so he could decide on a story flow and see what genre meshed.

What should I write about? If he was going to go for horror, then he definitely wouldn't want some paranormal bullshit. He wanted something that would make the audience question whether the things happening in the story were real or not. He looked out the window. It was sunny, but since it was October, he expected the temperature to be low. He put on his leather jacket and zipped it up.

He picked up his keys, cellphone, and earphones. He exited the apartment, locked the door, then descended the stairs—the building had no elevator. Dean lived on the third floor; climbing up and down was always sufficient exercise for him, except he didn't really go out that much lately.

As soon as Dean stepped outside, the sunbeam blinded him. He whipped his arm up to shield his eyes for a moment. It was warm despite his initial assumption that it would not be so. He wondered if global warming had anything to do with the warm weather because he remembered Oregon's freezing temperatures during this time of the year in his youth. He was only thirty-five, and he wondered if the effects of climate change would become significantly noticeable by the time he becomes an old man.

Dean unzipped his jacket because he knew he'd be sweating by the time he even reached Red Sunset Park. Although Dean preferred living in the downtown of big cities, the calmness of Gresham was often enjoyable. Dean didn't need to worry about crazy drivers or people shouting because they were in a hurry.

Red Sunset Park was only a few blocks away, and when Dean approached it, he put the earbuds in his ears and plugged the jack into his phone. He went to YouTube and searched "suspenseful music for reading." Plenty of results popped up, and Dean chose the ten-hour-long one to avoid interruptions. An ad about a certain juice played at the start of the video, and Dean hoped that the creator of the video wasn't a jerk who put ads in the middle.

The music muffled most of the outside noise—except for his footsteps—the cars whizzing by, and the occasional murmurs of people he walked past. Dean entered the park, overcome by a sense of tranquility. He could no longer discern the street's chaos. Barely any people were present at the park, so the only sound aside from the music that accompanied Dean was the occasional breeze blowing in his face.

Okay, let's brainstorm some ideas for the book, he thought as he put his hands in his pants' pockets.

No ideas came to him, though. It was as if they were right there in front of him, but each time he tried to reach for them, they eluded him like a carrot on a stick.

A story about a serial killer in the woods, maybe? No, I don't know what the premise would be. What about a story about a monster in the mountain, hunting a group of hikers? It would be a slasher, and slashers are boring. What about a story of a hermit living in a cabin in the middle of the woods? No, that's the serial killer one. Fuck.

Dean turned off the music, figuring that it was only interrupting his creativity. Even with nothing but silence surrounding him, potential ideas remained elusive. He sat on a bench and stared at the surrounding maples, tulips, and sequoias, trying to imagine a scenario of how a book would start. He didn't even care about the whole story itself; he just wanted a captivating prologue.

Nothing.

Even after spending an hour at the park, he was stuck at square one. Frustrated, he went home. He sat on the couch and rubbed his eyes, his brain frying from trying so hard to think of a story. In the end, it didn't matter if he had thirty days or three hundred. He was still stumped.

Dean turned on his laptop and browsed *Creepypasta*, hoping to gain inspiration from the stories on the main page. He used to read those in his early twenties, and some of the stories stuck with him. While most of them weren't particularly well-written—because they were short stories—the ideas were incredible. Dean could see some of the authors on the forum becoming famous writers one day if they'd continued to work toward such a goal.

It was the old urban legends that finally got something stirring inside him. Many unexplained—or fake—legends posted on the website intrigued Dean enough to research them.

The legend of the Russian Sleep Experiment: the radio that broadcasted Russian sentences on a loop for years. The legend of the man from a nonexistent country called Taured. Countless stories sat on the website, and while some of them were more appropriate for action thrillers, most of them served as great material for horror.

This was it. Dean was going to write a story about one of these urban legends. But which one? So many of them looked interesting, but which one could be used to write a story?

He was suddenly motivated beyond words. He wanted to dive into it and type away, but he knew that if he even tried it, he would only be staring at the blank white page, unable to write. He needed to conduct a thorough investigation first.

Dean went to his bedroom and rummaged through the nightstand drawers for a pen and notebook. He went back to the living room and wrote down every urban legend that he could possibly investigate. Eight of them were on his list, but the majority—if not all—would not be appropriate for a full-length novel.

Someone had already written about Taured and the Russian Sleep Experiment. The one about the woman called "The Expressionless" seemed great but not for a book that Dean had in mind. One by one, Dean scratched the legends off the list. With each one eliminated, and the list dwindling, despair formed inside Dean again. If he was left without a single possible candidate, he would need to look through the list again.

That was, unfortunately, exactly what happened.

With all eight urban legends etched out, Dean scratched his head in confusion, facing a dead-end once again. He went through the list again, giving undivided attention to each urban legend. He tried to imagine what kind of story he could write, but once again, he was overcome by another carrot on a stick.

The urban legends were interesting, but that was all there was to it. There was no grandiose story, no mind-blowing closure. Dean ripped the page out of the notebook, crumpled the paper, and chucked it across the room, suddenly overcome by insurmountable anger. It wasn't satisfying enough. He then grabbed the empty glass on the coffee table and threw it as well. The glass shattered, tiny shards dispersing against the wall and falling on the floor. With his laptop on the verge of falling victim by his hands, he thought twice about ruining it. He needed the laptop for work—if work would come to him.

Staring at the shards of the broken glass, he realized what he had done and calmed down. Skylar's voice faded into his memory, reprimanding him for his temper. *I'm sick of dealing with this! Don't you dare blame your temper on me! You know what?! I'm going to sleep at my mother's place tonight. I'll see you in a few days, Dean.*

Dean shook his head. He was glad that Skylar wasn't here to see him still breaking things. He hadn't done it in a while, and he had been controlling his temper, but when he shattered the glass, he realized how much anger had been bottled up inside him.

He was angry at everyone. He was angry at Alex for giving him this job out of nowhere, despite Alex knowing that he struggled with writer's block. He was angry at Skylar for leaving him when he needed her the most. He was angry at the public for "canceling" him after the incident. But he was angry the most at himself for not being able to produce a new story, even though it was his job.

His fury was a hurricane that ravaged everything on its way and left a mess for him to deal with, too vicious to be subdued in the spur of the moment. Each subsequent time he let it pass, it grew stronger.

Dean sighed and swept up the shards of glass. He cut his thumb while sweeping, which further exacerbated his anger, but he remained in control this time and didn't throw the dustpan with the glass. He inhaled and exhaled. "In and out, in and out," just like that instructor on YouTube said. Sometimes it worked, sometimes it didn't.

This time, it worked.

He swiped his laptop's touchpad to wake it up. He frowned at the screen. He was still on *Creepypasta*, but something snagged his attention.

The title of the story read "SUICIDE TOWN."

Chapter 3

All Dean could do was stare at the title. Was this just another story? Still, the title captured his attention. He clicked the link. *404 Page Not Found.*

"Shit." Dean pressed his lips together. He went back to the main page, then tried opening the link again. The same error greeted him. He tried pasting the link into a different browser but no luck.

He had to know more about this story. It could have been just the fact that he had no access to it, which made him want to know about it all the more, but Dean didn't care. He had to find out what this Suicide Town was. He went to Google and typed in "suicide town." Results for Jonestown, where the people poisoned themselves on the command of Jim Jones, popped up. But that wasn't it, was it? He continued looking through the other links and found a forum discussing it.

> *Has anyone read the Creepypasta called 'Suicide Town'?*

A plethora of various answers decorated the thread.

> *Yeah.*
> *Nope, the link is broken for me.*
> *I read it. Not too scary.*

The third comment got a lot of replies, where people asked what it was about. His response was not very detailed but enough to further interest Dean.

> *It's an apparent urban legend about a town where people massively commit*

> *suicide. Like, the townsfolk can't leave because their suicidal tendencies become too strong, and the ones who visit the town quickly off themselves, even if they had no history of depression or suicidal tendencies. Again, nothing too scary and I don't think it's true.*

People further asked the guy in the comments if he knew in what town the story took place, but he, unfortunately, didn't know.

A town where people committed suicide. That thought was intriguing. This was the right story—Dean was sure of it. It wasn't just a tingling sensation like he had with the other urban legends. No, he could actually envision a story here. Images too obscure to understand came and went like pieces of a puzzle that he couldn't put together just yet.

But that's exactly what he needed to do. He had to find out more to piece the puzzle to write something about it; he was sure of it. The motivation he felt was immeasurable. He felt like he could run ten miles without getting tired. Even if he didn't find out more about the town, he would write about it, that was for sure.

He wasn't giving up on his research just yet, though. He went back to the search engine, determined to find out more about the mysterious Suicide Town. The results for the rest of the pages were meager, too. Either the links were broken, the forums were deleted, or the information was scarce. Dean couldn't help but think that someone was actively trying to erase the existence of Suicide Town from the internet.

Hoping to find some urban explorers or horror enthusiasts who had perhaps been to the town or talked about it, Dean opened YouTube and looked up "suicide town." The results: a song called *Suicide Town* and documentaries about Jonestown.

Even with the lack of information, Dean wasn't ready to give up. The motivation gave him wings, and he was soaring high in the sky, going higher by the second. He hoped that he wouldn't plummet to the ground upon losing momentum, like the kites he flew when he was a kid.

One thing he could do was get on the deep web, dark web—whatever people called it—and try to find out more about Suicide Town there. He knew nothing about the deep web, save for the fact that he needed special tools to access it and that it could be dangerous. *First, exhaust the regular internet, then think about the alternatives.* Dean returned to the search engine, trying different keywords in the search bar.

> *Town where people kill themselves*
>
> *Small town where visitors commit suicide*
>
> *Suicide Town creepypasta*
>
> *Is Suicide Town real?*

None of the search results bore fruition. He ran in circles, only getting scraps of information here and there from either the posts or the comments.

> *I know a guy who went there, and he shot himself in the head two weeks later.*

I heard it's located somewhere in the middle of Texas.

Guys, it's just an urban legend. It doesn't exist. The fact that it's impossible to find information about it is exactly why so many people are intrigued.

It's supposedly not anywhere on the map. Even the GPS can't find it.

Dean opened multiple tabs on his browser, losing track of which was which. One by one, he closed them once he exhaustively read every sentence. He figured that no useful information would be on the page. But for each crumb of info, he wrote down notes in his notepad. He didn't feel like he was getting any closer to his goal, but the exhilaration of investigating an urban legend had not subsided, even after almost two hours of scouring various websites.

Eventually, he went back to the first forum where one of the comments briefly explained the story of Suicide Town. The activity seemed to be abundant on that website, so Dean made an account. He was going to post a thread about it himself, hoping to get some viable answers. He registered under a random username and posted the topic.

DOES ANYONE KNOW MORE ABOUT SUICIDE TOWN?

I first saw the story on the Creepypasta website, but I couldn't find any more information online. Apparently, there's this town where suicide rates are astronomical, and people who visit the

> *town end up killing themselves. If anyone knows anything about the town—name, location, anything—please let me know in the comments.*

Dean clicked the POST TOPIC button and leaned back on the couch. He intertwined his fingers behind his back, feeling productive. He hadn't done anything except search for information online for two hours, but when he was in the planning stage, research was his work, not writing.

Since it would probably be awhile until he got some answers, and his stomach rumbled to remind him the eggs for breakfast were not enough, Dean decided to go out and buy some food. He didn't really care what he ate; he just wanted to pass the time while waiting for answers.

As he stood from the couch, his phone rang. In the absence of any noise in the room—save for the laptop's low whirring—his phone startled him. An unknown number was calling him, and he contemplated answering. In the past, there have been situations when zealous fans managed to get their hands on Dean's number and incessantly called him. Dean enjoyed that kind of attention for the first six months or so. Then it became cumbersome.

After the accident, it happened again, but this time, it wasn't calls from fans exclaiming their love but death threats from angered people who had heard about the news. Dean ended up changing his phone number and even contemplated hiring a bodyguard, but even when he had tons of cash from his writing, it was expensive.

"Hello?" Dean answered the call, ready to hang up at the first sign of trouble.

"How's my favorite writer doing? Whatcha up to, D?" an obnoxious, magpie-like voice said over the phone in a buoyant tone.

Shit, Dean thought to himself, almost wishing that it was an angry fan making death threats.

"Hello, Iris," Dean said with a lot less gaiety than the caller, fighting the urge to ask her right off the bat what she wanted.

"How's everything been going, D? Any ideas coming into your head lately? Maybe a new book you could write about?" Iris asked jovially.

Her timing was too coincidental. She must have spoken to Alex, or maybe the publishers at Dark Curtains. Dean immediately knew why Iris had called him. Although annoyance simmered in the pit of his stomach, it would turn into anger if Iris got on his nerves too much. He closed his eyes, inhaled, and exhaled as silently as he could, bracing himself for what he was sure was going to be an unnecessarily prolonged conversation.

"What do you want, Iris?"

"Someone's a bit cranky. I can hear it in your voice, D. Not get enough sleep last night?" she joked. "It reminds me of this writer I had a few days ago. I specifically asked her to write a thriller book for me, and not only was she late, but when I got the manuscript back, she had turned the book into a frigging gory slasher! I was pissed! So, I told the editor to cut out all of the violent scenes and—"

"You know about the deal Alex made with Dark Curtains, don't you?"

"The what? Nooo, come on, D. What do you take me for? Okay, yeah, I know about it, but I only know the basics."

Dean put on his jacket and grabbed his keys. If he made it to the closest store or whatever place to buy food, he could make an excuse and end the call with Iris earlier.

"I know why you called, Iris. You want me to publish a book through your publishing house."

"What? Nooo. Why? Are you considering it?"

"I have to go, Iris."

"No, wait, wait, wait. D, just wait."

Dean stepped out of the apartment and locked the door behind him. He was on his way down the stairs. "I'm kinda in a hurry, Iris. Can we talk another time?"

"Just five minutes, D."

Dean let out an exasperated sigh. "Five minutes. And then I gotta go." Iris's five minutes were fifteen minutes, but he would do his best to cut the conversation short.

He stepped outside into the chilly afternoon air and turned right. He craved something sweet, so he decided he would buy some donuts at Sunny's Donuts. It wasn't too close to his apartment, though, so he went around the building into the parking lot to get his car.

"Okay, so . . . yes. I know about the deal with Dark Curtains," Iris said. "And I want to talk to you about it. Are you sure you want to publish your book with them?"

Dean unlocked his BMW and got inside. The interior smelled musty and sour, a testament that it hadn't been used—or cleaned—in a while. Two empty bottles of water sat in front of the passenger's seat, and Dean didn't even need to look at the backseat to know that more trash littered the car. He could hardly see through the dirty windshield. Would the car even start after not being used for so long?

"Well, I'm not too happy about publishing through them, but right now, I don't really have a choice." Dean inserted the key into the ignition.

"Oh, I'm sure you're wrong about that, D."

"If that's what you think, then you might want to check out my page on *Wikipedia.* Specifically, under the section 'Public Backlash,'" Dean said, feeling indignant.

He turned the key. After struggling, the engine turned on. Barely any gas remained, but it would be enough to reach Sunny's Donuts without a refill. Dean activated the wipers and gave them a moment to swipe the glass. At first, they further muddied the windshield, but then they swiped the mud away. Some of the incessant, crusted dirt stayed plastered on the glass.

"The fans still love you, D. You just need a new book, and they'll flock to the bookstores on release day. And that's what I'm here to offer you. What if you—"

"I'm not publishing through you, Iris." Dean backed the car out of the parking lot.

Iris went silent for a moment, at a loss for words. Dean turned on the speaker and put the phone on the passenger's seat. "I know that's why you called, Iris, but we already talked about this. The last time I published through you, the sales were a bust. I can't even eat a fancy dinner with the royalties."

"Now, now, just hear me out, D. Okay, yes. The sales were a bust back then, but things will be different now. The company is growing. We have a lot of talented authors now. We have a poet from Denmark who writes a poem for each book we publish. And we have a marketing expert. And a cover designer. I'm telling you, D. The company will be a big name in a couple of years! Just two months ago, we've had the release of this new book by our author who specializes in . . ."

Dean had stopped paying attention. It was safe to do so for the next five or so minutes. Maybe longer. He was focused on driving, and he really didn't care what Iris was saying; it didn't contribute to the conversation. He would be at the donut place in a few minutes, and that's when he would end the call. He needed to find a millisecond of a pause in Iris's incessant speaking to interrupt her and tell her he needed to go.

"And then this cover. I'm sending it to you now. This one is really grabby. People are going to love it. Oh, and then this one, too. Our cover artist has all these premade covers that I bought from her because I just know we're going to need them someday for a book. Hell, you could even look at them, and you might get an idea about the story."

"Yeah," Dean said, absentminded, disinterested.

Most of the covers Iris chose for her books were a miss. Either they were too generic, or they didn't fit the genre or description of the book. Dean had reached Sunny's Donuts and parked the car in front of the store. Iris was still talking by then. That was one of the things with her. When she talked about something, she'd jump from one topic to another without pausing, talking for so long that Dean could make coffee and drink it, and by the time he returned, she would still be talking—not that he ever tried doing that, even though he was tempted.

"Iris. Iris!" Dean interrupted her as he turned the car off. She continued talking for a few more seconds before stopping. "Listen, I really have to go now. Look, I have no doubt that Inkworld Publishing is getting better, but it's just not the right fit for me. You specialize in romance and cozy mysteries. I tried writing one romance for you, but it didn't work out too well. I'm gonna go with Dark Curtains and see how it pans out."

"You're making a mistake, D. They are notorious for their bad quality in formatting, editing, cover designs, and lack of marketing. You really should reconsider."

Dean got out of the car and looked at the red neon Sunny's Donuts sign above the store. An aromatic smell accompanied him; something savory deep-fried in oil that caused his mouth to water, despite knowing that it's bad for him.

"I'll think about it, Iris," he said, knowing she would not get off the phone if he outright said no.

"All right, D. Take your time. Oh, and I have to say, I read your book *Dark Fears* recently, and it was really creepy. I had to keep the lights on because it had some creepy moments. Especially the scene—"

"Thanks, Iris. I'll talk to you another time."

Dean ended the call before Iris could say anything else. If she tried calling again, he would not answer.

Chapter 4

The endless options of finely decorated, filled animal- and object-shaped donuts overwhelmed Dean. One would be enough to fill him up. Indecisiveness led him to buy the six-pack mystery box.

He thanked the lady as he paid, then left. Iris hadn't tried calling him again, much to his relief. He felt somewhat bad for talking to her the way he did, but it was the only way to cut the conversation short with her.

As soon as he was in the car, Dean opened the mystery box. He raised his eyebrows and nodded at the aesthetically pleasing donuts. They weren't just glazed with one color or sprinkled randomly. These donuts looked like they were the work of an artist. The meticulously layered hues of blue, pink, and yellow coated the donuts almost made Dean not want to eat them.

The sweet scent tickled his nostrils, tempting him to take a bite right then and there. He resisted the urge. There was no way around avoiding sticky fingers and making a mess in the car. Eating would have to wait. Sunny's Donuts didn't seem to get a lot of customers whenever Dean visited the place, and he wondered why because he thought they had the best donuts in Oregon—and the entire country. Not even Voodoo Doughnuts came close to Sunny's. Dean closed the box and started the car.

On the drive back, he remembered that it had been some time since he posted the question about Suicide Town on the forum, and that further raised his dopamine levels. He would eat first, though. Not only would he satisfy his cravings that way, but more time would pass until people answered his question.

Once Dean got home, he slumped onto the couch and placed the box of donuts next to the laptop. He opened the box, the heavenly smell once again permeating his senses. He took out a glazed, hippo-shaped donut and took a bite.

"Holy shit," he said, his mouth full of raspberry jam. The taste was orgasmic.

Dean finished eating the entire donut so fast that it induced hiccups. He went to the kitchen and drank two glasses of water. He was already full, which he expected would happen, so he took just one more bite out of a chocolate-glazed, ring-shaped donut and then closed the box. He went to the bathroom and washed his sticky hands and chin, dried them on a towel, then returned to the living room.

It was time to check the forum.

He put his laptop on his lap and woke it up. The screen turned on, the brightness piercing his vision. The battery was almost drained, but he still had some time until the laptop warned him to charge it.

The page was just as he had left it. Dean refreshed it. He held his breath as he waited a few seconds until the thread appeared in front of him again, only this time, it was different.

Dean's jaw dropped.

A red cross and a message replaced the body of the text.

> *YOUR POST GOES AGAINST THE COMMUNITY STANDARDS AND HAS BEEN REMOVED BY THE MODERATORS. NOTE: YOU WILL NO LONGER BE ABLE TO POST ON THIS FORUM.*

"What?" Dean said as he refreshed the page again, expecting the message to disappear. He refused to believe this was the outcome. The red cross and the message from the moderators remained.

Disappointment surged through Dean like electricity. *What fucking community standards?* He just asked about an urban legend. Maybe the word suicide was what ticked them off, and they didn't want that word on the forum. Often, website filters eliminated words that alluded to any sort of harm like rape, kill, guns, et cetera.

Dean scrolled to the comment section. People had posted comments, but the mods had removed them, too. "Fuck." He leaned back and put his hands behind his head. If it wasn't such a hassle, he would have contacted the forum's moderators to see what the problem was, but if they had removed his post and each comment, then they probably wanted to go out of their way to ensure no one talked about Suicide Town.

But why? Was this all just a part of an elaborate joke to stir more unease among the people following the urban legend? If it was, it was going too far, in Dean's opinion. He scrolled back to the top of the page, and that's when he noticed that he had a number two under his Messages icon.

Dean clicked it on a whim. The first message was an auto message from the moderators, informing him that his post had been removed. The second message was from *user51734*. Dean could only see part of the message from here.

> *Hey man, I saw your post about Suicide Town, but when I went to . . .*

Dean opened the full message. It was a paragraph, which got his heart racing. He darted his eyes across the message, breathless, hanging on to every word that *user51734* wrote.

> *Hey man, I saw your post about Suicide Town, but when I went to comment, it was already removed. I wanted to tell you that the name of the town you're looking for is Pineridge, also known as Suicide Town, and it's located somewhere in Southern Oregon. My friend who went there said it's close to Medford, but he wasn't specific.*

Dean reread the message multiple times. *Southern Oregon, close to Medford.* If that was the case, then he was lucky because he could reach the place in a few hours by car. He then reminded himself that he didn't even know where the town was, and he had barely any information to go on. Still, this was a good start. He replied to *user51734*.

> *Thanks a lot for the message. Do you think you could contact your friend to ask him where exactly the town is located? I need it for my research.*

He hit the reply button and waited. His eyes fell on the box of donuts, which tempted him to open it and take another bite, but his stomach reminded him that he was already full. He refreshed the page and a new message from the same user popped up.

> *I'd ask him, but he's no longer with us. Killed himself just two days after coming back from Pineridge.*

Dean froze. He wondered for a moment if *user51734* was fucking with him. Maybe he was in cahoots with the moderators, and they were trying to build dramatic suspense by pranking unsuspecting forum members. Dean chose not to reply to the person.

He noted *Pineridge, South OR, close to Medford* and exited the forum. He typed Pineridge into the search bar. He assumed that he would get a lot of results for small towns under that name, and he was right. All sorts of results under Pineridge and Pine Ridge showed up, so Dean looked up "Pineridge Suicide Town," instead. That immediately narrowed the results.

Just like with his initial search, most of the links were dead. But then he found one result that led to a Wyoming journalist's website. His name was Joshua Bauer. The website didn't seem relevant to Dean's search at first, but when he searched *Pineridge*, he found it on the page in an article.

> *The town of Pineridge, although populated with less than 4,000 people, is extremely deadly. Reports suggest that suicide rates in the town are high, especially among older generations. One interesting legend states that visiting the*

town will curse you, causing you to commit suicide.

Next week, I will venture to Pineridge, also known as Suicide Town, in hopes of finding out more about the local legends and putting them to rest, if possible. You will find the article, along with the pictures and videos, live on my website.

The article was dated four weeks ago, with it being the newest article. Looking through the history, Joshua Bauer had posted on his website consistently every week for months before, maybe even years. So, why did he suddenly stop after posting about Suicide Town?

"What the hell is going on here?" Dean asked, scratching his cheek.

He had to get to the bottom of this. The more he found out, the more he wanted to know. It was an endless maze, leading him deeper and deeper into the belly of the beast, promising to give him the answers he coveted. Any doubts he had about writing a book about Suicide Town had long since perished. This was going to be his big break. It wasn't even just about the book anymore. It was about pioneering a dive into the mystery of an urban legend that no one apparently knew about.

He looked for Joshua Bauer's contact information. He had an email, social media, and a phone number. As much as he wanted to call him, he opted to email him.

Dear Mr. Bauer,

My name is Dean Watson, and I'm a writer. You might have read some of my books like Dark Fears, No Time to Die, or Faithless and Dead. I have read your article about you going to Pineridge (Suicide Town), which happens to be the project for my next book. I was hoping to find more information about Pineridge from your website, but I can see that you haven't posted anything about it yet. I need to know how to reach the town, so I can do my research. I heard it's located close to Medford, OR, but I need your help in confirming the exact location.

Thank you so much, and I look forward to hearing from you.

Dean Watson.

With the message sent, Dean had nothing else to do right now for his research, even though he was itching to continue investigating. He aimlessly browsed Joshua Bauer's website and then looked through the other links that he had opened in new tabs. Aside from the journalist's website, he couldn't find anything else useful.

Joshua Bauer was going to be his lifeline.

He looked up the journalist online. He was present on all the popular social media websites, frequently posting his thoughts on Twitter about billionaires hoarding money and damaging the world, as well as the downsides of capitalism. His last post was almost four weeks ago. He hadn't posted a single thing anywhere since then, but he had been online four days ago on one of the sites.

Dean exited the browser and put his laptop on the coffee table in front of him. He went into his trademark hands-on-the-back-of-the-head pose and stared at the screen displaying the wallpaper of a beach. Dean's mind raced a million thoughts an hour. It was all coming together.

He envisioned his story: a group of young people in their twenties on a road trip, accidentally taking the wrong turn and ending up in a strange town. They would try to pass through but passing through would be impossible. Things would escalate, and before the main characters knew what trouble they had gotten themselves into, it would be too late.

What the premise of the story would be—Dean didn't know. He would figure that out on the go. Right now, this idea was the only one he had, and it was stronger than any idea he had had in the past two years, so he held on to it for dear life, like a drowning man. He had to ride the wave and maintain the momentum if he hoped to put words on paper. The urge to write was insatiable, but he couldn't start just yet. He had no story outline. He had to create that first, and the best way to do it would be to visit the infamous Suicide Town. It would also get his inspiration flowing better.

He ate another donut and then lay on the couch, staring at the cracked, moldy ceiling. In his mind's eye, Suicide Town would comprise idyllic, medieval, rustic elements such as a sprinkling of dilapidated buildings, two main avenues, and a bunch of alleyways slapped together, surrounded by grassy flatlands with a view of the woods and a small, rippling stream. Elderly people would wander the town—because why would young people stay there?

Dean's eyelids felt heavy. As he drifted into a half-dreamy state, he stepped into his fabricated town. He saw different things now, too. A congregation of gray clouds clustered above the town, nooses hanging from the trees and signposts, bodies swaying in the wind while townsfolk walked past them, going on about their business.

If anything else adorned his vision, he couldn't remember it.

Chapter 5

Dean found himself in his car, driving in the middle of the night through the tunnel. Skylar was in the passenger's seat, wearing a fancy red dress that fell taut against her curves. They were driving back to the hotel from the studio where Dean was a guest on *The Tonight Show*.

Jimmy Fallon was an entertaining host. Dean had never been on a big show such as that one, so he was nervous, but Jimmy made him feel comfortable enough for the two of them to end up cracking jokes. The audience loved them, and Dean felt like he was unstoppable with all the love he was receiving from the success of his latest release.

On the way back from the studio, Dean and Skylar had stopped at a restaurant for dinner and drinks. They ended up drinking a little more than they should have. Skylar stared at Dean the entire time with a proud smile, and once they finished the first bottle of wine, that look of pride changed into a look of prurience.

Dean and Skylar were impatient to arrive home.

Skyler ran her finger down Dean's thigh. "Climbing up in the world, are you, bestseller?"

Dean looked at her, then at the road. The moment they exited the tunnel, heavy rain battered the car. The drumming on the metal drowned out the engine. The wipers did nothing to make the visibility better against the pouring sheets between each swipe as if buckets of water were constantly being spilled.

A pair of headlights approached from the distance. The other driver had honked, but as the car drove past them, instead of the siren, a high-pitched ringing screeched from the car in passing.

Dean opened his eyes; his cellphone was ringing. He shot upright and blinked furiously. He felt heavy as if he had bricks strapped to every part of his body. He reached for the phone on the coffee table and answered without looking at the caller ID.

A robotic female voice spoke, and it took Dean a moment to understand that it was an automated message. He didn't care to find out what it was about, so he ended the call. He threw the phone on the couch in frustration.

He was relieved, though. He hated witnessing the end of that dream. He always knew what would happen, but he could never do anything to stop it. Sometimes, it was different. Sometimes, he'd dream about him and Skylar in their old apartment. The outcome of his dreams was never a happy one.

Dean went to his laptop and wiggled his finger on the touchpad to wake it up. The screen remained black. *Fuck, the battery.* He reached for the charger behind the couch and plugged it into the device. His eyes fell on the box of donuts. Dean gulped through his dry mouth. A sugar craving greeted him.

He didn't resist the urge. The donuts he ate today were far from a meal replacement, but he didn't care. He would probably need to ease off on the junk food because he was gaining weight, especially since he was getting older. In his twenties, he could eat whatever and however much he wanted, and he even struggled to gain weight.

Now, just looking at a burger packed layers onto his abdomen. He still looked slim when dressed, the muscles on his arms and pecs well-defined from his athletic days of playing football in college; however, when shirtless, he had a dad bod. He forgot all about those concerns when he took the first bite of the chocolate donut.

While eating, he pressed the power button on the laptop. The screen flashed to life, displaying the email page that Dean had left it on. With the charger plugged in, and with the absence of natural light through the windows, the laptop's screen was too bright. Dean repeatedly pressed the button on the keyboard to reduce the brightness, all the while squinting.

No new emails. He refreshed the page again, hoping that the website simply froze. Nope. Nothing. Dean looked at the clock. It was seven p.m. It wasn't too late in Wyoming. He went back to Joshua Bauer's website and located his phone number.

After inputting the number in the dial screen and double-checking to make sure it was right (he often wrote down numbers wrong), Dean dialed the number. By then, he had eaten half of the donut before tossing the other half back into the box. He wiped the chocolate off his mouth and swallowed the remaining bits of the pastry.

The phone started ringing.

"Yes?" a gruff, nasally voice answered after just two rings.

Dean suddenly found that he was at a loss for words. He opened his mouth and cleared his throat to let the person know that someone was on the other end. He finally managed to utter, "Hello. Is this Joshua Bauer?"

"Yes. Who is this?"

It was a voice that could have belonged to someone Dean's age or an old man. It was impossible to tell.

"My name's Dean Watson. I'm a writer. You might have heard about me before."

Protracted silence draped the line. "Sorry, I don't believe I have." Bauer said.

Dean felt stupid for expecting a red carpet roll-out, but it could have been worse; Bauer could have known about Dean from the backlash on the news.

"That's okay, Mr. Bauer. I sent you an email earlier, but I figured I'd call you since I need information urgently."

"What kind of information?"

Dean thought he could detect caution in the man's voice. The question sounded more like "What do you want?" Either Dean had called him at a bad moment, or he didn't appreciate getting random calls from strangers.

"I read your article about going to Pineridge, aka Suicide Town. I was wondering if you'd be willing to share the location of the town." Dean paused to let Bauer process the sentence. He thought he heard a low gasp coming from Bauer's end. Then, nothing. "Mr. Bauer, are you still there?"

"I don't know what you want with that information, but if you know what's good for you, you'll stop meddling in the business of that cursed town," Bauer said. He sounded like he was out of breath. It was clear that the topic agitated him. "Stay the hell away from Suicide Town!" he added to the last sentence with a raised tone.

"Mr. Bauer, I just—"

Beep, beep, beep.

Dean looked at the phone's screen to confirm, and sure enough, Bauer had ended the call. The journalist's reaction shocked Dean. Shocked him and angered him.

He dialed the number again. Call declined. He tried once more, only reaching an automated message. "The person you are calling is unavailable. Please leave a message after the tone."

"Shit," Dean muttered.

He contemplated writing a message to the journalist, but what good would that do? He wouldn't answer. What happened to Joshua Bauer in Suicide Town? Whatever it was, it must have been traumatizing to cause such an extreme reaction. But Dean wasn't going to let the journalist off the hook just yet.

He called Alex.

Chapter 6

At first, Dean baffled Alex at his desire to find out more about some journalist. Once Dean explained that he needed that information for his book, the literary agent was more than willing to assist him. Dean wasn't even sure what kind of information he was looking for, but he was hoping Alex could find out what had happened to Joshua Bauer in Suicide Town.

Alex assured him that he would do everything he can to find out where this Suicide Town was, then they ended the call. Dean did research of his own for the rest of the day. Later that night, he went out to buy coffee, energy drinks, and some food because he wasn't going to get any sleep tonight.

After hours of digging yielded miserable information, Dean managed to find out that Pineridge used to be more populated back in the seventies, but a mass suicide had vastly decreased the town's population. Nobody knew the cause of the mass suicides. He also found out that Suicide Town wasn't just one town.

It was actually two tiny towns put together, so in a sense, Pineridge was only a district, so to say. They called the other district Raintown. Dean didn't know how Raintown fit into the whole picture and why Pineridge was more prominently known.

He fell asleep around four a.m., wanting to do more research, despite his dreary eyes. He awoke to the sound of his phone ringing. Still half-comatose, he fumbled for it but couldn't find it anywhere. Eventually, he located it on the floor, tucked under the couch. He answered with a raspy voice and listened in confusion as Alex spoke in what sounded like a foreign language.

Dean told him to give him a moment to wake up, and then his brain slowly churned into action. The words that Alex spoke gradually gained some meaning, and Dean could finally understand the sentence.

"I couldn't get in touch with the journalist, but I have his wife's phone number," Alex said. "You might want to call her. I'll send you the number in a bit. If you want, I can also call her in your name."

"No, that's fine. I'll do it. What did you say her name was?"

"Marianne. If she's not responsive, then we might have to leave them alone because we're harassing them."

"Yeah. Thanks, Alex."

As tempted as Dean was to call Marianne immediately, he decided to give himself some time to wake up. He didn't want to come off as a drunkard, but he also wanted to react and defuse the journalist's wife if need be. He dreaded her reaction.

It was only nine a.m., and despite the lack of sleep, Dean felt okay for now. He brushed his teeth, put all the empty cans of energy drinks and empty wrappers into the trash bag, then brewed coffee. The only edible thing in the apartment aside from the eggs were the leftover donuts. Two were still intact, so Dean ate one for breakfast. By then, Alex had sent him a message with Marianne Bauer's phone number, and he was then ready for the phone call.

He dialed the number and held his breath. Outside his apartment, the occasional car driving by and a distant police siren echoed. The phone rang. Dean swallowed and licked his dry lips. A soft, feminine voice interrupted the fourth ring.

"Hello?" Marianne said in a small, barely discernible tone.

"Hi. Am I speaking to Marianne Bauer?"

"Yes, who is this?" Marianne asked, her tone still dead.

"My name's Dean. I tried reaching out to your husband, Joshua, yesterday, but he was unavailable. I was hoping to speak to you, instead."

"I'm sorry," Marianne said with a cracked voice. "My husband is no longer with us, as of yesterday."

An iron ball dropped to the pit of Dean's stomach. He was sitting, and it was a good thing, too, because his legs were wobbly, like cooked noodles.

His voice quivered. "I'm sorry . . . what did you say?"

"Joshua committed suicide yesterday," Marianne said as she sobbed into the phone. "I just don't . . . He hadn't been himself lately, but to do this . . ." She sniffled and gasped.

He killed himself?

Dean could not utter a single word. Marianne's crying came as if through a tunnel. His mind stopped working in an instant, like a house suffering a power outage. Thoughts clouded his mind. Could he have inadvertently caused Joshua Bauer's suicide by mentioning the town? No, that was ridiculous.

"Mrs. Bauer, I am really sorry for your loss. I had no idea. I know this is really difficult for you, but do you happen to know why he did it?"

Marianne stopped weeping and exhaled. Dean thought for a second that he might have crossed the line with that question. But then Marianne said, "No. That's the thing. Joshua was not suicidal. He was a happy man. We have a five-year-old son, and we're expecting another child, and . . ."

She broke into another sobbing fit.

Dean didn't know what to say to make her feel better. Nothing he said could have alleviated the pain of this situation. Her husband was gone, just like that, without any explanation, leaving her to take care of her son and unborn child. Her life was going to be very hard.

Things could have been worse, Dean thought. *It could have been her child.* As soon as that thought ruminated, he shoved it away, ashamed of himself for thinking that.

"You said that he'd been acting strange lately. What did you mean by that?" he asked.

Marianne sniffled a few times, the snorting loud in Dean's ear. "Ever since he returned from his trip to that town—"

"Suicide Town?"

"Yes," Marianne exclaimed with a calm voice. "Ever since he returned from that town, he hasn't been the same."

That town. Dean sensed hesitation in Marianne's sentence. She refused to call the town by its name. Perhaps she was afraid to utter "suicide" because it would mean facing reality. Perhaps she refused to believe that her husband, a happy family man, would do something so unspeakable, leaving her and their children alone to fend for themselves.

"Mrs. Bauer, do you happen to know where your husband went on that trip?" Dean asked.

"I don't know. It was somewhere in Oregon," Marianne said and sniffled again. She had stopped sobbing, and her voice was somewhat calmer, albeit still quavering.

"You don't happen to know the exact location, do you?" he insisted, even though the answer was already clear.

"I'm sorry." She confirmed his suspicion.

"That's okay," Dean said, disappointed. "Do you happen to know if he kept any notes or anything like that? Anything at all that might tell me where the town was located?" He knew that he was being pushy, but this was his last chance to find something out from Joshua's wife. Once the call ends, there would be no second chances.

"He kept all his work files upstairs in a folder on his laptop, but I don't understand why you would want to know more about it." Her voice became stern. "If you plan to sensationalize my husband's death—"

"No, nothing like that, Mrs. Bauer. I'm not after a good scoop. I simply want to get to the bottom of this. Other people who have gone to that place have committed suicide, just like your husband, despite not having a reason to do so. I need to know why."

He chose not to elaborate further. If Marianne asked him why he wanted to know more about the town, he would have to lie. He couldn't tell her that it was for his book. But in a way, it wasn't just for his book anymore. Now, more than ever, Suicide Town's mystery pulled him into the whirlwind, and the only way he would get out would be by getting the answers he sought.

Marianne remained quiet for a moment. She was going to refuse; Dean was sure of it. She was going to defend her late husband's honor and then end the call. What came instead was Marianne sucking in a sharp breath and saying, "I'll send everything my husband worked on to your email address."

Dean nodded, silently breathing in relief and excitement. He recited his email address to Marianne and then repeated it once more, just to make sure she got it right.

"Okay. I'll send it to you in a few minutes."

"Thank you so much, Marianne. If I find any answers, I'll be sure to share them with you."

Marianne sobbed a little more. She thanked Dean, and they ended the call. Dean lowered the phone from his face and stared into space. His ears were ringing with a distant echo. Did the conversation with Marianne even happen?

Joshua Bauer? Suicide? What could drive a man to do such a thing? Marianne claims that Joshua wasn't suicidal. Was it the town? Did it do something to him? No, couldn't be the town, but it might have been the people. Maybe Joshua saw something over there that scarred him so badly that he decided to take his own life. Or maybe the town has some noxious gases coming either from the ground or the mines, causing everyone to become suicidal or depressed.

Suddenly, Suicide Town seemed a lot more dangerous than the urban legends on the internet. Dean wasn't afraid of committing suicide. His instinct to survive was so strong that he doubted there could be anything in the world that would wobble his will for self-preservation.

What worried him was the townsfolk. Joshua Bauer had safely made it back from Suicide Town, but what if it was a close call? What if the townsfolk had tried to kill him, or worse? Maybe they tortured him, and once he was broken, they released him to go back home?

Dean was too far invested in this legend to back down now. He would see it through to the end. A part of him told him that he could simply write a story based on the information he had. He had more than enough material to go on, but Dean wasn't that kind of writer.

He wouldn't want to write some mediocre story because it sounded like a good idea. He didn't even want to write a good story. He wanted to write an amazing story that people would remember for years to come. To do that, he needed more research, and the best way he would get his research done would be by visiting the town.

Not to mention, he wouldn't be doing it just for the book. Once he returns from Suicide Town, he would answer the questions about Suicide Town that everybody on the internet has been asking all this time. It would no longer be a censored urban legend with fragments of information.

Dean would crack the mystery of why everyone who went to Suicide Town committed suicide.

Chapter 7

The email page displayed on his laptop's screen automatically refreshed, and a new message appeared in his inbox. Dean leaned forward with alacrity and clicked on the message. It was an email from Joshua Bauer. The message was devoid of text except one link.

Dean clicked the link, and it took him to a shared folder. His eyes widened, and he felt like he had won the lottery. A plethora of files beckoned him. Text documents, audio files, video files, pictures—Dean had access to all of it.

"Yes!" He rubbed his palms together and then put the laptop in his lap and leaned back on the couch.

Since the files were dated, Dean decided to check them out chronologically. The first one on the list was an audio file. Dean double-clicked to play it. No sound came through, so Dean turned up the volume. The familiar gruff voice of Joshua Bauer boomed from the speakers, startling Dean.

"I have just arrived in Pineridge, also known as Suicide Town. I don't see anyone on the streets, but it feels as though I'm being closely watched. It's rainy here, and only here. It was sunny up until the moment I crossed the threshold to the town. I will now proceed to find the closest hotel, motel, or bar, if there are any."

The audio file ended. Next in line was a picture. When Dean opened it, he saw a shot of a street curving to the right and disappearing downhill on the horizon. On the right side of the road was an array of short buildings huddled together like sardines. Parked cars sat in front of the building. The road was wet from the rain, and the sky was overcast. In the foggy distance, tree-covered hills stretched out of view.

The next picture showed another street shot. The road was empty, and what looked like shops lined both sides of the street. This time, the droplets of rain were clearly visible under the streetlight. Hundreds, if not thousands, of those streets riddled the big city. In a small town like Pineridge, it was probably the main avenue.

After closing the picture, Dean opened a text document, probably impromptu notes that Joshua Bauer took as he went around the town.

> *Finding the town was difficult. The GPS refused to cooperate. No matter how many times I pinpointed the exact location of Suicide Town, it refused to take me there. I had to follow the map I found online. On my way into the town, I was pulled over by a police officer. He warned me that the road ahead was blocked until I gave him the password. He then let me through, but reluctantly.*
>
> *PASSWORD: JUST PASSING THROUGH*

Dean frowned. Finding Suicide Town was more complicated than he originally thought. Not only would he need to find the exact location of the town, but he would need to complete certain steps to be able to get to it. He sardonically thought to himself how he hoped that he wouldn't need to complete a whole ritual that required sacrificing a goat or a virgin.

Another picture followed the document. This was a map. A small red cross marked a spot just West of Medford. The guy on the internet was right. It was, indeed, close to Medford. Coordinates were written below. Dean snapped a picture of the map with his phone and wrote the coordinates into his notebook. He then opened maps in a new tab and input the coordinates.

After comparing the location on the map with the one in Joshua's picture, Dean deduced it was exactly the same. Upon clicking the Directions button, the GPS estimated how long it would take him to get there by car, but the route cut off before reaching the destination. It took him West of Medford and then just stopped upon reaching the end of a road.

Dean decided he would circle back to that a bit later. Luck had it that Joshua's next file gave him detailed directions to the town. The text document explained in bullet points how to reach Suicide Town.

> *I-5 to Oregon RV Outlet, then turn left toward Merlin.*
>
> *Follow Galice Road to Rogue River Scenic Waterway.*
>
> *Turn left onto unmarked road.*

Multiple rows sat below the initial three, but Dean would study them in detail later. Either way, he had an exact route that would help him reach Suicide Town, and for that, he was grateful to Joshua. The next file was a video. That excited Dean even more because it meant he would get to see way more. He double-clicked, and it started playing.

The camera showed the interior of a bedroom. The lamp was on, casting a dusky light. The shot wobbled and became fuzzy as the person holding the camera panted and shuffled across the room with loud footsteps. The camera then pointed at the window. The blinds were pulled down so tight that not a sliver of light came through.

"I've been in the town for three days now," Joshua, who was evidently the cameraman, said. "I'm staying in the motel, room eleven. The people here are definitely hiding something. Every night, at the exact same time, something happens outside my window. There's someone walking outside, but I can't look. The townsfolk warned me that I can't, under any circumstances, look outside the window."

Joshua's short breaths made Dean wonder if it was from physical exertion or from something else. The camera momentarily shook, blurring everything in the image. It then stabilized and pointed to the corner of the room right next to the window.

"It's about to happen. Listen," Joshua said.

Joshua's breathing draped the background. Dean squinted on a whim as if to help him hear better. First, silence stole the show. But then he heard it. Something muffled in the distance. Something that sounded like a jingle. It rattled, stopped, then rattled again. Each time, it amplified. Dean held his breath.

It wasn't jingling; it was metallic clinking. Chains, maybe? They sounded like they were being dragged on the ground. The rattling was so loud that Dean half-expected whatever was causing it to appear in the camera's frame. Just as slowly as it came, it faded into the distance, each pause bringing it farther and farther from the camera.

"Listen," Joshua said.

The clinking stopped, silence enveloping the air. Dean became aware of his heavy breathing, so he slowed it down. An animalistic wail yanked the breath out of him. The scream sounded like it could have belonged to either a man or a woman. It drowned out all the other noises. It was drawn out and sounded tormented, maintaining a crescendo, sending shivers down Dean's spine.

He suddenly felt like the scream was warning him or bringing with it a danger, and he was compelled to look around the room, just to make sure he was still alone. The caterwaul descended in intensity until it faded into nothingness, but its echo still reverberated in Dean's head, bouncing inside his skull like a tennis ball.

The scream, whatever it was, left him feeling small and vulnerable. He looked around the room again. He was grateful that he watched the video in the daytime. That feeling seemed mutual to that of the cameraman, the camera trembling so violently that the frame became blurred. His breathing was more audible, too. He sounded like he had just finished a workout.

"You hear that?" Joshua asked. "I'm not crazy. It happens every single night. It's not always in the same place or at the same time, but I can always hear it. They told me not to look. Tomorrow, I'm going to sneak a peek. There's no way they will know."

The video ended, showing the frozen frame of the corner of the room. Dean stared at the blurry yellow walls and a dirty carpet. The aftershock of the scream still shook Dean's body. The temperature of the room had dropped by twenty degrees. The chill subsided, and he chided himself for reacting that way to a video.

It was a creepy video, yeah, but there was a logical explanation for it. The townsfolk of Suicide Town, who probably rarely—or never—get any visitors, decided to play a prank on the outsider and further feed into the urban legend. But then, why did Joshua commit suicide? What if it wasn't suicide at all but murder?

No, that was a ridiculous thought. It was one of those fleeting millisecond thoughts that had no logic behind them. Yet, for some reason, Dean wondered if it was the case. He reprimanded himself for being so paranoid. He hadn't slept enough, and he'd been investigating Suicide Town too much. Coupled with the fact that mystery had enshrouded the town, it was no wonder he had those kinds of delusional thoughts.

Dean went on to the next file. It was another audio recording.

"I'm seeing things," Joshua said. He sounded, again, like he was out of breath, and he spoke with an erratic and quickened tone. "I can't explain it, exactly, but I'm seeing stuff. Most of the time, I look at something and vividly see myself ending my life. For example, when a truck drove down the street, I could clearly see myself jumping in front of the truck and getting myself splattered. I hadn't even realized that I had taken a step on the road until Lawrence yanked me back. I would have continued walking, and the truck would have killed me. On top of that, I keep hearing a voice in my head. A woman's voice. I think it's her. I think it's her. She wants me to do things. Something is not right with this town, but nobody wants to talk about it. I don't think it's safe for me to stay anymore."

With the audio file reaching an end, Dean opened the next video. It was a ten-second-long video of the road in Suicide Town at night, filmed from a car's interior. The engine roared, indicating that the person driving was speeding too much. It was raining, and the visibility was poor. The headlights illuminated something as it ran past them at an incredible speed; the sound of screeching tires followed as the car came to a halt.

With the car at a standstill, someone's panting echoed in the car. Joshua's, Dean assumed. The camera picked up increments of shuffling noises, then the video stopped. Dean replayed the video. He refused to blink when the animal ran across the beams. It was too fast, and he couldn't tell what it was. A deer, maybe?

He replayed the video, slowing the playback speed to half this time. He still couldn't identify the animal. Too blurry. He couldn't even tell if it was on all fours. He paused the video the moment the silhouette came in contact with the headlights. Two glowing dots stared back at the camera. If Dean thought it was a deer, it could have been a deer. But if he imagined the figure standing upright, he could almost see a bipedal creature running across the beams and disappearing in the darkness off the road.

Dean closed the video. Only one more file remained, and it was a text document. He opened it.

STAY OUT OF SUICIDE TOWN

Dean rubbed his nose's bridge and stared at the sentence. He wondered if it was perhaps an encrypted password or something. No, more like the ravings of a man who had lost his mind. Something terrible happened to Joshua Bauer in Suicide Town.

Dean was determined to find out what it was.

Chapter 8

After informing Alex that he would be away for a few days on a small trip, Dean went out to buy brunch. He stopped at a nearby diner where he had pancakes and coffee. While eating, he looked up information about Raintown on his phone. As it was with Pineridge, and the entire Suicide Town, he found nothing concrete.

Dean felt like a new man. He felt like he had opened a new door that he didn't even know existed, and behind that door was what he was looking for this entire time. He had been stuck in a cesspool of self-pity for a long time after the accident, and at times, he thought he was never going to be able to write again.

He had tried writing stories in the past two years, but whenever he found himself in front of the laptop, he would stare at the blank screen. He tried to write in different genres. He wrote starting sentences, just to kick-start the story, but then he would delete them, and write another one that sounded wrong, and he would end up slamming his laptop shut in frustration.

One thing that worried Dean was what was going to happen after he finished the story of Suicide Town. He hadn't thought about it actively, but he hoped that finishing this book would cause a chain reaction and help him write more books after that. He refused to believe that he would suffer writer's block again after this book.

Upon returning from the diner, Dean went back to his laptop to double-check all the information that he had received from Joshua's email. He downloaded all the files so that he could view them without the internet. He didn't know what Suicide Town's internet would be like or if they even had it. From the pictures, the town seemed modern enough to have electricity, but Dean couldn't help but feel like it was a town frozen in a certain era.

If he immersed himself enough while he was there, he would stay to write. Dean generally liked visiting small towns, but he disliked staying in them for too long. Still, this trip wasn't for his own pleasure; it was for business but also for investigation. He owed Marianne some answers about her husband's premature death, and he planned on finding out everything he could.

It was a little late to go on the trip now, but Dean decided to pack the essentials and be ready in the morning. He didn't need too many things. He packed some non-perishable food and water, fresh clothes to last him a week, a flashlight, a portable charger for his phone, his notepad, and a dozen pens; he had no idea which ones would randomly decide to run out of ink.

After double-checking if he had everything in his suitcase, Dean closed it and put the suitcase on the floor next to the couch. Around that time, Iris called him. The screen hadn't displayed her name, but he remembered the phone number's final digits from her final call. He let it ring. Whatever it was could wait.

Not a minute later, his phone rang again. Dean didn't even bother looking at who it was. He went around the apartment, opening drawers, checking if he needed anything else for the trip. It felt foreign preparing for a trip since he hadn't had one in a while. Having thought about it, it had been months since he had left Gresham. The last time he had a trip was about six months ago, when he went to Oswego Lake for a hike for inspiration. But a multiple-day trip? The last one he had was with Skylar.

That was also one reason why it was so foreign preparing for the trip. Skylar was the one who did all the packing. She would always pack way too early, so Dean wouldn't even get the chance to help her. Eventually, it became a ritual for them—he would book a trip, and she would pack everything for the both of them.

At the same time, Dean had more control now. He would at least know where he put each item without having to rummage through the luggage to find it. And unlike Skylar, he packed light. Not to mention that he wouldn't need to stop for a five-minute coffee break whenever an interesting landmark on the side of the road caught Skylar's eye.

A million tiny things had irked Dean that Skylar had done during their trips. Yet, he couldn't stop a twinge in his heart at the thought of the two of them driving into Suicide Town together.

A ping came from Dean's phone, informing him that he had got a new message, so he checked it out. He rarely received messages, and when he did, it was from companies promoting products and informing him of discounts. As if the universe had heard his thoughts, when he unlocked his phone, he saw that he had a message from Skylar.

Please call me when you get the chance.

Dean checked the missed calls. One was from Iris and the other from Skylar. "Shit," Dean mumbled under his breath. *Please call me when you get the chance.* The message conveyed urgency, or at least that's how Dean had perceived it. Did something happen? His mind immediately raced to figure out what's the worst thing that could have happened to Skylar.

Maybe she was in an accident. Maybe one of her parents had died. Maybe she needed some financial help. *No, Skylar would starve before asking you for money.* Then maybe she just wants to . . . talk. About what? Dean killed his hope of her having a change of heart.

Since he was done packing, he wanted to focus on finalizing his research and arranging his notes before the actual trip. The problem was that the nagging sensation that something happened to Skylar would derail his concentration. He would finish the phone call first and then focus on his stuff.

As he tapped the button to call Skylar and pressed the phone against his ear, nervousness crept up on him. The phone rang once, twice, three times. Dean figured that Skylar was absent and would call him when she got the chance. Tentative relief flooded him when a click interrupted the fifth ring.

"Hello?" a gentle, feminine voice said on the line.

Dean had still remembered her voice in his mind's eye, but it was only a distant echo compared to the how it actually sounded. When he heard her voice over the phone after such a long time, it shoved him back into the past, into happier times, back when he and Skylar had a future together.

Her voice dredged up the regret that had been eating away at him for the past two years. With all the frustration and anger gone, the picture was clear; he wished he had acted differently when he had the chance. He wished for Skylar to know that. But that wouldn't change anything, anyway.

"Hi, Sky," Dean said, trying to sound as calm and as indifferent as he possibly could. "You called me?"

"Yeah," Skylar said. "I've been meaning to call you for a few days now, but things have been busy."

Things have been busy. It was the way she said it that caused something to stir inside Dean, forcing him to grit his teeth. Why didn't she just come out and openly say what that meant? He already knew, and he hoped that she would tell him, but it was obvious that, between the two of them, she was the one who had moved on.

"Yeah, I understand," Dean said, pushing down an otherwise passive-aggressive tone. He then chided himself for being so toxic right from the get-go. *It's no wonder she fucking left you,* a nagging voice in his head said. "So, um . . . why did you want me to call?" He asked, fumbling to find the right words that would not make him sound accusatory.

"Alex called me," Skylar said, and Dean knew immediately what this was going to be about. "He didn't want to tell me at first, but I hear you're about to start writing again. Congratulations."

Dean realized with another painful twist in his heart that it sounded so formal. It sounded exactly like what she would tell other writers with whom Dean was acquainted. It was how she spoke with strangers.

"Thanks. I haven't started yet, but I'm getting some inspiration, so we'll see."

He imagined himself going to book signings, talk shows, and award shows again, and the thought of going there alone further exacerbated the pang in his heart. Would any of it even be worth it without Sky by his side? These emotions were alien to him. How was it possible that he had managed to suppress these feelings for so long? He had concluded that he would never write again after the accident, and he believed in it one hundred percent. When he discovered it might change, it reeled in new emotions with which his brain hadn't dealt before.

"Well, I'm really happy for you, Dean. I'm sure this new book is gonna hit the bestseller list."

"Fingers crossed."

A moment of awkward silence deadened the conversation. That kind of silence didn't exist even on their first date. Back then, the silence between them was soothing. Dean realized that Skylar didn't call him just to congratulate him. That wasn't like her. No, it must have been something else.

"So, uh . . ." Dean started. "Yeah. How are things on your end?"

"Oh, good. You know, the usual," Skylar said.

The usual. Anger boiled inside Dean again. It was so obvious that she was hiding something, but she refused to tell Dean about it. Why? To not hurt his feelings?

"How are things with your new boyfriend?" Dean asked with a rictus. He knew that he came off as passive-aggressive, which wasn't his intention. Or maybe it was. He wasn't sure. Skylar paused. Noticing it, Dean jumped in to add, "It's okay. Alex told me."

"That snitch. He can't not spill the beans on anything," Skylar said with a nervous chuckle, but Dean knew her well enough to detect anger in her voice. "I'm sorry, Dean. I didn't want you to find out about it."

"Why? I mean, we both knew it was going to happen. It was just a matter of time," Dean said with a raised voice. He was standing by the window, his fingers wedged under the sill, pulling up at it in repetitive motion. The sun appeared from behind the clouds and hit Dean in the face, forcing him to gravitate his gaze toward the windowsill.

"I had to move on. You can't blame me for that," Skylar said.

"I don't," he said. But he did blame her, and as much as he wanted to tell her a million things, that would escalate the conversation as well as his anger, and it would end with both of them yelling over each other.

No, that's not how it would end. She would need to care in order to yell. She would drop the ball, let him yell as long as he wanted, then calmly end the conversation. He would then feel like shit. That's how every conversation they had seemed to end in the last days of their marriage.

You know what? You're right, Dean. Whatever you say, you're right. I can't deal with this shit anymore.

"Listen," Dean said. "I know you didn't call me just to congratulate me. Alex snitches on everyone and everything, so I assume he told you where I was headed. And that's why you're calling, right?"

Skylar paused again, then inhaled. "Yes, that's why I'm calling. He told me what happened to that journalist. Dean, I really think you shouldn't go to that place. It sounds dangerous."

The anger remained, stagnant and unwavering. He hadn't written in two fucking years, and when he could finally write, she told him not to go on with his research. It made him want to do it even more, just to spite her.

"It's going to be fine, ba—I'll be okay." He tripped on "babe" out of habit. He hoped she didn't notice it.

Skylar sighed. "All right. Just please be careful over there. Maybe you should get some protection, just to be on the safe side."

"All right. I'll see what I can do about it." He patronized her. If she still knew him, she would be able to tell that he was bullshitting her. But Sky didn't object.

"Okay. Well, I hope everything goes well with your new book. I'll be sure to preorder it as soon as it's available," Skylar said in a jovial yet somber tone.

"Thanks," Dean said. He wanted to say, "*You always were my number one fan,*" but he didn't want it to come off as flirting. "You take care of yourself, Sky."

"You, too, Dean. Be seeing you around."

The call ended. Dean noticed that his hand was trembling violently. The conversation with Skylar was so formal, so cold. What microscopic hope Dean had that his ex-wife still cared about him vanished with a phone call. He felt like a moron for even thinking the tiniest chance for them to ever get back together existed. He knew, of course, that it would never happen, but a tiny candle buried somewhere deep within him, its light flickering, fought not to get extinguished.

Now, it was gone.

Dean couldn't dwell on the past. He had a book to write, and he would see it through to the end, no matter how dangerous it was.

Chapter 9

He got little sleep that night, tossing and turning in bed. While he slept, images of Suicide Town visited him. Something decrepit and old, dragging itself through the streets, emulating the scream from Joshua's video plagued Dean's dreams.

His dreams shifted to the car scene with Skylar. They were driving down the rainy road after the talk show, but Skylar wasn't as affectionate as Dean remembered. She sat ramrod straight in her seat, staring ahead.

"There's someone else now," she said.

"So, you're just going to leave me? After everything we've been through?"

The rain was so strong that it flooded the street. The water level rose with each passing second.

"Yes. I can't deal with your shit anymore," Skylar said in a calm tone without looking at him. "All you do is yell and break things. You're not the same man I married, Dean."

Dean's tears contributed to the rain, elevating the water level, submerging the car. Muffled water acoustics filled the interior. A blue glow from the water cast onto Skylar's face, but she continued staring ahead of her. Dean cried harder and harder, but his cries fell on deaf ears.

Dean, covered in a cold sweat, opened his eyes to his dark bedroom. The dream almost felt real, and he was relieved to be awake. The reality was hardly any different, though. Skylar cared about someone else now. Dean was no longer the most important person in her life, and that thought hurt him like nothing else.

He couldn't fall asleep after that.

Eventually, he got out of bed and wandered into the kitchen to eat some sweets. It was four a.m., and even after eating until he was full, which usually made him drowsy, he couldn't fall asleep. He spent an hour tossing from one side to the other, replaying in his head his conversation with Skylar, as well as the dream.

There's someone else now, Skylar's voice hissed in his head. *Congratulations. I hope everything goes well with your book.*

Emotions often hit Dean too late. He would feel nothing at first, unaware that it would simmer inside him for a while until they suddenly started bothering him. That's what it was like regarding his phone conversation with Sky.

He thought he wasn't affected too much by it, but the lack of sleep was evidence that it bothered him more than he cared to admit. After more tossing and turning, he thought maybe sleep wouldn't come anymore. Even if it did, he would end up sleeping in, which meant he'd run late for his trip to Suicide Town.

He got out of bed for a cold shower. The icy water washed away the remnants of sluggishness that imbued him, and he was more than ready for his trip than ever. It was almost six a.m. by the time he ate breakfast—he had milk and cereal—and upon checking to see if he had everything, he was finally ready to go.

It was still dark outside. This part of Gresham was relatively calm, and during these hours, it was a ghost town. It felt empty but tranquil. Dean wondered if Suicide Town was going to be like that. He shuffled into the driver's seat and turned on the GPS.

He input Joshua's coordinates, and despite the GPS only leading him a part of the entire trip, Dean decided he would follow the I-5 until he reached the first checkpoint.

Since Dean's car was almost out of gas, he refilled the tank at the nearest gas station. Once he was on the interstate, he turned on the radio and flipped through the channels. It was too early for any talk shows or news, and since Dean didn't feel like listening to music, he ended up turning off the radio.

As soon as tall trees replaced concrete buildings, tranquility draped over Dean. It felt good to be driving on the freeway, surrounded by nature. His inspirational juices flowed, and he, once again, felt the irresistible urge to write.

Ideas saturated his creativity. Not only did he know what to write about, but the plot unfolded as his mind raced with ideas. They were all jumbled up at that moment, but once he organized them, the story would be more coherent. He wouldn't be able to use all his ideas, though. That was okay; he could use them at another time.

Dawn came soon, and Dean slowed down to admire the red sunrise on the horizon that bathed the scenery in shades of marigold. Dean wished that he was an early bird so that he could revel in the sunrise more often. He had tried doing that in the past, and he managed to do so three days in a row before becoming too tired from the accumulated lack of sleep.

Dean occasionally glanced at the map to check his progress. When he first turned on the GPS, it told him that he would need about five hours to reach the destination. That was probably going to stretch to around six hours, since Dean wasn't a fast driver, and he would take at least one or two breaks at gas stations for breakfast.

The sun crawled up the sky, the hues of red that colored the road gone. It was a nice day. Would Suicide Town project the same exuberance? With each mile closer to the town, he couldn't help but feel underprepared. How would he interview the townsfolk? He didn't even prepare questions, and if he wanted to ask about Joshua Bauer, he would need to phrase those questions in such a way to get the best possible answers.

A little after ten, on his way out of Canyonville, his phone on the passenger's seat rang. Dean took it into his hand while focusing on the road, and Iris's familiar number greeted him on the screen. He groaned as he flicked the button to decline the call and dropped it back on the passenger's seat.

"What the fuck do you want, Iris?" Dean said to himself. "Just send me a fucking message."

He was sure that Iris didn't want anything important. She might have been itching to persuade him to publish with her instead of Dark Curtains. Whatever it was, Dean didn't need to answer the call to know that the offer wouldn't be tempting.

A little before reaching Merlin, clouds swarmed the sky, blocking the sunlight that had grown somewhat bothersome by then. He was close to the RV Outlet where he would need to start following Joshua's instructions. With that in mind, Dean slowed down.

A gas station was on his right, so he decided to stop. He had already taken one break a few hours before, at a diner where he had coffee, but sleep was starting to creep behind his eyelids. He needed more coffee. He was too eager to arrive in Suicide Town, so he didn't stay longer than fifteen minutes.

By then, yesterday's phone call with Skylar had fallen into oblivion, and Dean was solely focused on

Suicide Town. As mesmerizing as the scenery was, driving on the I-5, Galice Road was even more interesting. Dean couldn't help but admire the enormous cabins on the side of the road, the ancient bridges, and the tree-covered slopes that extended upward on the rock wall on the right side and downward below the cliff on the left side. It all yielded material to write in his book, to make the story more immersive and realistic.

Dean followed the instructions that he had written in the notebook to a tee, double-checking each bullet point that Joshua Bauer had written. The asphalted road went farther on, curving to the right, but Dean had to turn on the unpaved narrow road on the left.

As soon as he got onto the dirt road, he had to slow down the car because it trundled and bounced violently. Dean wasn't sure if the car would even survive the journey because it'd been so long since he took it to a mechanic. The road would not get any better from here, so the car just needed to make it to Suicide Town.

The GPS on his phone pinged, warning him that he had taken a wrong turn. "In one hundred feet, make a U-turn," the female robotic voice said. Dean ignored it. Every couple of hundred feet, the GPS repeatedly dinged to inform Dean he was going the wrong way and then the lady's voice would suggest where to turn.

Dean picked up the phone to see where he was. The map displayed a blue dot that represented him, in the middle of nowhere, off Galice Road. According to the map, no road existed there, and he was in the middle of the woods, but so far, everything Joshua Bauer had written was correct. Dean had no reason to believe the instructions would lead him anywhere in the wrong direction. He turned off the GPS. It was of no use to him here. Not anymore.

He wondered why the GPS was trying so hard to turn him around. He didn't believe in the paranormal, so he assumed that there must have been a logical reason as to why he was being turned around. He was too absorbed in finding the right path to Suicide Town to care about that right now.

The road more and more became like a maze. Dean often had to stop and read the instructions multiple times to make sure he wasn't making the wrong turn. Most of the paths were unmarked here, and not only did he need to memorize where he turned but also what bullet point he was on. It was so easy to get confused.

Aside from the labyrinth, darkness enshrouded the road. Encroaching pines and mulberries allowed wisps of sunlight to pierce the foliage. By the time Dean had realized it, the path he drove through was so narrow that he feared he might need to leave his car and walk from there. He had no idea how much longer he had until he reached Suicide Town. Between some bullet points on the list, there was barely a hundred-foot distance, but for others, the road stretched for a solid ten minutes of driving before reaching another fork.

It was when Dean reached the second-to-last point on the list that the road widened and merged with asphalt again. The old road was beaten, overgrown with roots and grass, and riddled with potholes. A concrete road was good news; Dean was getting somewhere. He could also see past the rows and rows of endless tree trunks that blocked his view and left him in the darkness. The road climbed toward the horizon where it met with the rhino-colored sky. From this angle, it looked as if it ended there, only endless space stretching beyond.

Knowing that it was an intriguing but ridiculous thought, Dean sped up. The sharp jump off the road never came, and Dean, instead, found his car ascending a grade and then, just as slowly, descending it. With the road wider and the trees out of the way, the sky became clearer. Black clouds hovered in one particular spot in the distance. The rest of the sky had gray clouds thinly spread above the forested area.

Dean looked at the notes and read the final bullet point on the list. *Past the old gas station and then left.*

He was close now. Just a little longer. Buoyancy overwhelmed him at the thought of reaching his destination. He felt like he was in search of a long-lost historical city. The fact that the town hid from the maps made the sense of achievement even greater.

Dean looked at the watch. It was almost one p.m. He hoped that shops in Suicide Town didn't close early. He continued driving on the ramshackle road for another ten minutes before seeing a gas station on his left. He would have completely missed it had he not slowed down and scoured both directions.

The gas station—if it was even that—was a tiny, dilapidated house, overgrown with vines. The rotted door struggled to grasp its lower hinges, and boards covered the only window. Tall grass enveloped the area near the pump and the pump itself, and the roof had rusted beyond recognition. The view drew in his admiration. The scene looked like something straight out of an apocalypse movie.

A part of him expected that the gas station operate and that he would find one lonesome, awkward employee sitting behind the counter—someone who would give Dean directions to the town. This was way more interesting.

Once he had basked in the landscape, Dean drove off. A few hundred feet ahead, he ran into another forked road. One continued leading straight toward the horizon, and the other turned left. Both asphalt roads were equally in bad condition. Dean double-checked the note. *Past the old gas station and then left.*

Although intrigued as to where the road leading straight led, he didn't have the time or the patience to explore it right now. He steered left and sped up. The path led him across a bridge on a creek. The farther he went, the darker the skies became. He soon realized that he was driving toward the mass of black clouds from earlier.

Sure enough, the first tapping sounds came above him, informing him that he was driving into an area with rain. It was not strong enough for him to have to turn on his wipers, but the road here was wet, the potholes filled with black water. Dean swerved around them as much as he could, unaware of their depth.

He was so close to Suicide Town that he could almost feel it. He pressed his foot on the gas, impatience seizing the better of him. The rain intensified, forcing Dean to flick the windshield wipers on. Driving on this old, battered road during rainfall reminded him of that fateful night that changed his life forever.

How was he supposed to know it would happen? It was an empty strip of road in the middle of nowhere, late at night. That kid just came out of nowhere. For the first few months since it happened, it plagued Dean every night. He would wake up, covered in cold sweat, hyperventilating, but Skylar tried to be there for him.

She couldn't do much for him, though. He saw the look in her eyes. She had blamed him as much as he had blamed himself. In return, Dean retreated into himself, reluctant to express his feelings to her in such a vulnerable state. As a chain reaction, a gap wedged itself between their marriage, inducing coldness and detachment.

Bouts of anger riddled with Dean's depression that he'd never experienced before. He would snap at Skylar for the smallest things, and that soon escalated into breaking objects. When Skylar couldn't take it anymore, she left. She had a lot of anger in her, too. She had told him how it was all his fault and that he was dragging her down, making her miserable because he himself was miserable. That hurt more than facing the ramifications of his actions.

He hadn't even realized how fast his car was going until the flashing blue lights appeared in his rearview mirror.

Chapter 10

Where did the cops even come from? They must have had a secluded spot where they parked, waiting to ambush someone. There was nowhere adequate to park the car on the side of the road as far as Dean could see, so he slowed down to stop. The vehicle behind him stopped as well, and when Dean turned off his car's engine, the blue lights stopped flashing.

Dean rolled down his window, letting in a cool waft of air as well as the occasional droplets of rain. He put his hands on the steering wheel and stared at the side-view mirror. A figure stepped out of the police car and prudently walked toward Dean. Dean then remembered Joshua Bauer's notes. They weren't here to stop speeding drivers. They were here to make sure no one entered Suicide Town.

As the police officer approached, Dean could see that it was a tall, gangly man around his age.

He stopped next to Dean's car and stooped to see him clearly. "Good afternoon, sir." He smiled. "Do you know why I pulled you over?"

In other words, are you willing to confess to speeding?

"I'm not sure I do, Officer." Dean flashed him a PR smile.

"May I have your license and registration, please?"

Dean released the grip on the steering wheel and handed the documents to the police officer. The cop thanked him and straightened his back while scrutinizing the documents. He was so tall that, when he stood straight, Dean couldn't see him from the chest up.

A few moments later, the cop bent down again. "Dean Watson, correct?"

"That's what my ID says," Dean said. He was starting to become a little uneasy. This jovial police officer emanated layers of disconcertment you could cut with a knife. Dean didn't want to be around him for longer than necessary.

"Where are you headed, Dean?"

"Suicide Town, Officer," Dean retorted. The cop must have already known where Dean was headed, and there was no use skirting around the topic. He was headed in that direction, and Dean doubted that any other roads out of the town existed.

The police officer's smile drooped but then quickly returned. The officer cleared his throat, trying to mask his reaction, but Dean had already seen it.

"Suicide Town, huh? Why would you want to go there? There's nothing to see there."

Dean shrugged. "I like small towns."

The cop eyed him for a moment. Dean fully expected the officer to tell him to make a U-turn and leave the way he came—or worse, to tell him to step out of the vehicle. Instead, the officer nodded and said, "This town is not an ideal vacation spot, Dean. I hope you know that."

"I'm aware of that, Officer."

"And not only that, but as an officer of the law, I have to warn you that it's also fairly dangerous."

Dean gulped, staring at the cop, waiting for him to elaborate what he meant by "dangerous," but that explanation never came.

Seeing that, Dean nodded. "I'm also aware of that."

"So, then, why choose this location?" It was as if he was hinting to turn back. His rigid smile looked as if a pair of fingers stretched it back.

"I'm . . . just passing through," Dean said on a whim.

The police officer retained the plastic smile on his face. A droplet fell on his cheek, just below the eye, but he didn't even flinch, blink, or try to wipe it off. Dean froze; the look on the cop's face perturbed him. He was sure that the password he used must have been wrong—perhaps it was a keyword for something else and not to pass through.

After a long staring contest, where Dean refused to look away, the police officer handed the documents back to Dean, then tapped the rooftop of the car and straightened his back. He took a step backward so that he could see Dean and said, "All right, sir. You look like you know where you're going. You drive safely now. Have a great stay in Pineridge." His smile stretched farther, revealing pink gums.

"Thank you," Dean cautiously said and rolled his window up, muffling the pattering of the rain.

He felt the police officer's incessant stare on him from the middle of the road as Dean turned the key and stepped on the gas. Even when he was some distance away, looking in the rearview mirror, the cop stood in the same spot, soaking up the rain, following Dean's car with his gaze.

Dean frowned at the rearview mirror. That was one weird interaction. He couldn't help but feel like driving forward was the only way to go. Something told him that if he made a U-turn, the police officer would stop him and make him continue driving toward Suicide Town. That sense of not having a safe exit stirred trepidation into his stomach, but he pushed the foreboding feeling back to the deepest recesses of his mind. He came here, knowing full-well what the risks were, and he was not going to leave until he got all the answers he was looking for.

He glanced a few more times in the rearview mirror. He had seen the tiny figure sauntering back to the vehicle. The car remained entrenched until the moment the road veered to the right, causing the trees to block it out of view. Dean couldn't shake the feeling that the cop stared at Dean as intently as Dean stared at him until they were no longer in each other's line of sight.

Shrugging those thoughts off, Dean focused on the road ahead. He had completed all the steps in Joshua Bauer's notes, so he should arrive at Suicide Town soon, right? Dean slowed down as he swiveled his head left and right, looking for any landmarks that might tell him he was on the right way.

What? No grand "WELCOME TO SUICIDE TOWN" signs? No welcome signs with a drawing of the grim reaper next to the "ABANDON ALL HOPE, YE WHO ENTER HERE" message?

No sooner had he finished that thought did he see the first house to his right. As if on cue, more houses sprouted on both sides of the road from behind the trees. Foliage overgrew the houses, the leafless branches creeping above the rooftops, abrading the walls. The houses were disintegrated and abandoned, and Dean imagined he was arriving in a ghost town. Looking ahead, the road suddenly became wider and perfectly smooth. His car rolled onto a well-maintained road, decorated with a yellow line that separated both lanes. Driving on such a smooth concrete surface felt unusual.

Before Dean knew it, low buildings on either side of the road replaced the tall skeletal trees, making for an actual street. The forested hills through which he had driven just minutes ago seemed hours away, as they occupied the distant horizons. The rain had weakened to a drizzle, the pattering turning into silence, but Dean paid no attention to it whatsoever.

Dean slowed down to twenty miles an hour and pivoted left and right to observe Suicide Town. Parked cars were on the side of the street; trees that served as street plants stood fastened in their spots off the side of the road. The residential houses and the shops that occupied the road were, undoubtedly, Suicide Town's main avenue. Adjacent streets and alleys connected to the road piqued Dean's curiosity; he wondered if there was anything to see there or if those were just alleys with clustered households. With the lack of tall buildings, Dean couldn't help but feel like the sky hung too low, pressing down on the town. A woman exited a building with a grocery bag, her gaze following Dean. As Dean drove past her, she turned around to walk in the opposite direction, rubbernecking him.

Great. Now everybody in the town is going to know there's a new visitor.

Dean knew that it wouldn't take long for rumors to spread in a small town like this one. He wondered what it was like living in a place where the community was so tiny that you needed to be careful about doing something that would get you judged by the whole town. In bigger cities, you could make a fool out of yourself every weekend and not have to worry about that. In towns like Suicide Town, one gaffe would probably cost you your reputation for a lifetime.

Since he knew that this must have been downtown Suicide Town, Dean parked the car on the side of the road in front of a barber shop. He killed the engine and peered through the glass door with the OPEN sign hanging on it. A silhouette in the darkness of the shop slinked around, craning to see who the new visitor was.

Dean grabbed all the relevant items from the car, opened the door, and stepped into the cold afternoon air, ignoring the tickling droplets of rain. He barely had time to close the car door when a deep voice came from behind him.

"Afternoon," the person said.

Dean shot around to face the voice. In front of him stood a bulky man wearing a sheriff's hat and a raincoat. On the chest of the raincoat, it said "POLICE." Dean first noticed the person's round, protruding belly, and only then was he able to focus on the facial features under the rain-battered hat. He was around Dean's age, maybe a couple of years older. His head was round, his baby-shaved face devoid of blemishes. The tiny blue eyes and wide grin displayed goodwill, so Dean figured he wasn't in trouble . . . yet.

"Hey there," Dean said with formality in his voice.

"Are you looking for someone?" the sheriff asked, still smiling. Dean couldn't help but think of the cop back on the road who had pulled him over. The sheriff had his hands in his pockets, showing his relaxed demeanor, but the way he stood in front of Dean gave the writer the impression that the question was more of a demand.

"Yeah, actually." Dean looked at his car and locked it before facing the person. He was trying to portray that the cop wasn't a threat and that the conversation was only in passing. "Can you tell me where I am?"

The man blinked a few times and then said, "I think you already know that, don't you?" Dean sensed animosity in the man's tone despite the retention of the smile on his face.

"Nobody accidentally wanders here."

"You make it sound like I'm not welcome here."

The sheriff stared at Dean for a moment and then put one hand forward so fast that Dean had to fight the urge to recoil. When Dean looked down at the man's hand, he realized that he was holding it out for a handshake. Dean shook it firmly, trying to show the man that he was no pushover.

"I'm Sheriff Donovan Moody," the guy said. "Welcome to Suicide Town."

Chapter 11

"Name's Dean. I'm a writer," Dean proclaimed. He didn't use the title of writer to brag but rather to give the sheriff an idea of why he was visiting a small place like this one.

"Dean? *That* Dean?" The sheriff widened his eyes.

"Not Dean Koontz, if that's who you mean. My name's Dean Watson."

"That's what I meant. The author of *No Time to Die*, right? Boy, Jayden is going to lose his shit when he sees you. He keeps your books in the window display of his bookstore, which says a lot."

"I'm flattered," Dean said with a frown. The information took him aback. He didn't think that anyone from this small town would have heard of him, let alone be a big fan of his books. At the same time, it made him feel good because he felt like he had some leverage in his investigation.

"Well, since we already know you're not here for sightseeing, mind if I ask why you came to our cozy little town?" Sheriff Moody asked. "Plan on writing a book about Suicide Town?"

Although the tone was friendly, Dean couldn't shake the vibe of a subtle interrogation. He decided to play along for now, stay friendly, and hope it yielded results.

"Actually, yes. I was planning on writing a book directly inspired by Suicide Town, if the people of your town won't have anything against it, of course," Dean said.

"Nah, they'll be pleased to have someone interested in it." The sheriff took one hand out of his pocket and flicked his wrist. "As long as you follow the rules of Suicide Town, no one will bat an eye."

"What rules, Sheriff?" Dean pulled his suede jacket's hoodie over his head to shield himself from the annoying droplets of rain.

"We'll discuss those a little later. Just a few whatnots you need to be aware of. I assume you planned on staying more than a few days, yeah?"

"Right." *I need to if I want to find out what happened to Joshua Bauer*, Dean wanted to say, but he kept that information to himself to stay friendly with Sheriff Moody.

"I reckon you'll need a place to stay, then. Come with me, Watson, I'll show you where Baxter's Motel is." The Sheriff motioned over his shoulder and turned around. Dean followed him across the street toward an alley. "We never got any writers in the town before. Mostly, it's just curious teenagers and urban explorers," Sheriff Moody said as he waddled into the alley. His pace was slow, and Dean had to slow down to keep him in the lead.

"You get a lot of visitors?" Dean asked.

"Not so many these days. As I said, no one wanders here by accident. So, whoever comes here does so knowing the risks." He slung an accusatory glance over his shoulder at Dean. Dean didn't read into it too much.

When they broke out of the alley and onto the other side of the street—just as Dean assumed, it was a narrow one-way street, nothing like the main avenue—Sheriff Moody pointed at a huge vertical Baxter's Motel sign to the left.

"This place is owned by Nelson Baxter. He's a retired miner who inherited a lot of cash from his pa. It's the only motel in the town. Since we rarely get any visitors, you can choose whichever room you like. Go on, head inside."

It sounded like the sheriff said, "My duty here is done, and I'll be on my way." Dean wanted to stop that from happening. If anyone could give Dean the answers he was looking for, it would be the sheriff of Suicide Town.

"Sheriff, I have a lot of questions."

"Don't you worry. I'll be waiting. You go on and book a room." Sheriff Moody flashed him a smile.

The sheriff himself must have been thrilled to have a visitor, too. He probably had nothing to do all day long, so guiding the visitors around the town must have occupied him. Dean speculated what led Sheriff Moody to become a sheriff in Suicide Town. Was he born and raised here and wanted to protect his town? Did he want to have an easy life, where he could just drive around the town, stop at a diner for a break, and get paid for it? What was it like having to arrest the people he knew all his life, if arrests even happened in Suicide Town?

Dean decided he would ask the sheriff those questions more intimately later. For now, he pushed the motel's wooden door open, striking a chiming bell. The interior was dark, the gray light peering through the window, the only source of illumination. On the right-hand side was a reception desk cluttered with tall stacks of juxtaposed, disheveled papers, an ashtray full of cigarette butts, and a desk lamp.

Initially, Dean didn't even see a person sitting behind the reception until movement caught his eye. A round face, not dissimilar to Sheriff Moody's, peeked at the visitor around the mess. As soon as his eyes fell on Dean, the man shot up to his feet, kicking the chair on which he was sitting back with a loud scrape and thud.

"Good afternoon," the man said with a smoker's voice that gnawed at Dean's ears. He stood directly in the light coming through the window, his facial features clearly coming into view. The top of his head was bald, save for a few long strands of hair combed to the side. The bags under his eyes were heavy and dark, and red speckles dotted his puffy cheeks, perhaps from reckless shaving. Just like the sheriff, Nelson Baxter smiled at Dean.

"Hi. Sheriff Moody showed me here. Do you have any available rooms?" Dean asked with an equally friendly smile, even though he already knew the answer to the question. He took off his hoodie; the temperature in the motel was almost as low as it was outside.

"We do. Let me just check which ones we have available," Baxter said. Dean had to press his lips tightly to avoid laughing out loud. The motel owner opened a notebook, licked his fingers, then flipped through the pages that were most likely empty. "Okay, we actually have a few rooms available. We have room four . . . room six . . . room seven—"

"Do you have the room that Joshua Bauer stayed in available by any chance?" Dean interrupted Baxter's slow reading, impatient.

The motel owner looked up from the notebook, his lofty eyebrows furled all the way to where the bald scalp started. He still had the smile on his face, but Dean detected intrigue on the man's face.

"Room eleven? Any . . . any special reason you want that room?"

Dean rubbed his chin, the sharp stubble pricking his fingers. He had to have known why Dean would choose that room, so there was no use lying about it. Soon, the entire town was going to know that Dean Watson had visited, and they would discover his motives.

"I wanted to retrace Joshua Bauer's steps. You don't mind if I do that, do you?" Dean flashed the motel owner a smile.

"No, not at all," Baxter said, reciprocating the grin. He turned around and traced a stubby finger along the wooden key rack mounted on the wall. He ran his finger slowly from number one and onward as if expecting the number eleven to pop up out of nowhere.

He's stalling.

Sure enough, when Baxter reached number nine, he suddenly snapped his fingers and then turned around to face Dean. "You know what—I just remembered. We have a luxury room available for the same price as the other rooms. How about I give you that one?"

"Thank you," Dean said. "But I would really like room eleven. It's important for my investigation."

"Investigation?" Baxter asked, rubbing his hands together.

"Yes. I'm a writer."

"Oh." Baxter visibly relaxed. The sudden change was almost comical. He let out a wheezy laugh in relief and lowered his hands. The only thing needed to complete the gesture was Baxter facepalming himself. "Okay, well, here. You can have room eleven," he said as he picked the key from the number 11 hook.

Dean thanked him and paid in advance for five days. He wasn't sure if he was going to stay longer than that, but he knew that he wasn't going to stay less than five days. Even if he managed to question everyone within a day, he would conduct his own investigation based on Joshua Bauer's notes; he didn't trust that the townsfolk would necessarily tell him the truth.

"All right, then. Let me show you to your room," Baxter said.

He led the way through the hall in the back on the right side and past the rooms lined up left and right. He was already out of breath. The way Baxter's entire body lolled left and right with each step told Dean that he might have a shorter leg or a deformity that was causing the limp.

The motel owner stopped and pointed right to the room with the copper 11 on it. Dean unlocked the door and pushed it open, revealing a dark room. He stepped inside and flipped the old light switch up. A sallow light bathed the room, how Dean expected it to look from Joshua Bauer's video.

The room was minimalistic. It contained a bed and a nightstand with a landline phone on it. Above the nightstand was a wall-mounted lamp. On the left was the door to the bathroom. Opposite of the entrance were windows, draped by thick blackout curtains. A moldy, musty odor percolated in the air like clothes that had been left in the washer for too long.

Baxter's hoarse voice broke the silence. "You can use the phone to call me if you need anything. It can't call outside, though. If there's anything not to your liking in your room, let me know, and I will be happy to change it."

"That won't be necessary. Thank you so much, though," Dean said. He stopped in the middle of the room and turned around to face Baxter. The motel owner stood in the doorway, blocking it. He raised a chubby hand and scratched his double-chin, once again, looking like he was uncomfortable.

"I assume the sheriff told you about the rules, right?"

"No. What rules?"

"Well, he'll fill you in on the details, all right? I'll let you have some privacy now. If you need anything, I'll be at the reception, okay?" He hooked a thumb behind himself and left, panting.

Dean scanned the room for a moment. As he looked at the bed and the pale yellow walls that might have been white a long time ago, he didn't see a comfortable place where he would sleep. No, this was a crime scene in his mind. Joshua Bauer had stayed in this room while in Suicide Town, and he might have left some clues for Dean to find. He would thoroughly inspect the room later, right after he made sure his privacy was safe from any possible spy cameras inside. He normally didn't check for hidden cameras unless he booked an Airbnb, but this town was shady as hell.

When Dean went back outside, the sheriff was still there, his thumbs tucked in his belt. His head snapped toward Dean when he heard the chime of the bell above the door.

"All good?" He smiled.

"Yeah. I got a room. Nice guy," Dean said as he put the key in his pocket. "I still need to get the things from my car and take it to the room."

"I'll help you with it. Just bring the car around."

Dean didn't object. He went back to the car on his own and drove it back to the front of the motel. By then, more people had seen him. A woman walked past him on his way to the car and said hi in passing, two men saw him driving and turned their heads to face him, and when he parked the car in front of the motel, a family of four waved to the sheriff and shot curious glances in Dean's direction.

The sheriff assured Dean that he could leave his car on the street and that nobody would be writing him a ticket or towing it away, and since the motel had no parking of its own, no other convenient place was available.

"If you want, you can take it to the gas station to protect it from the rain. Everything in Pineridge is so close, you could crawl to it in a matter of minutes," Sheriff Moody said.

"That's okay," Dean said as he opened the trunk of the car. By then, the rain had intensified, the droplets heavier and more aggressive. "Is it always like this here?"

"What do you mean?" Sheriff Moody asked as he took Dean's suitcase to help him unload.

"I mean the weather," Dean said.

Sheriff Moody threw his head back and heartily guffawed. "Oh, this is nothing, Watson. You should come during spring. The downpour doesn't stop for days. People become even more suicidal then."

"Is it true what they say about Suicide Town?" Dean asked. He had to raise his voice over the rain.

"What, exactly? About people killing themselves?"

Dean nodded as he closed the trunk of the car.

"Well, why do you think they call it Suicide Town?" The sheriff chuckled. "Certainly not because the town is a happy place with sunshine and rainbows."

"How often do people commit suicide here?" Dean asked as he and the sheriff walked to the motel's entrance.

"Depends. It's mostly the elderly people killing themselves."

Sheriff Moody pushed the door open and greeted Baxter before making small talk with him in passing, stalling Dean from asking the plethora of questions. They took the things into room eleven and placed them on the bed. The sheriff then tucked his thumbs into his belt again and asked, "That all?"

"Yeah," Dean said.

"All righty, then. You said you had questions, right?"

"Yes." Dean nodded as he patted his pockets to make sure his notepad and pen were there. He was eager to get some answers, and the sheriff seemed more than willing to talk.

"All right, but I can't talk on an empty stomach. Come on, let's go to Susan's Diner. Lunch is on me," Sheriff Moody said.

Chapter 12

They went to the Rainy Days diner in Sheriff Moody's patrol car. The diner was on the main avenue farther down from where Dean initially stopped. The owner, Susan Bennett, was a woman in her fifties who looked like she came out of the fifties. She had one of those old-fashioned hairstyles that Dean only saw in old movies, and the ton of makeup she put on her face didn't complement her looks at all; it made her look like a zombie, if anything. Her purple eyelids looked bruised, the crimson cheeks that looked like she had just come inside from a raging blizzard, the bright lipstick that matched the rest of the makeup but not her face—garish against Susan Bennett's shriveled facial features.

"Howdy, Sheriff. See you've brought a new friend. What's your name, handsome?" Susan asked as she obnoxiously chewed the bubblegum, ogling Dean like he was a nice piece of steak.

"My name's Dean Watson, ma'am."

"Sounds like the name of an important person. Are you a government official, darling?" she asked.

"No." Dean chuckled. "I'm a writer."

"Ooh, a writer. Fancy."

Dean couldn't figure out if she was ironic or not. She leaned on the side of the seat where the sheriff was and asked, "So, what will y'all boys be having?" Dean's eyes fell on the long fingernails on bony fingers and the veiny hands.

"The usual for me, Susan," Moody said.

"What about you, sugar? We got some mean burgers on the menu today." She winked and blew a pink bubble. The bubble burst with a quiet pop, and Susan put the mangled gum back in her mouth and continued chewing. The way she eyeballed Dean made him wonder whether she just thought he was handsome or if she was trying to read his mind. Either way, it made him uncomfortable.

"Yeah, that sounds fine," Dean said.

"You want fries with that?"

"Sure."

"Okay, hun. Should be ready in fifteen minutes. Holler if you need anything." She winked at Dean before leaving to tend to the other guests.

Dean expected the diner to be empty, but quite a few guests occupied it. The sheriff greeted every one of them, and they greeted him back, but their attention was mostly focused on the visitor. Dean tried his best to ignore their incessant gazes, pretending he didn't notice them.

With the waitress gone, the guests' chatter and the soft country music playing from the jukebox rose to the surface. Dean fished the notepad and pen out of his pocket and placed them on the table. The sheriff leaned forward and interlocked his fingers.

"Now, then. I'll answer all the questions you have, but there are a couple of things we need to get out of the way first," Sheriff Moody said as he took the hat off and placed it on the table. He had short blonde hair, and it took Dean a moment to get used to him without the hat.

"I'm listening," Dean replied.

Moody stared at Dean as if trying to detect if he would be compliant. The stern facial expression didn't suit the sheriff one bit; or maybe it was strange to Dean because he had only seen the sheriff smiling until then.

"Okay," Moody said. "You know where you are, Watson. You found this place because you wanted to find it. No one stumbles into it on accident. And I reckon you know the dangers of Suicide Town."

"Everyone who visits ends up committing suicide. Right," Dean said. He opened his notepad and clicked the pen, ready to jot down notes.

"No, the visitors are safe unless they do dumb things, which they often tend to do. Suicide Town consists of two towns." Sheriff Moody raised a fist. "Pineridge." He showed his forefinger. "And Raintown." He unfurled a middle finger. "This is Pineridge. This is where most of the folks live. You can roam Pineridge wherever you want. No place is restricted. Raintown is a few hundred yards down the road, but it is strictly off limits. Not just to you but to us as well. You never ever go to Raintown under any circumstances. Are we understood, Watson?"

The strict manner in which the sheriff said that made the situation seem like Dean's life depended on it—and somehow, he knew that was exactly the case. He nodded as he wrote *RAINTOWN OFF LIMITS* in his notepad.

"Okay," Moody said. "And don't try sneaking there, either. You wouldn't be the first one to try it. We have people watching the road to stop any dumbasses from going there. Trust me when I say that Raintown is restricted for your own safety."

"Understood," Dean said.

He was tempted to write something along the lines of *ARE THEY HIDING SOMETHING?* but didn't want Sheriff Moody seeing it. He needed to stay in his good grace if he wanted to progress with his investigation.

"Okay," Moody said. "You're a smart man, Watson. Well-read, I assume. Gotta be if you're a writer. You understand that trespassing to Raintown can be extremely dangerous. Not like those kids who went there. By the time we found them, it was already too late."

"What kids? What happened to them?"

Moody dismissively waved Dean off and said, "Some curious kids came here to film videos for their online channel or something. They ended up sneaking into Raintown. That was over four years ago, and the people are still shaken up about it."

Dean opened his mouth, confused. He jotted some notes down and then asked, "They died there?"

Sheriff Moody closed his eyes and shook his head. "Some things are best left alone, Watson. Trust me. Anything about Raintown should stay in Raintown. Got it?" He took a moment to pause and then continued, "But I didn't lay down all the ground rules yet. So, rule number one is, don't go to Raintown. Rule number two is, be inside your motel room by midnight at the latest."

Dean wrote so fast that his hand started to hurt. The handwriting looked more like footwriting, and he hoped to be able to decipher later what he wrote down. Already, he could envision his book coming to life. He suddenly found himself feeling like the main character. He had never put himself in his books before, but maybe that wouldn't be a bad idea this time, especially because he would be able to write the character better.

"Rule number three," Sheriff Moody continued. "By one a.m., at the latest, the blinds on your windows need to be pulled down, and the curtains pulled over. You will perhaps hear sounds outside. No matter what you hear, you are to remain inside your room and under no circumstances look out the window. This rule is perhaps the most important one, and it is imperative that you follow it, no questions asked."

The grotesque scream that came from Joshua's video echoed in Dean's memory. Dean had completely forgotten about it until the sheriff mentioned the rule and then, like a suppressed memory, the video of the motel room flashed before his eyes.

Back when he was in Gresham, he watched the video from the safety of his apartment. But now, Dean would be in Joshua Bauer's shoes. The thought of putting himself in danger had been on his mind this entire time, but it was only a theoretical thought. The actual thought of dying hadn't really hit him until now.

He dismissed that thought, chalking it up to the paranoia caused by the research he conducted online and the sheriff's words.

"Watson, you still with me?" Sheriff Moody asked.

"Yeah." Dean nodded.

Moody leaned back on the seat and put one hand on the table. He gave Dean a solicitous look, his face no longer rigid as it was when he explained the rules. "Look, Watson," he said. "I know you're probably here because of that journalist. Am I right?" Dean nodded. "I'm willing to tell you everything you need to know, give you all the names of people who spoke to him, but you need to promise to follow the rules."

The sheriff's polite attitude was only a guise. The sheriff would most likely not hesitate to kick Dean out of town if he broke a rule. Dean would play along—for now—and if his investigation got stumped, he would look for alternatives.

"All right," Dean said. "We got a deal. I first want to know more about Suicide Town."

"What about it?"

"Everything. Every single small detail that you think is relevant for an outsider like me to know, I want to know it."

The sheriff leaned forward and interlocked his fingers again. His face was no longer slack, Dean noticed. "You already know the legend," Sheriff Moody said. "Whoever visits the town commits suicide. But it's not just the visitors who die like that. Most of the people here die by committing suicide. It's as normal as saying "good morning" to your neighbor. Of all the deaths that have occurred in this town; death by suicide takes up more than ninety-five percent."

"Wow," Dean said as he scribbled that down before flipping to a fresh page. "I wanna know more about that. What's causing these suicides?"

Moody shrugged. "It's just always been that way. It goes so far back that no one even remembers anymore. The people here believe it's something supernatural, even though these things can probably be explained with logic."

"So, what exactly is going on?"

"People here have suicidal tendencies . . . more than the rest of the world. They're like these black clouds that constantly hover above us, you know? You get used to it after a while, but it's always there, like a nagging sickness."

Just then, Dean smelled something savory. Susan Bennett walked up to their table moments later, carrying two trays. She placed the tray with the humongous burger, fries, and milkshake on Dean's side while placing the tray with a Reuben sandwich on the sheriff's side. Dean wasn't in the mood for eating, and he didn't appreciate Susan interrupting the interview.

"Here you go, darlings," Susan said before leaning on the table and turning to Dean. "The milkshake's on the house." She winked at him.

"Thanks, Susan," Sheriff Moody said with a polite smile.

Susan turned around and left, much to Dean's relief. He felt relieved not being in the woman's proximity. She made him feel uneasy with those flirtatious remarks.

Sheriff Moody began eating, and Dean did the same, leaving the questions for after the meal. He hadn't realized how hungry he was until he took the first bite of the burger. It was greasy and packed with too many toppings, leaving Dean to finagle his way around it to bite. The burger was tall, and Dean imagined it being made for snakes who were able to unhinge their jaws to such size.

Nevertheless, despite its gigantism, and the grease that poured onto the tray with each bite he took, the meal was delicious. The fries were perfectly done, not like in most of Gresham's places where they came out either too shriveled and hard or too salty. The milkshake was just the right amount of sweetness. By the time the sheriff finished his sandwich—which was also enormous—Dean hadn't finished even half of his burger. He was already full, too, so he decided to leave the meal aside and continue the interview.

"So, about the suicides . . ." Dean said with his mouth half-full, wiping his greasy hands on a napkin. "You mentioned that the suicide rate is over ninety-five percent and that mostly just elderly people off themselves. Can you tell me more about that?"

"I wish I could," Moody said as he leaned back. He silently burped into his hand. "No one knows exactly what happens, but as I said, everyone who lives here has that . . . sickness. The ones who are naturally suicidal have a much stronger desire to kill themselves living in this town. And they do end up killing themselves earlier; some even doing it as early as in their teens. But most people end up committing suicide when they're old. It's been talked about many, many times, and the conclusion that we were able to come up with was that the old folks who are old are more susceptible to the sickness. They become senile and demented or simply worn down, and then they do it."

"I see," Dean said as he wrote everything down. "This sickness. Do you think it's a physiological disease or something else?"

"By 'something else,' I assume you mean something supernatural, right?" The sheriff smiled. "We don't know. I personally believe that people here are suicidal because of the weather."

"That doesn't explain some of the other things. The unnatural tendency to kill yourself, the fact that the town is so well-hidden, and so on . . ."

"As I said, I believe there's a logical explanation for all of that, Watson," Sheriff said sternly.

Susan had arrived to take their trays and gave Dean a sad look. "Aw, hun. You didn't like our house special?"

"It was amazing, ma'am. I'm just full, is all." Dean flashed her a grin.

"Aw, too bad. Well, let me pack it for you, huh?"

Before Dean could answer, Susan took the trays and left. Dean's fake smile drooped, and he looked back at the sheriff, who was staring at him. He felt embarrassed about letting Sheriff Moody see that he was irritated with Susan, but he chose not to say anything about the topic. He cleared his throat and looked down at his notes.

"The rule about not looking out the window after one . . ." Dean looked up at the sheriff. "What is going on out there at night, Sheriff?"

"It's tradition, Watson. Now, I know you're curious about it, but that right there is a very private tradition for us here in Pineridge. All you need to know is that no foul business is going on, and nobody is getting hurt. You understand?"

"Is looking outside the window illegal?"

The sheriff's lips tightened into a slit, but then they relaxed. He looked like he was trying really hard not to say something offensive to Dean. "No, not illegal," he said. "But very dangerous to your well-being. I'm trying to be a hospitable host to you, but if you plan on breaking the basic rules—"

"It's not like that, Sheriff. I'm only curious, is all." Dean lied.

"I understand. Well, your curiosity better not get the better of you. Or you might be the next one we bury behind the church. And the graveyard's already full as it is."

"He's right, hun," Susan chimed in just as she returned with Dean's packed food in a grocery bag. She placed the bag on the table in front of him and said, "It's just a boring town tradition, is all it is. Not worth losing sleep over it. Don't you bother your pretty little head with it."

"Everyone in town will tell you the same thing, Watson," the sheriff continued. "Nothing to see out at night. But if you do happen to look . . . we'll know."

"How could you possibly know?" Dean asked.

"We just do," Moody said.

"He speaks the truth, hun," Susan interjected with a fervent nod. "My friend, Mindy, looked when we were in high school. She was never the same after that. Ended up drowning herself in the canal." Just then, someone called out to Susan. She turned her head to see who it was and what they wanted and then looked

123

at Dean before saying, "Looks like I'm needed somewhere. You stop by anytime, sugar. Except after midnight, of course." She winked and left.

A moment of silence ruminated while Dean processed everything Sheriff Moody and Susan Bennett had told him. He stared blankly at the scribbled notes.

"You heard her, Watson," the sheriff said. "Now, since I've explained the rules to you, and I need to get going soon, I'll answer a few more questions you have and then I'll be on my way."

Dean went straight to the point. "I want to know more about Joshua Bauer."

"The journalist? Why don't you ask him?"

"I can't. He killed himself two days ago," Dean said.

"I see. A shame," the sheriff said, coldness laced in his tone. The lack of reaction made Dean question whether the journalist's death came to the sheriff as a surprise at all. "All right, give me that notepad." The sheriff gestured to the notes. Dean hesitantly slid the notepad and the pen to the sheriff. Moody spent a minute writing on a new page, stopping for moments to think, before handing the items back to Dean. "There. These are some of the people who spoke to Joshua Bauer. You can go talk to them if you like."

Dean glanced down at the notes to see if he could make out the words. They were clear. "Thanks, Sheriff," he said a moment later and put the notepad and pen in his pocket.

Sheriff Moody stood and put his hat on. He took some cash out of his wallet and placed the money under the empty cup. Then he and Dean exited the diner. By the time they did so, the rain showed no signs of subsiding. It even seemed stronger, slowly turning into a downpour. The sheriff drove Dean back to the motel, even though it was a minute of driving away with the one traffic light that the town had.

On the drive back, a notice board plastered to the wall of the motel with black and white pictures caught Dean's eye. It took him a moment to realize that he was staring at obituaries.

"That's a lot of dead people," Dean commented in passing.

"Yep. You'll see new names there at least once every month."

Dean rubbernecked at the obituary as they drove past it.

"If you have any questions, feel free to find me," the sheriff said as he pulled up in front of the building. "Just ask anyone; they always know where I am."

Dean nodded and stepped out of the car. He held the open door for a moment and then stooped to look at the sheriff inside. "Hey, Sheriff?"

Moody raised his chin in Dean's direction.

"You said that all the residents in Suicide Town end up committing suicide, but I'm a visitor. What's going to happen to me?" Dean asked with a raised voice in the thundering rain. The heavy droplets drenched him.

The sheriff's chest slowly rose and then fell. He leaned toward Dean and said, "Follow the rules and you won't have to find out." He leaned back.

Not understanding the sheriff's words, but not wanting to ponder them in the rain, Dean closed the car door and watched as the sheriff drove off.

Chapter 13

The conversation with the sheriff replayed in Dean's head over and over.

Raintown is off limits.

Be inside by midnight.

Do not, under any circumstances, look out the window.

Raintown is off limits.

What the fuck is Raintown? Dean looked down the road where it gradually descended and tapered in the distance. Pineridge ended where the bare road surrounded by trees started, but no sight of another town from here. Dean envisioned a shantytown out there, full of dirty people and ramshackle makeshift huts slapped together from rusted metals and discarded shipment containers.

Dean got into his car and looked around. One person with an umbrella sauntered into an alleyway. The streets were empty other than that. While listening to the pitter-patter of the rain against the roof of his car, Dean pulled his notepad out and stared at the notes he had written at the diner.

Just one conversation with the sheriff yielded a lot of information about Suicide Town, yet Dean was unable to shake the feeling that what he got was only the tip of the iceberg. He wanted to dive deeper and get the full picture; all the shameful details that the townsfolk could possibly be hiding.

When Dean got to the sheriff's notes, he read them multiple times. Names and addresses were written. People who had spoken to Joshua Bauer. The first one on the list was Denise Lamar, who worked in the bakery on North Street. With the list of "suspects" who he needed to interview, Dean suddenly felt like a detective rather than a writer.

He put the key in the ignition and turned it. As soon as the engine turned, he blasted the heat and made a U-turn. When he reached the traffic light, he turned right onto the wide intersecting street. He had seen that street on his way to the diner with the sheriff, which proved that the town was bigger than Dean had initially thought. The two big streets went North to South and West to East and intersected in the middle. The rest of the town consisted of narrow streets, one-way streets, and alleyways.

Dean drove slow to spot the bakery among the bevy of stores that occupied North Street. It soon became apparent that Suicide Town had pretty much everything it needed right here, whether it was a butcher, supermarket, convenience store, or anything else. How did the townsfolk get their supplies imported? They had to come from somewhere, and he doubted that they produced everything right here on their own.

The Lamar Bakery was right next to the Suicide Meat butcher. Dean parked his car in front and entered the bakery. It was a small place, barely big enough to fit three customers at the same time. When Dean entered, a man was inside, buying bread from the overweight lady working behind the counter—both looked in Dean's direction.

"Thanks, Denise," the customer said as he took the bag with the bread, paid, and turned around to leave. The person shot Dean a curious glance before hurriedly leaving the place.

"Good afternoon, Mr. Watson," Denise said. "How nice of you to visit my humble bakery. What can I get for you today?" She smiled, showing crooked teeth. The fact that she knew his name cemented Dean's assumption that everyone was already aware he was here. He must have been the talk of the town by now. He approached, casting an aloof glance at the dry-looking goods behind the glass display and then raising his gaze to Denise.

"Hi. I was actually hoping to ask you a few questions, if you don't mind," he said.

"No, not at all, Mr. Watson. Ask away," the woman said in a friendly tone.

Dean took out his notepad and turned to a new page. He started with the most basic questions. "Can you tell me more about the town?"

She chuckled. "Oh, not much to tell. You probably already know the gist of it. People kill themselves, and the weather is horrible."

"What was life like growing up over here?" Dean asked.

"I really can't say, Mr. Watson. I'm not from here."

"You're not?"

"No, I come from Portland. I only work here."

Dean raised his eyebrows in surprise. "Oh, interesting," he said. "So, you still live in Portland?"

"Yes." Denise nodded. "I work here, but I live there."

Dean took a moment to write everything down. He looked up at Denise and asked, "How does that work, exactly?"

"Well, depends," Denise said as she looked around and then at Dean. "I usually go home on the weekends, sometimes not even then; it depends."

"I see. Which part of Portland do you live in?"

"Oh, it's a remote neighborhood. You wouldn't know about it." Denise flicked her wrist and chuckled. Dean detected nervousness in her tone, and her hand gestures became just a little more erratic.

"What's the neighborhood name?" Dean insisted.

"It's Overlook," Denise said after a pause that she probably wasn't even aware she had made.

"Oh, I know it. It's the neighborhood all the way South, in Portland, right?" Dean smiled.

"Yes, that's right." Denise nodded with a fervent smile.

Dean smiled back and wrote in his notes, *DENISE LAMAR LIED ABOUT WHERE SHE CAME FROM.* Overlook was on the West side of Portland, not South.

He wanted to probe with some more questions about Portland or to simply ask her why she was lying, but he didn't want to get confrontational just yet. He would talk to some other people first.

"What can you tell me about Raintown?"

Denise's shoulders relaxed. Her eyes weren't as wide as before, her voice no longer shaky, her gestures not as erratic. "I've never seen it. All I know is it's a bad place," she said.

Dean nodded. He could not know for sure if Denise was telling the truth about that, but he would ask other people to find out. "Recently, a journalist called Joshua Bauer came to the town. The sheriff told me that you spoke with him?" Dean said.

"Only in passing. He came here a few times to buy some goods. We never really spoke in detail."

"Did anything about him kind of stick out to you? Maybe something he said or did while he was here?"

Denise shook her head from left to right in one mechanical motion. "Not that I can remember. I'm just trying to make a decent living with my bakery, Mr. Watson, that's all. I don't meddle in other people's affairs, so I didn't pay too much attention to Mr. Bauer."

Dean understood that would have been the case if Denise came from a big city like Portland. But Denise was not from Portland, and anyone who has lived in a small town like this one for such a long time would be interested in so much as a stray dog wandering to the town, let alone a journalist with a bunch of questions.

"Do you happen to remember how long he stayed in town?" Dean asked.

"A few days, maybe. Like I said, I didn't really pay much attention."

"Thank you for your time, ma'am," Dean said as he put away his notepad. Denise's eyes followed the notepad, and the woman further seemed to relax when he put it away.

"No problem at all, Mr. Watson. If you need anything else, please let me know. I'm always here from seven to six."

Upon exiting the bakery, Dean wrote more about Denise. She was suspicious as hell, that was for sure. Dean would come back to question her more aggressively next time if he didn't find out anything from other people in the meantime.

The next person on the list was Robert Kutcher, the butcher who owned Suicide Meat. Dean wondered if the name of the shop impacted his sales in any way but then remembered that this was Suicide Town. Suicide Meat was probably the only butcher in town.

Just like the bakery, the butcher's shop was small. It was much colder in here, due to the refrigeration of the meat, and it smelled as such, too. Robert Kutcher was a man in his late fifties from Dean's assumption, and he wore an apron stained with shades of pink and red.

"Ah, the writer, huh?" the butcher said with a friendly grin.

"Dean Watson. Robert Kutcher, I assume?"

"Kutcher the Butcher, that's right," the butcher said and guffawed. The laughter was contagious, and Dean couldn't contain his own laugh.

"Say, did you become a butcher because of your name? Or did you change your name because you're a butcher?" Dean joked once Kutcher stopped laughing.

"It's just a coincidence, son," Kutcher said. "But works really well, doesn't it? It all started with me and my dad finding roadkill. We took it home, and I spent some time learning how to skin it. We cooked it, and the family ate fine that night. Been selling roadkill ever since."

Dean and the butcher stared at each other with blank faces. The butcher threw his head back and laughed again, his voice booming in the small room. "I'm just kidding, son!" Robert Kutcher said, continuing to laugh. Dean laughed along with him. He already liked the butcher.

"Hoo boy." Kutcher wiped a tear from his eye once he came down from laughing. Still red in the face, he looked at Dean and said, "I assume you're not here to buy meat, right? So, what can I do you for, son?"

"You got me. I was wondering if you have a few minutes to answer some questions."

The butcher nodded. Dean pulled out his notepad on a new page and wrote *BUTCHER* at the top. He started with the basic questions about Suicide Town. He got pretty much the same response as from Denise Lamar: shallow descriptions and no concrete answers about Joshua Bauer.

"Why do you think so many people here commit suicide?" Dean asked.

"Well, a very popular theory is because the town was built on a wetland."

"Wetland?" Dean asked. "You mean this entire region used to be a marsh?"

"Marsh, swamp, bayou. Call it whatever you want. But nothing good comes out of the wetlands. Why someone would decide to build a town here is beyond me. But anyway, they did, and people speculate that the vapors from the swamp are affecting the people's psyche."

"Just like the toxic gas from the mines in Centralia, Pennsylvania."

"The what, now?"

"Never mind. Just talking to myself. Have you noticed anything strange about Joshua Bauer while he stayed here? The way he behaved or anything like that?"

"Nope," Kutcher said. "I mean, he looked kinda weird to me from day one, so maybe I just didn't notice the difference.

"Has Joshua Bauer broken any of the rules while he was here?"

Kutcher shot a pensive gaze at the ceiling. He shook his head a moment later and looked down at Dean. "Probably not. He was here for a few days and then left. Nothing special to it."

"I see. What can you tell me about Raintown?"

"Nothing," Kutcher said in a curt manner. "Never been there. It's foul business over there, so we don't like to speak about it too much."

"Are you from here?"

"No."

The butcher's humorous attitude became aloof and reserved when Dean fine-tuned his questions about the town and where he was from, so trying to get information out of him was futile. Dean thanked him for his time, and the butcher's joking nature returned.

"Stop by anytime," Kutcher said. "I have a good selection of pâté made from monkeys. Imported directly from Brazil."

"Really?" Dean squinted.

"No, I'm just joking," the butcher said and laughed again.

This time, Dean didn't find the joke funny. He said goodbye to the butcher and left. He wrote the same things about the butcher as he did about Denise: both lied about not being from Suicide Town. The question was, why?

The rain outside had reduced to a light sprinkle by then. Dean returned to his car and went through the notes once more. The people here were hiding something. Maybe not about Joshua Bauer per se, but they were definitely hiding something. Dean still had a few people to question. The next person on the list was Jayden Price, the owner of Price Books, also conveniently on North Street. Dean exited the car and looked for the right address.

The bookstore was easy to miss. It consisted of a tiny glass door and a book display squeezed between two buildings. The sign above said Price Books, which made Dean wonder if everyone in Suicide Town named their business after their last names. Dean parked the car in front and approached the store. Through the glass display, among the myriad of books, Dean's own book caught his eye. *No Time to Die* occupied the honorary spot, right in the middle of the display. Pride overwhelmed him at the realization that he was still remotely popular somewhere in the world.

A bell not dissimilar to the one in the motel chimed above his head as he opened the door. The smell of fresh paper brought him back to the good ol' days when he had book signings. The bookstores where he had signings were not as narrow and cluttered with shelves as Price Books—here, he wouldn't even have enough space to do book signing—and were much better illuminated, but this bookshop was cozy.

"Oh, my Lord!" a petulant voice said on Dean's left behind the counter.

Dean jerked his head in the direction of the voice in time to see a skinny man in his early twenties with glasses stand from his seat. His mouth was agape, his eyes wide in awe as he stared at Dean as if looking at a naked woman rather than a washed-out writer.

"I can't believe it," the young man said. "Sheriff Moody said you were here, but I thought he was pulling my leg. Oh, my God." He clasped a hand over his mouth.

"Hi. You must be Jayden Price," Dean said as he put his hand forward, flattered to get such a reaction but unable to match the enthusiasm. "I'm Dean."

Jayden took Dean's hand with both of his and vigorously shook. "I am your biggest fan, Mr. Watson! I've read all your books! I have them all on the shelves right here! I keep telling the other folks that they gotta read your books, and they don't know what they're missing out on! I even thought about tattooing a quote from your book on my arm!"

Dean released Jayden's grip and pulled his hand back as gently as he could without showing his discomfort at Jayden's cult-like enthusiasm. Back when he was still a thing, he met a couple of obsessed fans, but security quickly intervened to get them out of the way. Here, he was alone in a tight-knit community in the middle of nowhere, without anyone to be on his side.

Jayden continued speaking rapidly. "I've been waiting for you to write the next book for some time now. I check your website almost every day. When Sheriff Moody told me you were here to write your next book, I thought he was screwing with me, but you're actually here in the flesh! And to think you'd come to our shithole of a town—pardon my French—and to write your next book!"

"Well, I haven't started writing my new book, so don't get your hopes up just yet, Jayden."

"But you're working on one, correct?"

"Perhaps," Dean said and then got an idea. If Jayden was really such a superfan, then he was perfect for Dean to get some information out of him. "You know, I'm actually looking for someone to be a beta reader for me. Since you're such a big fan . . ." He winked.

"Oh, my gosh, no way! Dean Watson wants me to beta read a book for him? I must be dreaming! You honor me, Mr. Watson!"

"Please, call me Dean. I will definitely need some beta readers, and I'll put your name at the top of the priority list. But to write my book, I'm going to need your help, Jayden."

"Anything you need, Dean, just name it!" Jayden said with a big smile.

"Well, you remember that journalist who visited recently, Joshua Bauer, right?"

"I remember. Never spoke to him, though."

"You never spoke to him?"

Jayden shook his head. *Shit. Why would the sheriff put Jayden Price on the list, then?* And then it hit him. He was on the list because he wanted to do the kid a favor and help him meet his favorite writer. As angry as Dean was, he couldn't blame the sheriff. The last thing he wanted was to present himself as an ill-tempered asshole who would completely destroy Jayden's image of his idol.

"Does that mean I'm off the list?" Jayden asked with a hint of disappointment in his tone.

"No, no. Not at all. You'll still get to beta read for me. But I'm still going to need your help," Dean said.

"Whatever you need, Mr. Watson—I mean, Dean."

"Can you start by telling me if you're from the town?"

"Yes, I am. Born and raised here, unfortunately."

Dean raised an eyebrow. "You don't like living here?"

"Not one bit. I planned on leaving, but unfortunately, that's not an option." Jayden shrugged.

"Financial problems?" Dean asked.

"That, and some other things," Jayden muttered.

Dean didn't want to pry. It was clear that the issues that were stopping him from leaving Suicide Town were not what he wanted to discuss, so Dean steered clear of it.

"I spoke to some other people here, and they told me they're not from here. Now, I know for a fact that they're lying. But I wanna ask you, why would they do that?"

"Why would they lie, you mean?" Jayden asked. "Well, it's obvious. They're embarrassed. They don't want any outsiders knowing that they've spent their whole lives living in a small dump like this one. Who was it that lied to you? Was it Denise? She also lied to Joshua Bauer about it, I heard."

Jayden's astuteness impressed Dean. He jotted that down in his notepad. "So, about Joshua Bauer. Anything about him that I should know? Anything unusual he did or said while he was here?"

"Well, I know for a fact that he snooped around, and a lot of folks didn't appreciate that."

"Was he trying to find out more about the town?"

"I think so. I heard him and the sheriff having an argument one day, but I couldn't hear what they were saying. I suppose Joshua disobeyed one of the rules."

Dean nodded while taking notes. He stared at the half-filled page of notes and then looked around the bookshop. Although the counter area was a mess, the rest of the store was neatly arranged. The piles of books that sat behind the counter were separated into piles of new books and old, tattered ones with ruined hardback and paperback covers. Perhaps Jayden ran out of shelf space and couldn't part with the books, or maybe he couldn't find the right genre on the shelves to put them in.

The hideous decorative carpet that muffled the footsteps gave a library-like vibe, making Dean feel like he needed to keep quiet. The overhead lights that illuminated the store were dim but hurt Dean's eyes. He would have trouble picking out a book in such dimness.

"What can you tell me about Raintown?" he asked after a moment of listening to the rain outside. Jayden had been patiently waiting in silence for Dean's next question, like a soldier awaiting his next order.

"Nothing, really. Never been there. Only heard stories."

"What kind?"

"Just things about how all the bad kids get sent there. How it's a place for the damned. How people who got there never go back. How some people who went there—"

An incongruously loud beeping resounded in the bookstore. It took Dean a second to realize it was his own phone. "Excuse me," he said as he pulled the phone out. It was Iris again. Frustrated and on the verge of answering to tell her to fuck off, Dean declined the call, put the phone in his pocket, and focused on Jayden again.

"Sorry about that. You were saying?"

"Well, that's pretty much it about Raintown." Jayden scratched his shoulder.

"But those are just stories, right?" Dean asked.

"To tell you the truth, I have no idea, Mr. Watson. No one ever gives a straight answer over here."

"Seems like it." Dean ripped out a page from his notepad and wrote his email down. "Okay, Jayden. I don't have any more questions right now." He handed the piece of paper to Jayden and said, "Here. Email me here, and I'll send you the beta version of my book as soon as it's ready."

"Oh, wow! I can't believe this!" Jayden said as he gently took the paper with both hands as if it were a delicate flower that needed nurturing. "I won't let you down, Mr. Watson, I promise!"

"You've already been a great help. Thanks for that, Jayden." Dean put a hand on Jayden's shoulder and turned toward the door. He grabbed the doorknob and then turned his head to Jayden.

"Oh, by the way. Do you want me to sign any of your books?"

Jayden's jaw dropped as he flashed Dean a Cheshire Cat smile.

Chapter 14

After visiting the bookstore, Dean questioned the remaining three people on the list. The first of the three was Father Walter, who worked as a priest at the church in Suicide Town. The church, although not impressively big—just like everything in the town—was nicely decorated and well-maintained on the inside.

Father Walter was a stern old man who gave curt answers to every question Dean asked. He looked at Dean with visible disapproval and spoke highly of Suicide Town. Dean asked him what religion they were practicing here, and the priest looked at Dean like he got slapped. He said that the religion was a version of Catholicism that didn't shun acts of suicide.

Dean was an atheist, so no matter what the religion was, he found it ridiculous, but the fact that the Pineridge townsfolk practiced Catholicism by choosing to ignore the commandments that didn't work in their favor was even more ludicrous. Dean didn't openly say anything about that to Father Walter, but he did shamelessly pry about what they believed happens in the afterlife, especially with those who commit suicide.

Father Walter gave a vague response that didn't answer Dean's question. When asked about Raintown, Father Walter warned him that even thinking about the topic was abominable. Dean left the church with no new information.

The other two people he questioned were Harriet Woodward from the laundromat and Marshall Chandler, who worked at the pharmacy. They proved to be useless since they gave him no information. He wasn't losing hope just yet because he had only talked to a few people, and he still had a lot to do and see in Suicide Town.

On his way out of the pharmacy, Sheriff Moody waited in front, posing in his signature thumbs-in-belt stance as he leaned on his cruiser. Something about the way he stood told Dean the sheriff was waiting for him. The rain had weakened by then, and night was falling, even though it was not even five p.m. yet.

"Investigation going fine, Watson?"

"Not too great," Dean said.

"So, I heard. Got complaints from people that you were asking private questions, Watson. Couldn't even wait a day, could you?"

The sheriff wasn't going to throw Dean out of town or arrest him. He would have already done it if that was the case. No, he either wanted to give Dean a fair warning, or he was here for an entirely different reason. Whatever it was, Dean stood his ground.

"I'm just trying to find out relevant information for my book, Sheriff. And I'm already finding out things you somehow forgot to tell me. Why's that?" he taunted.

The sheriff pushed himself away from the car and went around to the driver's side. "Get in," the sheriff said as he opened the door and stepped inside.

Dean wondered what game the sheriff was playing. Maybe he started to realize that Dean might be a threat to the town, so he was going to try another strategy to get him to stop asking around. No, he was too friendly. He was going to tell him something that he hadn't told him back in the diner; he was sure of it. Dean got in the car and put the seatbelt on.

"Where are we going?" Dean asked, impatient.

"Just for a short ride," the sheriff said as he turned the key in the ignition. He looked at Dean and said,

"Don't worry, Watson. You're not in trouble. Yet. We're just going to drive round the town so you can get a better idea of where you are."

"I already know where I am."

The car lurched forward. "No, you don't," the sheriff said. "I mean, you do in theory, but that's just it. The legends are way different from reality over here. Usually, the legends are exaggerated. Like the stories my momma used to read to me about that one heroic soldier who single-handedly managed to defeat an entire army of invaders. In reality, he died in the battle. But anyway, here, in Suicide Town, it's the opposite. The legends are mellow compared to the reality."

The sheriff drove past the traffic light and continued down North Street toward the edge of the town, where the road slightly ascended. Soon, the commercial street was behind them, and the few households that occupied the streets were gone as well, leaving Sheriff Moody and Dean on an empty stretch of road surrounded by the tall pines. With the absence of the streetlights, it became much darker, and the sheriff turned on the high beams.

"You meet Jayden Price yet?" the sheriff asked.

"Yeah. Good kid," Dean said.

"Sorry for misleading you. You don't look approachable, no offense. And the kid's been jabbering about you for a while now. I just wanted him to meet his role model."

"I'm not angry," Dean said.

"He wants to become a writer someday, you know? He already wrote some crime fiction that he printed and sold in his bookshop. It sold pretty well, but he doesn't understand that, in this town, everybody supports everybody. Out there, selling his books could be harder. You know how it is as a writer."

Dean agreed. Becoming a full-time writer was difficult. Not only were there too many vanity presses that wanted to publish books from aspiring authors without offering any quality services, but even the big publishers often had bad marketing. Either that, or the book wasn't popular at the moment, or all the big publishers who released books at the same time drowned new releases out—not to mention the authors' low royalty percentage rates, which never surpassed thirty percent.

Dean had managed to make a name for himself, but that was a combination of talent, hard work, and a lot of luck. He had published multiple books in his twenties with small presses, then went on to self-publish a few books, but that turned out to be too costly and inefficient. It wasn't until he wrote *No Time to Die* that he found Alex on a literary agent website. From there, he managed to get published and hit the bestseller ranks. At that moment, his career as a writer soared, and he could finally quit his day job as an accountant.

He had been dating Skylar for a year at that time. She worked as an English teacher in an elementary school in Portland, and the entire time, she believed in Dean and told him that he would catch his big break one day.

You just need one book that'll get published by the big shots and then you'll become famous, she told him over and over, but he didn't really buy it. He was sure that even if he got published, the sales would dry out after some time, and he would have to go back to the drawing board.

Reminiscing the bouncy road that he traveled to get to that fame, he wanted to help future writers, like Jayden Price, reach that goal more easily than he did.

Dean was once in Jayden's place, admiring big authors like Bret Easton Ellis and James Lee Burke, wishing to become like them.

"I could help him out a little bit," Dean said. "I know literary agents and publishers. I can take a look at Jayden's writing and coach him. He'd have no trouble getting published. Besides, he wants to leave town, anyway."

"Yeah. And that's the biggest problem," the sheriff said. "That's why he's never going to become a big writer like you, Watson."

"What does that mean?" Dean frowned, not liking the sheriff's smug tone.

The sheriff stopped the car in the middle of the road and pulled the handbrake. The headlights illuminated the misty road, merging with the impregnable darkness ahead. The sheriff opened the door and stepped outside. Dean sat for a moment, perplexed, then followed the sheriff out. Cold air swaddled his face and neck the moment he stepped out. It was freezing.

Sheriff Moody sauntered in front of the car about fifty feet ahead and then stopped. Dean stopped next to him and looked around. For a moment, he thought that Sheriff Moody really was going to execute him here in the middle of the road. Maybe that was exactly what Suicide Town was all about—not suicide, murder.

"This is as far as we can go," Moody said, turning to Dean with a shuffle. His breath dispersed into a billow of mist, swept away by the night air instantly.

"Is the road blocked ahead?" Dean asked, squinting against the illuminated road.

"No. In fact, if you follow the road, you'll eventually end up in Portland," Moody said.

"So, then, what's the problem?"

The sheriff pointed down the road while tucking the thumb of his other hand in his belt. "About fifty feet down from here was where they found little Tom's dead body almost twenty years ago. His head was cracked open so badly that his brain fell out of his skull." He lowered his hand and tucked the other thumb under the belt before looking at Dean.

"What happened to him?" Dean asked.

"He tried to leave town is what happened."

Dean ogled the sheriff, waiting for a punchline that never came. He snorted in laughter and shook his head in disbelief.

"You're screwing with me, Sheriff," Dean said.

"I wish I was. Remember what I told you about the sickness earlier, at the diner?"

"You mean how it always looms above your heads?"

"Exactly. Well, that sickness is not restricted only to growing up in the town. If you try to leave the town, it gets stronger. It gets so strong that the urge to kill yourself becomes tempting, sweet even. I tell you, I've been a sheriff here for almost fifteen years, and I've lived here my entire life. I have never seen anyone leave Suicide Town and live to tell the tale."

Dean looked down the road where the supposed death occurred. He imagined a little boy facedown on the road, blood and bits of brain pouring out of the gaping hole in his skull and onto the concrete. He looked back at the sheriff and asked, "You're telling me you can't leave the town because you'll end up committing suicide?"

Sheriff Moody nodded. Dean looked down the road again at the threatening, perpetual darkness ahead as if it would swallow him up if he took another step farther. Something changed about this place with nightfall. Dean couldn't tell what, but the darkness brought with it something ominous that he couldn't explain. He wanted nothing more than to retreat to the car and go back to the safety of Suicide Town.

"You don't believe me," Moody said, breaking the silence.

Dean looked at him. It was a statement and not a question. Dean thought about denying it but decided to stick to his guns instead.

"It's like you said earlier, Sheriff. It can probably be explained by logic." He wanted to add that perhaps the people who had tried to leave the town and ended up killing themselves did so under the influence of mass hysteria or a placebo effect. It sounded offensive in his head, so he chose not to say that. "Have you ever tried to leave Suicide Town, Sheriff?"

"Once," Moody said after a moment of hesitation.

"And then you wanted to commit suicide?" Dean asked.

"Yeah. Can't even get farther than this without wanting to floor the gas pedal and veer into the trees. Some people, who I've known for years, ended like that."

"So, this kid, Tom. What happened to him?"

"It happened about twenty years ago, back when my pops was still a sheriff. Tom wanted to leave the town and talked about it openly all the time. Everybody told him he was crazy, of course, including myself. One night, he just up and disappeared. The entire town organized a search party, but we couldn't find him. My old man found him on this road the very next morning. They determined that he ended up bashing his own head on the road. It was a huge tragedy, that one. Everybody in town gathered for the funeral. In a small town like this one, you don't get to ignore something like that."

Jayden's words echoed in Dean's head. *I planned on leaving, but that's not an option.* That explained a lot. Dean guessed that the younger generations were taught that staying in your hometown was a completely normal—and expected—thing.

"Nobody has ever left Suicide Town?"

"Nobody who has ever lived here has left and survived the hour. The visitors like you . . . they come and go. But if they break the rules, they think they'll be fine when they leave the town. They never are," the sheriff said in a somber tone.

That only confirmed Moody had already known what had happened to Bauer, even before Dean had told him about it. Dean looked down the road again. He couldn't help but imagine piles of bones littering the road ahead, just out of the headlight's reach. How many souls have tried to escape Suicide Town, desperate for a better life or a clean slate? How many of them knew the risks, and despite that, put themselves in danger? They must have really hated living here.

Dean put himself in their shoes for a moment. After living in a small town like this for more than thirty years, who was to say that he wouldn't do the same thing? It was made up of two streets that were populated by the same people, with nothing ever new to see and no one new to meet. Townsfolk were unable to travel, trapped under their neighbors' judgmental gazes, neighbors who were itching for the next rumor, desperate to kill time. Suicide didn't seem like such a bad option anymore.

"Come on," Sheriff Moody said, breaking toward the car. "Let's get back to town."

Dean didn't need to be told twice.

Chapter 15

Back in the motel room, Dean replayed the day in his head. The voices of the people he spoke to swirled in his head like a tornado, mixing into one big amalgamation of incoherent thoughts. Yet, despite the army of thoughts that occupied his mind, Dean was able to isolate what he thought was important.

Something was definitely off about this town. Although the sheriff's words stuck with Dean more than the rest of the townsfolk's, he had to give credit to Robert's wetland theory. By far, that seemed like the most logical explanation. If the residual vapors coming from the dried swamp affected the people living in the town, by making them suicidal, coupled with the teachings and beliefs they passed on to younger generations, it was no wonder that the residents of Suicide Town believed they were stuck here.

What about the ones who tried getting out? Sheriff Moody said that he hadn't seen a single person surviving the hour, but he couldn't know that for sure. For all he knew, the ones that left never returned. Maybe they had no family in Suicide Town to keep in touch with, either.

Jayden's words returned to Dean. *I planned on leaving, but that's not an option.* On the drive back, Sheriff Moody told Dean that Jayden's dad committed suicide when Jayden was only four years old and that his mother went missing a few years after that. Jayden's grandma took care of him for the time being, and since she hung herself a few years ago, it's only Jayden now.

Dean felt sorry for the kid. He wanted to help him and others like him in the town who were in the same position. To do that, he needed to prove to the townsfolk that the reason for such a high number of suicides had nothing to do with the supernatural. He was aware that failing to convince them was a big possibility, but he didn't need to solve the mystery right away. He could gather enough evidence, write the book, and once it became a hit, people would flock to Suicide Town. The legend would be revealed as only an old wives' tale.

Dean tossed the notepad on the nightstand. The glowing orange light in the tiny motel room wasn't bright enough. Depression seeped into the jaundiced room, especially since night had fallen. Dean rummaged through the drawers, hoping to find something that Joshua Bauer might have left before leaving, but no luck.

After organizing his thoughts, Dean ate the leftover burger from Rainy Days. Even cold, it was still heavenly. That would be his dinner for tonight because it was getting late, and everything probably closed early in Suicide Town.

He slid the curtains aside; the blinds were down. These weren't the typical blinds. They looked like hurricane shutters, heavy and sturdy. Except these were inside, and not outside the window. It was as if someone went out of their way to install blinds like these.

He pulled the pull cord, but the blinds remained stuck. Dean tried harder, but it wouldn't budge. He didn't want to mess anything up and have to pay for it later, so he returned to the reception where Nelson Baxter was reading a book, his feet propped up on the countertop.

"Excuse me," Dean said. Nelson swung his legs off the desk and stood, focusing on Dean. "I can't pull the blinds up. Are they stuck or something?"

"Oh, right." Baxter scratched his round chin. "I forgot to mention that the blinds are fixed and can't be raised. We had some incidents in the past, and I had to nail them down."

"I see. Are all the rooms like that?"

"Yup."

"No wonder you guys are so suicidal," Dean joked. "How about letting in some natural light? I'll pull the blinds down by midnight."

"No can do, mister. The sheriff and I made this decision. It's for the best, given what happened in the past."

"You mean . . . someone looked outside when they weren't supposed to, right?"

Baxter froze but said nothing for a moment. "It's for protection," he finally said.

"I get that, but protection from what?"

"That's private matters, Mr. Watson. I'd appreciate it if you didn't pry into something so delicate."

Dean gave Baxter a tight-lipped smile. "Point taken." He sauntered back to his room. It was getting late, so he got ready for bed. He opened his laptop. No Wi-Fi hotspots. No surprise there. The internet on his phone worked, but only selectively, prompting Dean to suspect certain websites were censored in Suicide Town. Perhaps the townsfolk was trying not to let information about the town leak to outside sources? He sent Alex a message to test the connection.

> *Arrived to the town earlier today. This is one weird place.*

151

He put his phone on the nightstand and got under the coarse blanket. No sooner had he done that, his phone buzzed with a message. Dean took it, fully expecting an error notification informing him that his message couldn't be sent. Instead, it was a reply from Alex.

> *Good luck out there. Let me know if you need anything.*

Communication with the outside world—at least to that extent—gave Dean some assurance. Earlier, he had sent all the relevant info to Alex in case something happened to him and if the police needed to be involved. Dean was doing all this for the book and to find out what happened to Bauer, but if it got too bad, he could always pull out and write the book based on the information he had gathered.

Dean flipped the switch on the wall to turn off the lights, engulfing the room in void-like darkness. He turned his head in the direction of the curtains. He wondered what went through Joshua Bauer's mind when he slept in the same motel room, in the same bed. With those thoughts, he quickly drifted into sleep.

***

He wasn't sure how long had passed since he fell asleep. It could have been five hours or five minutes, but when he opened his eyes, the same darkness that he fell asleep to awaited him. He was wide awake. That happened often ever since his accident; he'd have difficulty falling asleep despite being dead tired, then he'd jerk awake in the middle of the night, unable to fall asleep again for hours.

Dean must have had the same nightmare that jerked him awake, but when he awoke, he needed to use the bathroom. He fumbled for the switch above him and turned on the lights. He went to the bathroom and checked his phone when he returned. It was a little past two a.m.

He got into bed, turned off the lights, and turned on his side. With the absence of his shuffling, silence impregnated the room—for a moment. A sound caused him to open his eyes.

A tap on the window.

It was only for a fraction of a second and light enough for Dean's calm breathing to drown it out, but in the absence of all the other noises in the room, it might as well have sounded like a thunderclap. Dean froze and held his breath, his eyes wide open. Silence. He waited so long that his eyes burned from the lack of blinking.

Maybe the tap on the window was his imagination or maybe a heavier droplet of rain—

The rain had stopped, Dean thought, hence the absence of noise. This was unnatural. No, not just unnatural. Wrong. Dean couldn't shake the feeling that the absence of rain in Suicide Town was never a good thing.

A low shuffle came just outside his window. Or maybe it was a scrape or a scratch? Dean couldn't tell. The darkness in the room was no longer as blinding as it was before his eyes had adjusted. He could see the vague shape of the curtains, but nothing more.

Tap.

The tapping was so loud that Dean jerked upright. With his eyes still fixated on the window, he blindly patted the wall until his fingers touched the smooth switch. He flipped it on and bathed the motel room in the light's weak glow. At that moment, that light seemed brighter than a pair of high beams down the road.

Silence stepped in again. Dean gently moved the blanket aside and touched the floor with his toes before planting his feet down. He stood as slowly as he could, his head still craned to stare at the window. The bed creaked under his weight. Dean tiptoed around the bed toward the window and turned his head to listen.

His shallow breath and the pulsating in his neck stole the spotlight until a dragging sound came from the wall to the right, causing Dean to jerk his head to the sound and freeze in place. The sound crept from the window toward the corner of the room. Dean imagined a person standing on the other side dragging a stick along the wall.

Maybe it's an animal? Dean tried to rationalize, but suddenly, he remembered the deer from Joshua's video. *That was no deer.*

Dean followed with his head as the dragging reached near the corner of the room, then stopped. Accompanied by that came another sound that erased any doubts Dean had it was an animal.

A faint squeak came from the other side of the wall. Just like the tap on the window, it happened in a fraction of a millisecond, but Dean was sure that the squeak came from a gasping human throat. He leaned his ear against the cold wall, hoping to discern the sound.

Deafening silence permeated the air.

He deduced that the continuous dragging and tapping was all in his head. He wanted to pull the curtains aside and yank the blinds up to see what was outside.

He barely had time to finish that thought when a high-pitched wail erupted in his ear. Dean flinched back from the wall as if burned by a warm stove. He listened as the howl filled every inch of the room. Dean's memory transported him to the moment he first watched Joshua Bauer's video. *It was the same motel and the same room.* The hairs on his arms pricked as the agonizing screech echoed, a screech that seemed endless.

The howl weakened and faded, like a person running out of breath, until it ended with a similar squeak as before. And just like that, it was gone. Silence returned. Dean's fear paralyzed him. His fists were clenched, and his toes pressed hard against the floor like talons.

As much as he hated averting his gaze from the wall with the window, it compelled him to spin and scan the room. He looked back at the window and then got on his knees to peek under the bed. Nothing was there. No monsters lurking under, no pairs of eyes staring back at him, no hairy claws reaching out from the darkness.

With that, the gentle pattering of the rain returned, and Dean felt his entire being relax. At that moment, the tapping, dragging, and screaming was a million light years away. Dean took another look at the window and then shook his head.

"They're fucking with me," he said to himself. "The motherfuckers are trying to prank me."

He pushed down the urge to storm out on the street and yell at whoever was bothering him to fuck off, but he quickly gave up on that idea when he realized he would need to get dressed and probably fight Baxter if he was still at the front desk. Dean returned to bed, no longer unnerved but rather pissed.

Yet, whenever he closed his eyes, he couldn't help but imagine a ragged, monstrous figure standing above his bed, staring and grinning. Dean opened his eyes and looked around the room multiple times to put his mind at ease.

He didn't fall asleep until much later.

Chapter 16

It was still dark when he woke up, but his phone's bright screen told him it was nine a.m. Despite his exhaustion, Dean got out of bed. He had people to question. Last night's events hadn't struck him until he started brushing his teeth. He wondered what that was all about and who would do such a thing.

He understood that Suicide Town's people must have been bored out of their minds, so playing a joke on a new visitor was the perfect way to pass the time. Not a lot of people lived here, so it would be perfectly easy to keep the plan secretive. But Joshua Bauer was dead, and this was no laughing matter. Dean would get to the bottom of this, no matter what. On his way out, he saw Baxter seated at the front desk. He might as well have been fused with the chair with the amount of time he spent on it.

"Morning, Mr. Watson," Nelson Baxter said amicably.

Dean greeted him back. "Hi."

"Heading out already?"

"Yeah. Got a lot of work to do."

Dean was already at the door with his hand on the knob when Baxter called out to him. "Well, hang on a second." Dean turned to Baxter. "You want to find out more about our town, correct?"

Dean let go of the knob and faced Baxter. "Go on," he said, his voice flat.

"Try talking to Lawrence. He's the local mechanic on Wilton Street," Baxter said. "He actually works as an Escorter, which means it's his job to make sure no one breaks the rules. He'll have all the answers for you."

"Thanks. Anyone else?"

"He's your best bet. Try him, and if you hit a wall, come back, and I'll give you some more names if I can think of them."

"Appreciate it," Dean said as he pulled his notepad out and wrote down *LAWRENCE MECHANIC, WILTON STREET*.

Once Baxter explained to Dean how to get to Wilton Street, Dean was on his way out. Outside, it rained again. His stomach rumbled, and he didn't want to start his day on an empty stomach. The first place he thought of was Rainy Days.

On his way past the diner, he glanced at the obituaries. Most of the people in the pictures were old, except for two faces, who were middle-aged, and one woman in her thirties. Not only were their names and dates written but also how they committed suicide. Dean found it morbid.

He sped past the board, then something caught Dean's eye.

When he walked past the motel rooms overlooking the street, he noticed a horizontal black streak on the wall between two windows—it was between rooms ten and eleven. Dean got closer and squinted at the black stuff. Tiny droplets slid down where they dried on the wall, but it wasn't black paint, Dean figured when he got even closer. It was somewhat transparent, like black paint added to water. More of the stuff was on the windowsills and on the floor—

A black handprint on his room's window paused all thoughts. Lowering his gaze, Dean's eyes fell on a distinct shoe print in the remains of the black puddle. Even as he stared at it, the rain bleached the black substance, further diluting it. It would be gone soon. Dean looked up and down the street to see if any of the townsfolk were having a good laugh at his reaction.

The street was empty. With hurried steps, Dean continued walking to Rainy Days.

***

"Mr. Big Shot Writer," Susan said with buoyancy in her tone as she approached Dean's table. "Looks like this place has stolen your heart. Or maybe it was something else." She winked.

Dean smiled back and said, "I assume you serve breakfast."

"Sure do, hun. How does eggs and bacon and a couple of toasts sound?"

"Sounds good. And a cup of coffee with that, please."

"You got it, sugar."

"Thank you."

People came and went while Dean waited for his food. Sheriff Moody entered at one point, and after greeting everyone in the diner, he approached Dean. "How'd the first night go, Watson?"

"I didn't look, if that's what you're asking," Dean replied.

"I know you didn't. I meant, did you have any trouble sleeping?"

"Aside from the scream of whoever was trying to prank me, you mean?"

The sheriff let out a chuckle and shook his head. He looked like he didn't know what to say.

"Look, I don't know what exactly is going on here, Sheriff, but if you think you can scare me into running off, that's not gonna happen. I'm not leaving until I get to the bottom of this."

"Here's your coffee, Sheriff," Susan said as she put the steaming plastic cup on the counter and retreated to the kitchen.

"I gotta go, Watson. You stay out of trouble, you hear?" Sheriff Moody said. He eyed Dean a second longer before turning around and leaving with his coffee.

Dean wrote a note that the sheriff was hiding something. A few minutes later, Susan arrived with two platters of food. "Here you go, hun," she said with a smile as she put one platter on the table in front of Dean. "Enjoy."

Just then, a man bumped into Susan, causing her to teeter. The other platter slipped from her hand and fell to the ground. The ear-splitting crash attracted the other guests' attention, who immediately stopped talking to each other and stared at the commotion. Susan opened her mouth in a silent gasp as she stared at the shards of glass and food scattered on the floor.

"Oh, my. I'm so sorry, Elliot," Susan said to the man, but the person simply strode out of the bar without looking at the waitress, let alone muttering an apology. Dean followed the person with his gaze as he walked past the window. He wore a cap and a thick, dirty jacket. He had a thick beard, and his facial expression conveyed frustration and enmity.

"Everything's okay, folks," Susan said. She then turned to Dean. "Don't worry about that, hun. That's Elliot. He hasn't really been himself since his wife, Rachel, died."

"His wife died? Killed herself?" Dean asked.

"Um . . . yeah. Sorry. Forget I said anything. I gotta go clean this up," Susan recited and headed out of there.

Dean wrote *ELLIOT AND RACHEL. RACHEL DIED* in his notepad. It might not be of any significance, but Dean still wanted to investigate it, especially if only one person in town acted like an asshole.

After finishing breakfast, Dean paid for his meal and thanked Susan before leaving. He located Wilton Street, which was close to North Street. The mechanic was easy to locate, thanks to a rusted metallic post embedded in the ground that simply said *MECHANIC* with faded letters. A fence guarded two adjacent garages; one was closed, the other one was open.

In big cities, visiting a mechanic usually meant constant loud noises coming from the place. This one was quiet. Dean prudently walked onto the property and looked around. He doubted that whoever worked here left the area unattended.

"Hello?" he tried calling out.

No response. Dean walked further ahead and peeked inside the garage. The smell of oil, gas, and something else Dean couldn't identify filled the interior. "Hello?" he shouted again. Upon entering, he noticed that no wall separated the garages, giving him the freedom to peek toward the other one. An oil-stained desk occupied the inside, with messy stacks of papers on top.

"Hey!" a coarse voice said behind Dean. Dean shot around. A gaunt man faced him, who stared back at him with a frown. "Need something?" he asked, sounding more like *get the fuck out of here before I call the cops*.

"Hi. I shouted, but you probably didn't hear me," Dean said, refusing to apologize. "My name's Dean. I'm—"

"Yeah, I know who you are," the man said. "I asked if you need something."

Dean stared for a moment at the man's thinning V-shaped hairline and the protruding cheekbones above the sunken cheeks. His eyes bulged out of his skull, which made Dean think of a humanoid frog.

"Lawrence, right? Nelson Baxter gave me your address. I just want a few questions answered, then I'll be on my way."

"That fat fuck," Lawrence muttered under his breath.

He walked past Dean without even looking at him and entered the garage with his hands in his pockets. Dean followed Lawrence, not caring that he got no permission to do so. He felt like any wrong move could make the mechanic angry, and if that was the case, acting polite wouldn't get him any answers. He would need to be aggressive with Lawrence; that's what he sensed.

Lawrence walked up to the bench by the wall where a tool belt hung. He put the tool belt on and turned to Dean. "Well, go on. Ask and then scram because I have a lot of work to do. I'm a hard-working man trying to make a living, and I don't have time to play detective."

Starting with basic questions would yield no results with Lawrence. His hunch told him that the mechanic would dismiss the questions, might even call them stupid, or tell Dean to bother someone else with them. Dean would need to ask Lawrence questions that he'd believe were not a waste of his time.

"How about you tell me why I can't look out the window at night?" Dean asked.

"Rules are rules," Lawrence said. "You don't follow them; you get punished like every person living here would. Like I said, I'm too busy with my own work to be bothered with any nonsense. You think I became the most successful mechanic in Suicide Town by wasting my time chasing rumors and urban legends?"

The most successful mechanic in Suicide Town. More like the only mechanic in town, Dean thought to himself, suppressing laughter. *Okay, so going into details is out of the question. I'm going to need to ask about other things, instead.*

"Have you lived here your entire life?" he asked.

"Yeah," Lawrence brusquely retorted. He walked to the desk and pulled a rickety wooden chair out. He slumped into it and looked at Dean with impatience in his eyes. Any moment now, he was going to ask Dean to leave.

"Have you ever tried to leave?"

"No."

"Why not?"

"Why would I?" Lawrence shrugged. "I'm respected here. I run a successful business, which helps me earn good cash. Thanks to this job only, I was able to buy a house in less than a year."

Dean nodded. It was impossible not to notice Lawrence bragging with every opportunity he got. But was he really bragging, or was he just trying to look more glamorous than he was in front of Dean? He must have felt threatened, maybe even envious. He probably knew how successful Dean used to be, and his ego got the better of him and was forcing him to prove an insignificant point.

Lawrence's not-so-subtle boasting fell on deaf ears. The business he ran as a mechanic was probably lucrative for Suicide Town's standards but not enough to live a luxurious life. Lawrence oddly reminded Dean of Morgan from high school.

Morgan was a huge anime fan who ended up being the butt of many jokes in school. Every time someone made fun of him, he would theatrically claim how he was going to show them all one day.

A few years after high school, Dean got a friend request on Facebook from someone named Morgan Underdog. He accepted the request, and he sure had a lot of stuff on his profile. Morgan had become a reseller—or what they called a scalper—and he made money from buying rare goods, like limited edition electronics or sneakers, and reselling them at an inflated price.

He constantly posted before and after pictures of himself with quotes about how he made it in life despite nobody believing in him. While managing to earn money as a scalper was impressive, Dean knew that he realistically wasn't earning more than a five-figure salary from it. Lawrence was the same. He was a cat pretending to be a lion, and Dean saw right through him.

"Baxter told me that you work as an Escorter. What does that mean?" Dean asked.

"Means I make sure troublemakers like you don't go breaking any important rules."

"Is that all you do?"

"Yes," Lawrence shot back.

"So, you just patrol around the town and make sure everybody is inside before curfew?"

"Right."

"And then what? You go inside as well, or you stay out?"

"No one stays outside after curfew."

"What if they wait until you're all out of sight and then get out?"

"There's only one kind of person who would do that. Outsiders. The people who live here don't need to be told twice not to look or go out after curfew."

Dean nodded. He looked around the garage while thinking. Lawrence was very defensive, and it was impossible to tell if it was because he hid some information or because of his aversion toward visitors.

Either way, he wouldn't answer anything that he thought would be unfit for someone like Dean to know.

"What can you tell me about Elliot and Rachel?" Dean asked.

"Rachel Wood, you mean?" Lawrence raised an eyebrow.

"Is there another Rachel associated with an Elliot?"

Lawrence remained silent for a moment as if realizing he was the one who asked a stupid question this time. He shrugged again and said, "Nothing much. They were married. She died. End of story."

"How did she die?"

"You ask a lot of questions."

Lawrence and Dean locked eyes in a staring contest for a moment. Dean refused to look away. Was Lawrence like this with everyone in the town or just the outsiders? Dean was willing to bet that it was the latter. He could almost imagine Lawrence laughing at jokes with his neighbors in a bar on a Saturday night. Dean knew the kind of person Lawrence was. He was good to the people he knew and trusted, but to everyone else, he was hostile. A man who would give his arm for his neighbors but take one from anyone else, Dean assumed.

"What are you guys hiding so much?" Dean provoked.

"You're a writer; I know that. And you need information if you're going to write a new book, but I'm not going to help some outsider pretending to care about us, when we both know that all you want out of this is a story that can earn you cash."

Dean thought about disagreeing with the mechanic, then stopped himself when he realized it would not help his case in any way. If anything, it would only stretch the tension between the two of them.

"All right," Dean said. "One final question. What can you tell me about Joshua Bauer?"

"What about him?"

"He came to your town, first of all. He left in a hurry, then soon after, he committed suicide." Dean paused to gauge Lawrence's reaction. The mechanic didn't seem to flinch. Not even a slight change in his facial expression; nothing to indicate shock.

"Okay. So, what do you want from me?" Lawrence asked.

"Something happened to him while he was here. Something that changed him and made him commit suicide. That's at least what his wife said. But you know what else she said? She said that his suicide came out of the blue. He was a healthy man with no history of drug abuse or mental illnesses. So, what happened to him?"

"Are you suggesting someone killed him?"

"Those are your words, not mine."

Lawrence transfixed his gaze on Dean as if trying to think of what to say. Slowly, he leaned across the table so that he was closer to Dean. "You wanna know what happened to him?"

Dean said nothing. Lawrence was smart enough to know the answer to that question without Dean having to say it.

"He looked," the mechanic said with a sense of simplicity and finality. He stood and walked past Dean. "Now, if you'll excuse me, I have work to do. You know the way out."

The discussion was over.

Chapter 17

After his talk with Lawrence, Dean wandered the town's streets in search of random shops. He wanted to talk to someone who was not recommended by the sheriff and the motel owner because they easily might have given Dean names of the people who had their stories straight and would not arouse any suspicion.

The more Dean talked to the townsfolk, the more it solidified his theory that people were hiding something. Everyone seemed to have the same story, as if they had agreed to what they would say to any outsiders, word by word; those were the ones who were willing to talk. But on rare occasions, Dean ran into people who refused to exchange more than a few words with him.

When he entered a locksmith's shop, the woman working there warned him that she was closing, and he should be on his way. He told her that he only wanted to ask her a few questions, to which the woman responded by becoming erratic, telling him she was in a rush. Even when Dean assured her it would only take two minutes of her time, the woman refused to cooperate.

By late afternoon, Dean managed to find out from Jayden Price that the person he was looking for, Elliot Wood, lived on Park Street. All he knew about the guy was that he had been married to Rachel Wood and worked in the town hall in administration. Jayden Price also told Dean that Rachel died just recently and that her death came as a shock to everyone because she was so young.

Dean thanked the bookstore owner and went to visit the address. It was a regular house, no different from the neighboring ones. Dean was a little apprehensive about speaking to Elliot Wood because of his attitude at the diner. If he behaved like that with people he had known for years, what could Dean expect?

He rang the doorbell and waited. The rain that day had gone from bouts of drizzle to bucket-full downpours. Now, it was a steady pelleting that made Dean regret not going by car or at least bringing an umbrella. As he waited for Elliot to open, he noticed on the lawn more of the same black substances as in front of the motel. It was close to the door, just under the roof where the rain couldn't reach. Some shapes were smeared, others simply looked like they had splashed onto the grass.

Instinctively, Dean looked up at the sky. It was gray and becoming black fast. He put out his palm and observed the droplets that landed on his skin. They were colorless, and not black, like he had expected them to be. Earlier, he spoke to some people about the rain and what it was like during other seasons. He learned that the rain never really stopped. The best they had was a light drizzle for days. Even during winter, they either had rain and snow at the same time or just rain—never just snow.

Dean also learned that everything in the town stayed wilted throughout the year, as it was at that moment. The trees never bloomed, yet they refused to die. The meager imagination of Suicide Town being a more perky place during summer quickly abandoned Dean, and he started to understand more and more why people were so suicidal here.

If the rain really was so incessant and forced people to stay inside most of the time, they would have probably developed cabin fever and signs of depression. The people here had probably made up all the stories about wetland vapors and being unable to leave the town to cope.

Dean turned to the door. He rang the doorbell again, and after some waiting, he knocked on the door. No response. Either not home or didn't give a shit enough to answer the door. Dean turned around and stepped off the property, ready to return to the motel.

"You're looking for Elliot Wood, right?" an old man asked him in passing.

"Yes. Do you know where he is?"

"He's usually at the bar around this time. Try looking for him there."

Not only did the people here know each other, but they also knew where everyone was at any given time. Dean cringed at the thought of living a life like that.

***

The Protector was a bar about as small as Dean expected. The owner and two guests were in there, and as soon as Dean entered, they turned their heads to face him before resuming their chatter. When Dean asked about Elliot Wood, they told him that they hadn't seen him since morning.

Dean bought a drink and waited a little at the bar. Around that time was when Iris had called him again. He let the phone ring without picking up, telling himself once again that, if it was an emergency, she would have sent him a message.

While waiting, Dean went through his notes once more. Right now, he had more questions than answers, and with each conversation, more questions arose like a many-headed Hydra. Who was Rachel Wood? Why did she die so young? What happened to Joshua Bauer? What was with all the rules? What was with

Raintown? What was with the black substances that he had found around the town?

An hour had passed when Dean decided he was done waiting. He paid for his drink and returned to the motel. The black substance had been completely washed away by then—from the floor and the wall and windows. He sat on the bed of his motel room, listening to the shower outside the window. Although his inspiration for writing was still up in the sky, he felt like he had reached a dead-end with his investigation. Someone—everyone—was blocking him from finding out more than they wanted to allow him.

Dean looked toward the window. The black handprint on the glass flashed before his eyes. *Wanna know what happened to him? He looked.* The screech from yesterday. *He looked.* The scratching. *If you look, we'll know.*

"This is bullshit," Dean said as he stood. He wasn't going to let them play him like this. He walked up to the curtains to yank them aside, then stopped. His resolve to move the curtains had suddenly drained. As much as he wanted to pull them, it felt wrong to do so.

Dean looked over his shoulder, toward the door. He imagined Baxter standing there, staring at him, ready to jump in if Dean so much as thought about breaking the town's precious rules. He had locked the door, so there was no way Nelson Baxter could barge in. Just as quickly as that thought infested Dean's mind, he forced it out.

What the hell are you thinking? It's just superstition. The townsfolk here are bullshitters.

With that, he faced forward again and grabbed a clump of the old, thick curtains. They might as well have served as a blanket. They had a tenuous sour smell to them, which told Dean that Baxter rarely—or never—cleaned them. Without further mulling over the dos and don'ts of why he shouldn't do it, Dean yanked the curtains aside and looked at the indoor blinds on the window.

They were roller-type blinds that blocked out even a sliver of light from peering inside. Dean tried the cord once more, but the blinds wouldn't budge. Dean wedged his fingers between the tightly compressed rolls of the blinds and tried prying them open a crack, but it felt like trying to open something that was cemented—which very well might have been the case, he realized.

He turned around and looked at his jacket splayed on the bed. He rifled through the pockets until he found the keys and clutched them. He went back to the blinds and gripped the key with the blade facing forward between his forefinger and middle finger, ready to thrust.

At first, he tried wedging the key between the rolls, just as he did with his fingers. The tip of the key produced a scraping sound against the plastic but did nothing to penetrate. Dean moved the key up and down to find a better angle, but to no avail. The blinds had rattled, producing an alarming noise in the absence of any other sounds in the room.

Dean looked back at the door, then at the blinds. Frustrated, he squeezed the key so hard that his palm hurt. With one swift motion, he thrust the key at the blinds. Scraping and rattling ensued for a moment, too loud for comfort. A scratch marked one of the rolls now. Dean had to aim between the rolls.

He readjusted his grip on the key, aimed, and then thrust forward. A loud pop and rattle ensued, and the key was stuck in the blinds. Dean had to wiggle the key left and right to pull it out. Once free, he looked at his work.

The key cut a tiny horizontal slit in the blinds. A weak orange beam of light peered through it. The hole was around Dean's chest height, so he stooped to look. Immediately, the building across the street came into view.

Hell yeah!

Dean swept his gaze from left to right to get a full scope of the view. Despite the relatively obscured view, he was able to see enough. Dean tried once more to pry open the rolls from the new hole, but they wouldn't budge. He wondered if they truly had been cemented to stop people like him from looking.

What happened to Joshua Bauer? He looked, that's what happened.

Tonight, Dean was going to follow in his footsteps.

Chapter 18

After nicking the blinds, Dean pulled the curtains back over the windows, but for the remainder of the night in the motel room, he checked on the hole multiple times just to make sure it was still there. It was a foolish thing to do, and he knew it, but he couldn't help it.

The town is already starting to get to you, he thought to himself with a scoff.

Dean spent more time sifting through all his notes to check if he had missed something of relevance. He knew that he would never find out anything of significance if he tried getting the information from the townsfolk. He needed to do something unorthodox to get his much-desired information. The townsfolk would hate him for it if they found out. They might even kick him out of Suicide Town, but it was a risk Dean had to take—for his own sake and for the sake of Joshua Bauer's wife.

It was getting late, but Dean didn't feel sleepy yet, so he opened his laptop and compiled his notes there. The more he wrote, the more he started to believe that one ruined writer would not be enough to crack this case. This was much bigger than him and might even require involving the police. Right now, though, he had no evidence of any foul play. He needed to find something concrete that would confirm whether this town was as dangerous as he thought.

He set his alarm to five minutes until one a.m., even though he suspected he might not need it if the sounds from last night returned. He double-checked if he had locked the door and then went to bed. Excitement surged through him, rendering him unable to sleep.

In those quiet moments, his mind often inadvertently drifted to places he didn't want to be. Right now, he thought about Skylar and the life they had together before the accident. He never learned to appreciate her the way he should have, and that regret ate away at him like a malignant tumor spreading across his organs.

Maybe if he had behaved differently, things would have been different between them. Maybe if he hadn't been so ill-tempered. There were times when he had hurt Skylar with his words so badly, she cried. At the time, he was too angry and too selfish to care. It even brought him joy that he could affect her that way. He was miserable, and at times, he was angry at her for not reciprocating the misery. So, he often unconsciously or consciously went out of his way to bring her down to the shitty pit that he was in.

Looking back on those memories, he wished more than anything that he could take it all back. Skylar stayed with him in the most difficult period of his life to support him, even though it brought her down. She stuck with him through the lawsuits, the cancel culture, the death threats, the termination of his contract with the publisher, his inability to write . . .

It all lasted until she couldn't take it anymore. As much as Dean's soul ached at the thought of Skylar being happy with another man, he wished her the happiness she hadn't experienced with Dean.

The pitter-patter of the rain soothed Dean, his eyes losing the battle to stay awake.

***

He had the same dream of his drive back from the show with Skylar. Dean was driving over the speed limit, but it was okay because this was an empty strip of road.

He leaned toward her side of the seat and kissed her. One kiss turned into a make out session. Dean glanced at the road every couple of seconds just to make sure he wasn't swerving toward the railing.

The rain was so heavy, obscuring everything around the car, ramping up the sensuality for Dean. He leaned toward Sky's neck and gently kissed it, caressing his lips against her skin, drawing out Skylar's moans. Then, in an instant, her entire body became rigid.

"Dean!" she screamed.

Dean's head pivoted toward the road, but it was too late. The high beams illuminated a little boy on a bicycle in a raincoat. In that sliver of a moment, between Dean heeling the brake pedal and the car colliding with the child, Dean caught a glimpse of the boy's face, and it would haunt him most nights. His big eyes stared at the car in confusion.

He probably didn't even have the time to understand what was going on until it was too late. The kid's limp body fell on top of the hood, slamming against the windshield so hard that it spider-webbed and then rolled above the car's roof.

The car screeched to a halt, leaving the rain shower outside as the only discernible noise. All Dean could do for a moment was white-knuckle the steering wheel while staring at the cracked, bloodstained windshield. The rain washed off the blood, and Dean remembered thinking that, if the rain washed the blood off, then everything would be okay; it would be as if nothing ever happened. The windshield was cracked, but those were easy to change, right?

He looked at the side-view mirror, and through the darkness, he could make out the crushed bicycle and the mangled, limp body of the boy. He was lying facedown, a pool of blood from his head fusing with the heavy rain on the concrete.

The blaring alarm on Dean's phone woke him up from the dream. Thank god. He snatched the phone from the nightstand and turned the alarm off. Darkness engulfed the room, but his eyes were able to make out the shape of the curtains. Dean got up and put on his clothes, unaware of what to expect.

Instead of moving the curtains aside, he got behind them and located the perforation he had made. He squinted through it, and the empty, illuminated street greeted him. He expected an eye to stare back at him for breaking the rule, but he didn't break the rule just yet. He still had a few minutes until one a.m. Dean sat on the bed and waited in darkness and silence. He didn't want to turn on the light to avoid attracting any unwanted attention. He wanted to break the rule and prove to the people that nothing was going to happen to him.

Dean nervously glanced at the clock on his phone over and over, watching the minutes tick by, slow and painful. When one a.m. finally came, he returned behind the curtains and peeked again, his heart practically hammering against his chest. Nothing was happening.

No, that was wrong. Something *was* happening. The rain had stopped. Dean watched the droplets that fell from the sky and battered the street . . . just stop. One moment, the rain was here; the other, gone as if someone had flipped an off switch. That was weird. It was almost as weird as seeing *no* rain in Suicide Town.

The newfound silence felt strange, almost unnerving. He stared at the street from various angles, hoping to detect something, but aside from the lack of rain, nothing was going on. Dean wished that he had a chair he could drag to the window to sit and wait for something to happen; his body was slumping from being in the stooped position.

He returned to the edge of the bed and waited. He figured he'd hear something outside, like scratching or squeaking, just like last night, but he still peeped through the hole in the blinds every few minutes to make sure he didn't miss anything.

Dean tried to remember what Joshua Bauer had said in the video. Didn't he say that something happens outside every night? What time was Dean awake last night when he heard that scream? A little after two, maybe? Either way, he was too wide awake to go back to bed. He wondered if Baxter was still awake, and if he wasn't where he was right now.

Dean unlocked the door as quietly as he could and peeked into the hallway. It was empty and quiet, and even his breathing seemed too loud. Dean tiptoed down the hall and stopped near the corner. The entire building was dark. He perked his ears in hopes of detecting any sounds coming from the desk, and sure enough, he heard something almost immediately.

Snoring.

Dean peeked around the corner and saw a bulky figure sitting in a chair, its belly rising and falling. The window that overlooked the street had been covered with something, but Dean couldn't see with what because it was too dark. Either way, Baxter went to lengths to ensure that the guests couldn't look outside. Dean was sure that the door was locked as well, preventing him from leaving.

He returned to his room, gently closed the door, and locked it again. As soon as the lock clicked, a sound nearby snatched his attention.

Shuffling.

As excited as Dean was, he couldn't shake the feeling of looming dread. Something told him that he should just go back to bed and forget about breaking the rules, but his logic refused to believe that something supernatural was going on in the town. He was determined to prove it.

Dean went behind the curtain and leaned down to peer through the hole. Everything was still, except for the low shuffling that came just to the right outside Dean's line of sight. He moved to the left and squinted on one eye to take a better look, but nothing came into view.

He then noticed tiny bits of black mottling the road. When did that appear? Something came into view, and the street disappeared, replaced by darkness. He couldn't see anything. The splashing of the rain had started again, but he was more focused on whatever was blocking his view. He wiggled a finger into the hole to see if it was still there. It was. Dean looked through the hole from various angles and then froze when a moan came just on the other side of the glass.

On cue, the darkness washed aside, and Dean realized that it was a person blocking his view of the street. The window was getting battered by dark droplets. For a moment, Dean thought that the rain simply looked like that due to the streetlight, but then he took a closer look at the glass. *Is that black fucking rain?* And then it stopped, but the dripping somewhere to the left still droned in Dean's ear.

The silhouette of a person came into view from the other side of the street. It was out of reach of the streetlight, and Dean was unable to discern any details. What he could see was that the person shambled as if drunk, and in his mind, he was already concocting ideas of how he was going to tell the townsfolk that they were assholes for closing him inside the motel while they're outside. The person took a step forward, bathed in the streetlight.

"Shit!" Dean breathlessly shouted and jumped backward.

He stepped with his heel on the long curtain and felt his body losing balance as he stumbled backward. A *clip-clip-clip* that came above him warned him too late that he curtains ripped off the clamps from the metal rod. Dean fell on his back, hitting his head against the floor. Pain exploded in his skull, and he spent a moment disoriented, grabbing at the back of his head to soothe the pain. The image of what he saw outside just moments ago made him forget all about the pain.

What the fuck is that?

He was breathless, but he had to know. Dean stood, ignoring the toppled curtains, and tentatively approached the peephole again. He peered through it, holding his breath, careful not to get too close out of fear of losing his eye. The person in the streetlight was still there, and more details became discernible.

A woman stood under the streetlight, facing forward. The first thing Dean noticed was the soaked rag over the woman's head. It hugged the woman's facial features so tightly that Dean could almost make out a face—everything on it except the eyes.

The woman wore a drenched and muddy blouse and jeans. No, not just muddy. It looked stained in black. A frayed rope bound the woman's wrists in front of her. She slouched, and her knees slightly bent as if she was too exhausted to hold her weight.

Dean hadn't noticed it by then, but the black rain fell on the woman, and only on the woman in one concentrated area. The black rag and her clothes absorbed the inky droplets.

Dean stared in horror and fascination at the sight. If this was a prop or a prank, then it was a damn good one. Yet, despite not believing in the supernatural, Dean could not deny that something otherworldly was going on here.

"What in the holy fuck?" he said to himself, unable to pry away from the sight in front of him.

Up until then, the woman remained motionless under the streetlight, but the moment Dean spoke up, the head under the rag slowly turned until the eye sockets were staring directly at Dean. She didn't see him—he was sure of that. She couldn't possibly see him, not just from the rag, but because the small hole in the blinds would be impossible to spot, especially at night.

Yet, the woman took a shambling step toward the window. And then another one. It looked as if she was exerting herself to walk and would collapse at any moment. The black rain followed her, constantly looming above her, merciless droplets battering her.

The woman gasped and reached toward the window with her bound hands. Dean stepped away from the hole, his heart leaping in his chest. His body tensed up as he waited for what would happen next. The sound of the rain grew closer, just as the shuffling did.

As the shuffling reached the window, it stopped, but the rain persisted. Dean held his breath, his hammering heart pounding in his eardrums. He desperately wanted to cover the hole in the blinds for much-needed protection. He didn't even have the curtains to shield him from the figure's gaze.

Then he heard a voice.

It was low, and had he not focused as hard as he did, he would have missed it. It came from the other side of the window, and it sounded like whispering. The words were indiscernible, and despite not wanting to approach the blinds for his own safety, Dean was too intrigued by this to let it slip. Maybe it was the skeptical part of him that didn't believe any of this was real and made him feel like he wasn't in any immediate danger, except the danger of Suicide Town shunning him.

Dean took a step closer, his eyes fixated on the hole, the hole that looked like a weak link in a fortress in need of defending against an enemy attack. Just staring at the crack made Dean feel like he was allowing some unspeakable evil to infiltrate his motel room, like toxic gas leaking from a pipe. Despite his gut feeling telling him not to get closer, he ignored it because Dean was not a believer in the supernatural.

He stood in front of the blinds, listening to the whispering, but it was too slurred for him to understand the words. Was it even in English? He stooped, but before he could level with the perforation, a bang came on the window. Dean jumped backward.

The whispering stopped. Dean felt like he was in a zoo and that he had gotten too close to a dangerous animal's cage. The skeptical part of him chided him for getting scared so easily, while the small part of him that wanted to protect him from danger urged him to put more distance to the window. Instead of obeying either of those instincts, he remained entrenched in one spot, unable to move out of fear that permeated his bones.

The woman outside spoke with a quavering voice, barely above a whisper, but this time, the words were clear as day.

"Help me."

Chapter 19

A knock on the door woke Dean up. He was a heavy sleeper, but this morning, the small sound got him sitting ramrod straight in bed. Whoever was at the door, they weren't looking for Dean to invite him to breakfast. Three more knocks, these louder and more urgent.

Dean rubbed his eyes and threw the blanket off. He had no idea what time it was, but his brain, for some reason, told him that it was morning despite the thick darkness in the room. Dean stood on heavy legs, and the events from last night rushed into his mind like a train.

He looked toward the window. Last night, after the sounds outside the window had stopped, Dean spent some time putting the curtains back on the clamps. His shoulders were killing him by then, but he was so focused on replaying what he saw out on the street that the pain hadn't registered until later. When he went to bed, he saw the woman with the rag on her head staring at him, the sockets that had the fabric tightly stretched across them gazing at him.

The fear and anxiety ran through him so heavily that he couldn't fall asleep for about thirty minutes. He kept looking around the room, thinking he would see the woman standing at the foot of his bed. He was tempted to turn the lights on and sleep like that, but his ego wouldn't allow it.

Now, as Dean stared at the curtains, a passing thought occurred to him.

He imagined ripping the curtains down again, tying a knot around the curtain rod, and making a noose. He envisioned himself hanging and choking, since the curtains were too thick to break his neck on impact. The thought dissipated just as quickly as it entered, and Dean furiously blinked, wondering what the fuck he was thinking.

Three more raps on the door shot him back into the present. "Okay, I'm coming," Dean said. He put on his pants and approached the door. Whoever was outside, they were here to tell him that they knew what he did—he was sure of it. Dean unlocked the door and swung it open.

He expected Nelson Baxter's scowling face to greet him, informing him that he would need to leave the motel. He also expected the sheriff to tell him to come with him. Instead, the woman who stood in front of him caused Dean's jaw to drop to the floor.

"About time, D! Where the hell have you been all this time?" Iris said as she spread her arms. "I've been calling you for days!" she slapped her arms against her sides and then pointed behind Dean. "Mind if I come in? Okay, thanks."

"Iris . . ."

Iris squeezed between him and the doorway before he could answer. "Damn, what a dump. I thought you had class, D."

"Iris—"

"So, this is where you get your inspiration, huh?" she said as she turned to face him. She looked around the cheap room and then shrugged. "Okay, I get it. This is one of your stories where nothing makes sense until the end, where all pieces fit in the puzzle, right? Clever, keep your audience guessing."

"Can you just—"

"By the way, you wouldn't believe what a pain in the ass it was for me to get here. I mean, the digging I had to do? Geez Louise. I should get into private investigating; maybe I picked the wrong career."

"Iris, will you shut up for a second?!" Dean raised his voice.

Iris's smile dropped, and her face went slack, but she didn't look like she was offended. "You're right, sorry. I'm probably talking your ear off. It's been a lonely ride here, you know? And the townsfolk here aren't very talkative. And they give you these weird looks as if you—"

"Iris." Dean pressed his lips together, his timbre stern this time.

"Okay, sorry." Iris pinched her thumb and forefinger and motioned across her mouth.

Dean took a deep breath. For a moment, he thought he was still asleep. He *hoped* he was still asleep.

"What the fuck are you doing here, Iris? And remember the one-hundred-words rule?"

The one-hundred-words rule was a rule Dean set for Iris when she talked about irrelevant things, where she would need to say what she wanted in one hundred words or less. The problem was, Iris often forgot about that rule and then Dean would need to interrupt her in the middle of her speaking to shout "One hundred words!" The problem was, instead of explaining in fewer words, Iris would speak faster.

"Okay, one hundred words. Let's see," Iris said as she looked pensively at the ceiling. "So, I tried calling you to tell you about the new releases our publishing house has. You weren't answering, and I really wanted to show you the marketing plans for the future. You would love it. We now have horror authors and rom—"

"One hundred words!" Dean interrupted.

Iris cleared her throat. "Right. Anyway, you weren't answering, so I got worried. I called your ex-wife, and she told me what you planned on doing. So, I called you again to wish you luck, but you weren't answering, so I got even more worried. Decided to fly out to Oregon and find this," she curled her fingers to gesture quotation marks, "so-called Suicide Town."

"How did you find this place?"

"The town, you mean? Oh," Iris snorted, "Alex sent me the instructions."

"That son of a bitch," Dean said.

"Well, what did you expect, D? You have a ton of people who care about you. But no one cares more than I do. I mean, who else would risk their life to come all the way out to a dangerous town in order to save you, huh?"

"I don't need saving, Iris."

Her phone rang. "Hold on a sec, D," she said as she fished it out of her pocket. "Hello? Okay, I already told you, I don't want any sex scenes in the book. No, not even a peek. Uh-huh. Okay. Listen . . ."

Dean turned around. Just like she did with Dean, Iris conveyed too many redundant details to the author on the phone. Dean rubbed his eyes and then ran his hands down his face. While he had his eyes closed, he saw the woman from last night standing in front of him, inches away from his face. He could almost imagine the damp smell that would emanate from the rag. He imagined a shriveled old woman's face under the rag with protruding cheekbones and sunken eyes.

"Help me," Iris said, clear as day.

Dean turned and faced her, blinking furiously.

"Did you say something?" Dean asked. Iris looked at him and shook her head while she talked.

Help me.

Not Iris. It was the woman's voice. It wedged its way in his head, as clearly as it did last night. Dean's eyes fell on the notepad and pen on the nightstand. He walked toward the pen, grabbed it, and stabbed himself in the eye, jamming the pen deeper into his skull with the palm of his hand.

He blinked. The pen was still on the nightstand, both of Dean's eyes intact.

The appeal of that daydream felt like the most natural thing in the world.

Dean squeezed his eyes shut, then opened them and looked down. He had taken a step toward the nightstand with his wobbly legs. He needed to sit. He lumbered to the bed and slumped onto it just as Iris finished her phone call.

"I swear to God, some people I work with are total idiots!" Iris said, but her voice came from inside a deep barrel.

Dean focused on controlling his breathing, trying not to look at the pen that jabbed his peripheral vision. *Help me.* Dean closed his eyes, but whenever he did so, the ragged woman from last night appeared in front of him. Iris was still talking, but she might as well have spoken in a foreign language, because Dean couldn't understand a thing.

Go away, go away, go away, Dean chanted. The mantra worked. The intense sensation gradually diminished, and Dean could open his eyes again. He was exhausted and nauseous like after an intense jogging session.

"D, are you okay? You look a little pale," Iris said.

Dean looked up to see her standing in front of him. He had no idea how long she'd been standing there. He looked at the pen on the nightstand. The suicidal ideation disappeared. Whatever had happened to him was gone.

"Yeah, I'm fine," Dean said, only just then realizing how winded he was. He raised his head toward Iris to see her glowering at him with suspicion.

"Are you sure? You don't look too well. Have you been sleeping enough lately? Maybe this trip was a bad idea after all."

"I'm fine, Iris," Dean said, forcing himself to stand. He was out of breath, and although he was still somewhat fatigued, he felt his strength slowly returning. "Listen. There's something really weird going on in this town. The people here are hiding something." Iris opened her mouth, but Dean raised his hand to stop her from interrupting. "I think something really bad is happening here. I don't think Joshua Bauer killed himself just like that. The townsfolk did something to him, and I need to find out what."

Iris eyeballed Dean for a moment as if weighing whether to believe him. She then snapped a finger, and a grin stretched across her face. "Oh, I get it. This is one of those get-immersed-in-your-book moments. Okay, D. I can play along. If it'll help you write your new book, I'm all for it."

"No, darn it. Listen to me, Iris," Dean snapped. "This is real. It's not a joke. Okay? If we're not careful, we can get in a lot of trouble."

Iris retained the grin for a moment and then her face slackened. She nodded. "Okay, D. I believe you. Tell me everything I need to know."

Dean took a deep breath. He told Iris everything he managed to find out while in Suicide Town. Iris tried to interject a few times, but Dean stopped her from doing so because, if she got a word in, it wouldn't be just one word. When Dean was finally done explaining, Iris continued nodding, making Dean think that she wasn't paying attention.

"Okay, so . . . what do you want to do? If the townsfolk are really up to no good, like you believe they are, then we'll have to be extra careful, D."

"Agreed. There's bound to be something in the town that'll give us the answers we're looking for."

"Maybe that Raintown place?"

"Maybe, but we can't go just yet. They'll be keeping a close watch on us. We need to split up, find whatever information we can find, then work things out from there."

Help me.

The voice wasn't just in his head now. Dean looked around the room, expecting to see a person standing behind him. He swore he heard the voice right there.

"Something wrong?" Iris asked.

"No." Dean shook his head.

"Okay, well anyway, you go and talk to Elliot Wood. I'll see what else I can dig up, all right?"

"Sounds good."

"All right, then it's settled." Iris clapped her hands together. "This is so exciting! We're like detective partners! We should come up with a name!"

"I'll leave that to you," Dean said with a slight frown.

"Awesome, D! I'm gonna head out right away." Iris opened the door and stepped out but then peeked back inside. "Oh, and D?"

"Yes, Iris?"

"If this turns out to be a success, would you consider—"

"I'm not publishing a book through you, Iris."

Iris pressed her lips tightly together and nodded, uncomplacent. "Well, we're not done negotiating yet, D. You'll change your mind by the time this is all over."

With that, she left the motel room. Dean shook his head and let out a scoff. He still couldn't believe that

Iris was here. He could not imagine a person he would hate investigating with more, but at the same time, a sense of relief overwhelmed him. As annoying as Iris was, her presence helped in not only in the investigation, but alleviating the loneliness in such a hostile environment.

Dean put on his clothes and looked at the nightstand. After careful contemplation, he decided not to take the notepad and pen with him.

Chapter 20

"Good morning," Dean said to Nelson Baxter in passing.

The motel owner didn't greet him back. Dean was already at the door with his hand on the knob, but he turned his head to see why he got no response. Baxter was still in his rickety chair, engrossed in a newspaper, or so it seemed. His body was rigid, and he gripped the edges of the paper way too hard. He fixated his stare on one spot on the page.

Dean went outside, deciding not to say anything else to Baxter. It was almost nine a.m.; the drizzle outside was bearable today. The sky took on the color of abalone.

The first thing Dean did was look at the ground. He thought he detected specks of black on the concrete, but that easily could have been his imagination. He stopped in front of his room's window and stared at the tiny traces of watered-down black liquid sliding down the pane of glass across his elongated reflection. That left no room for doubt in his mind whether what he saw last night was real.

Don't believe what they say, said the voice in his head. An inky black head full of disheveled, straw-like hair, peeked from behind Dean and gently put its spindly fingers on his shoulder. Two incongruous white orbs stared back at Dean with tiny black dots in the center that represented the pupils.

Dean shot around with a gasp and swatted at the figure, hitting nothing but air. Dean looked left and right. An old woman across the street gawked at him before turning into an alley. Dean swallowed and turned toward the window.

Just his own startled reflection, nothing more. Dean bolted from the window, feeling like he had bugs crawling all over his shoulder, where the thing had grabbed him. He kept swatting at his shoulder. Whenever he looked down, he expected to see a black hand digging its fingers into his jacket's fabric.

They forced me to do it, the voice said.

Dean hurried his pace as if walking fast would leave the voice behind. He constantly looked over his shoulder. The streets were empty, but he had the distinct feeling of invisible eyes watching him through the opaque windows. A few times, he thought he caught a glimpse of the same black figure in those windows, and it made him pause. But the moment he blinked, the figure was gone. No matter how long he focused on the window after that, nothing appeared.

He entered a store to buy an energy drink that he desperately needed. While waiting at the cash register, a woman dropped a bottle of Corona, causing it to shatter on the ground. She swore and apologized, and the cashier told her it was okay. The employee excused herself from the cash register, presumably to fetch something to sweep the mess. As Dean stared at the mess of shards and the spilled beverage, he visualized picking up a piece of the broken glass and plunging it into his neck over and over until he bled out.

The cashier returned with a duster and broom a minute later and swept up the glass. The clinking and crunching of the bottle tempted Dean to chew the glass and swallow it, to choke on the glass as it embedded itself in his throat. He facepalmed himself to chase those thoughts out of his mind.

"Are you okay, sir?" the cashier asked, but the voice came as a muffled whisper.

Help me.

The urge to grab the glass and do something hurtful to himself became irresistible. Dean left the energy drink on the counter and stumbled out of the store, ignoring the confused cashier. The cold rain helped him feel a little better, so he let it shower his head. Even when he walked away from the store, the images of him mutilating himself remained in his mind a moment longer.

"Pull yourself together, Dean. You're imagining things," he said to himself.

He had to sit on a nearby bench to prevent himself from collapsing. Not having to be on his feet was an immense relief to his body and mind. The thoughts of killing himself were gone now, and he scolded himself for even thinking of such a stupid thing. Yet, when he remembered looking at the pen and the shards of glass, he realized that he was actually close to doing it. If he had stayed a little longer, he would have done it on a whim.

Robert, the butcher, walked past Dean. Dean greeted him, but the butcher shot daggers at him and left without a word. The same happened with Marshall Chandler later that day and then with Susan when he had breakfast at the diner. Susan made no small talk, witty remarks, or called him hun but instead asked him what he'll be having and slapped it on the table for him minutes later.

The eyes of the other guests in the diner occasionally focused on Dean, no longer curious as to who this outsider was but rather judgmental glares that looked like they wanted to hang him on the gallows.

They knew.

There was no denying that they knew he looked. Dean had no idea how they knew, but they did. He even stopped trying to explain it logically because there was no point. When the sheriff arrived at the diner, he looked over in Dean's direction, but didn't so much as bother to raise a hand in greeting. He might as well have been looking at an empty table.

After Susan gave him the cup of steaming coffee, Sheriff Moody thanked her and walked up to Dean. He took off his hat and sat at the table. He slurped his coffee and nodded.

"Good coffee," he said as he placed the cup on the table. "My wife has been trying to make coffee the way Susan does, but she never manages to do so. I think Susan has a secret recipe that she's not willing to share with the others."

Dean took a bite out of his pancake but said nothing to the sheriff. He expected a scolding to ensue, and he was mentally preparing himself for it. The sheriff must have noticed Dean's aloof behavior.

"Look, Watson. No need to pretend. We know you looked."

Dean chewed on the pancake, but the taste was suddenly bland, and he had difficulty swallowing the food. He gulped some water to moisten the dry bite in his mouth.

"What are you talking about?" Dean asked as he stabbed another piece of the pancake with the fork. He put it in his mouth and watched as the sheriff stared at him with a reticent glare.

Moody leaned forward and interlocked his fingers. "I don't think you understand the situation you're in, Watson. I gave you a list of simple rules, and you already broke one of them. You probably don't realize it or believe in it, but you put yourself in a lot of danger when you looked."

Dean focused on chewing at the sheriff's last sentence. He wanted to play the "innocent until proven guilty" card. For all he knew, the sheriff was just probing him for a confession on a baseless assumption.

"I tried being a nice guy, Watson," Moody continued. "I warned you about the rules. If you put yourself in danger, that's on you. I don't give a damn about that. But we have our annual Survival Festival coming in two days, and I will be damned if I'll let you fuck that up, you hear me?"

Dean swallowed with great difficulty. He refused to avert his gaze from the sheriff. He couldn't show him that the sheriff's threats offended him.

"You're free to stay during the festival," Moody said as he jabbed a finger downward at the table. "But I'm going to keep a close watch on you from now on. Both you and your friend. If you so much as blink the wrong way, I will drag you out of town myself. You understand me, Watson?"

Dean looked over the sheriff's shoulder; curious heads faced their direction. They looked away upon meeting their eyes with Dean's. Dean took another sip of water and leaned back, trying to assume a relaxed position.

And how do you plan to drag me out of town when you can't leave town yourself, Sheriff?" Dean asked. "Whether you like it or not, you're stuck with me until I decide to leave."

"We're definitely stuck, Watson," the sheriff said in a whisper. "But so are you—now that you looked. Just like Joshua Bauer was."

Before Dean could ponder whether to take that as a warning or something else, the sheriff put his hat on, took the coffee, and stood. He tucked one thumb in his belt and cleared his throat while looking down at Dean.

"Stick around for the festival. You'll like it," he said with a smile and left the diner.

Dean looked down at his unfinished pancakes. He was no longer hungry, and instead, a motivation to get to the bottom of the investigation burned within him with white-hot intensity.

He paid for the meal and exited, ignoring the guests' hostile eyes.

Chapter 21

Time seemed to slip away much faster in Suicide Town. Dean couldn't tell if it was just the byproduct of his imagination or if the town had some kind of distorted physics. The weather was already weird as it was, and so was everything else. Whatever Dean thought science and logic could explain was slowly disintegrating after last night.

Something was wrong with him, and he couldn't deny it. It wasn't the lack of sleep or the stress or the stories from the town. The feminine voice in his head occasionally came to him, just enough for him to hear it. It would usually be just one word or sentence, but he'd hear the voice loudly enough to get startled. As for the visage in the window he had seen earlier . . . he didn't even want to think what that was.

Dean visited Elliot Wood's house after eating at the diner, but the guy was not home again. He was not at the bar either, so Dean, instead, spent his time asking about the upcoming Survival Festival. He had forgotten about it and thought of it as insignificant until he heard one of the patrons at the bar mention it.

The more he learned, the more he realized what a big deal it actually was to the people of Suicide Town. It wasn't just some gathering of twenty people downtown. No, everyone in the town was involved in preparing for the Survival Festival. Dean got bits and pieces of information from each person, but it was Jayden Price who told him the story in full when Dean stopped at the bookstore.

"How's it going, Jayden?" Dean greeted the young man upon entering the store.

Jayden's gaze had been lowered toward a book in his lap. When the bell chimed, and he saw his favorite writer walking in, he stopped reading and stood to greet Dean.

"Hi, Mr. Watson. I mean, Dean," he said with a wide, courteous smile on his face. No, it wasn't a smile. It was a rictus. Dean didn't even need to guess why the sudden change occurred in the kid. He hoped that it wouldn't impact his extraction of information.

"Slow day?" Dean asked.

"Usually is, but not today."

"Why's that?"

"People are preparing for the Survival Festival."

"I keep hearing about that. What is it?"

Jayden grimaced flippantly. "Oh, just some historical reasons why we celebrate it. I don't personally like it, but you know, it's tradition."

"Yeah, I get it." Dean nodded. "I actually wanna know more about that. All I know for now is that you guys celebrate something, but that's pretty much all I've been able to get from the others. Mind telling me more?"

Jayden scratched the back of his head and shrugged. "Sure, if you're really interested in knowing. But it's kind of a long story."

"Oh, bummer. I hate long stories. Good thing I'm not a writer." Dean flashed Jayden a half-smile. Jayden reciprocated the smile, but his eyes conveyed confusion. Dean sighed in laughter and said, "It's a joke, Jayden. I don't mind listening to the story. I wanna know more about this town."

"Okay," Jayden said, awkwardly scratching his cheek before sitting down. He placed a bookmark between the pages of his book, closed it, and then gently placed the book on the counter. "Well, the

Survival Festival is something we celebrate every year because we managed to survive for the whole year."

Jayden paused, and Dean gave him a swift nod as approval to continue.

"We honor the ones who died from suicides in the past year and the ones before that by doing various activities. It lasts from noon until midnight. So . . . yeah."

"Give me a structure and some descriptions, Jayden. A writer needs to hook the reader and maintain their attention throughout the story by helping the reader visualize the scenes. Let's take it from the top."

Jayden shifted in the seat and let out a peal of nervous laughter. He cleared his throat, looked at Dean, and started anew.

"No one knows how long Pineridge has existed. We don't even know if the suicides have always been common here, but the first historical records date back to nineteen sixty-four, when Pineridge was a bigger city and more populated. It wasn't special for anything. It was just a small town founded by a person everybody forgot about. In nineteen seventy-one, suicides were recorded as more common in Pineridge. People started to suspect a curse. Various priests and witch doctors have been called to the town, but everyone who visited mysteriously ended up committing suicide."

"Good so far. I'm intrigued. Go on," Dean said, impressed with Jayden's eloquence and captivating diction.

Jayden continued, "The number of people who committed suicides became more and more frequent. The records say that the rain wouldn't let up for days, then months, then years. In nineteen seventy-five, a mass suicide occurred in East Pineridge. Over one and people died at the town square in various ways—some poisoned themselves, some cut their throats, some shot themselves, some crashed their cars into buildings. Either way, something happened that drove the townsfolk to kill themselves."

Dean nodded. The story seemed like something out of a fairy tale so far, but Dean had no reason not to believe Jayden, especially if the story came from historical records.

"Witnesses said that the town square was littered with dead bodies. No one wanted to approach to carry away the dead. Even the animals and insects avoided getting close. The rain never stopped, and the bodies were left there until they decomposed. No one has ever set foot there out of fear of contracting the curse that killed the ones in East Pineridge. That place became known as Raintown."

"That's how Pineridge got the name of Suicide Town, right?"

"That's right." Jayden nodded. "Ever since then, we've been celebrating survival in order to give thanks and to prevent the curse, sickness, whatever it is, from coming back and causing another mass suicide."

"Wow," Dean uttered. "It sounds like it could make a great book. Have you ever considered writing it?"

"No, I'm sick of living here. I wouldn't want to write about Suicide Town as well. If I do, it'll be about leaving."

He paused for a moment, but the intent gaze told Dean that Jayden wanted to say something—only he wasn't sure if he should say it.

"What's up?" Dean encouraged.

Jayden scratched his forehead. "I was just wondering. What's it like out there in the big cities? Is it like what we see in the movies? Big streets, lots of cars, tall skyscrapers, and all that?"

"Pretty much like what you see in the movies."

"I always wanted to live in a big city. If I could choose, I'd live in New York."

"You'd hate New York. The people are rude, and traffic is horrible. I hate having to sit—or worse, stand—in public transport for forty minutes to get where I want to be."

"Huh," Jayden said with a pensive expression. "I'd still like to visit New York, at least. I don't think I'll ever become a good writer like you if I don't get familiar with the big cities."

Dean flashed him a smile. The kid had big dreams, and Dean admired that. At the same time, it made him sad because he was no longer so sure if he could help him. What if it was true that he couldn't leave the town without the urge to kill himself overwhelming him? Dean could help Jayden get published, but if he was truly stuck in Suicide Town, then that would pretty much be in vain.

They used me, the voice said in his head. Dean ignored it this time. Although Jayden was staring at him, he didn't seem to notice Dean's perturbance. "So, tell me about the festival," Dean said, trying to get his mind off the voice.

"Well, we have a lot of food, we have Father Walter giving a speech and prayer, we have people wearing nooses around their necks in a parade, let's see, what else . . . Oh, we can't bring umbrellas or cover our heads with anything. We're supposed to let the rain fall on us."

"Why?"

"I don't know, to tell you the truth. But anyway, we have more prayers in the evening, a minute of silence, and then we have fireworks and then we eat whatever the ones assigned to cooking have prepared."

"Sounds fun," Dean said. "So, what about Raintown?"

"What about it?"

"Does anyone ever actually go there anymore? Is it just an empty town?"

"I wish I could tell you, Mr. Watson." Jayden shrugged. "No one is allowed to go there. Venturing to Raintown is punishable by death."

"Wait, death?" Dean raised his eyebrows.

Jayden nodded. "Whatever is in there must be dangerous because they are so strict about it."

"Why do you think they're stopping people from going there?"

"I don't know." Jayden shook his head. "I think they're afraid that they could contract the same curse that killed all those people fifty years ago and bring it back to Pineridge."

"I see."

Dean couldn't believe Jayden's words. Execution for entering Raintown? Why didn't anyone tell him about it? He could have wandered into Raintown by accident and ended up dead because of it. He was sure that, as an outsider, he was not exempted from such stringent laws.

"Jayden, do you know anyone who has been executed throughout your life here?" Dean asked.

"Not that I know of."

"Do you think it was possible that they executed Rachel Wood and made her death look like suicide?" Dean was aware of how outlandish his words sounded, but they had already left his mouth.

Jayden raised his eyebrows momentarily, and his face went taut, but then, just as quickly, it relaxed. "I mean, it would be possible if they had done it in secrecy, but executions have never been done like that; that's at least what we learned in school. The rule that I've been taught says that, whenever someone is to be executed, an announcement is made, and the whole town gathers at the edge of Pineridge in North Street. The guilty person is then forced to walk out of town."

"That . . . that's it?" Dean asked.

"Well, I mean, they never make it far; that's what we were taught. They died before getting out of sight of the townsfolk who ostracized them."

"Suicide?"

"Nothing other than that."

Dean looked down and put his hand over his mouth, assuming a pensive stance. He had no doubt that Jayden told him everything he believed in, but the question was whether his knowledge was the truth. It could have been stories made up to scare the townsfolk into staying.

No, it's not just stories. After last night, can you really say it's just stories? As difficult as it is to believe, something is happening here that cannot be explained with any physical evidence and scientific tests or experiments.

"One more question, Jayden," Dean said.

Jayden nodded.

"How does everyone know I looked?"

Jayden raised a hand and rubbed his forehead for a moment while looking around anywhere except at Dean. "It's difficult to explain to someone who doesn't live here. I mean, it's difficult to explain in general because . . . hm, I don't know. You wouldn't believe me, anyway."

"Just tell me," Dean pushed.

"Well, all right. It's like there's a change in the atmosphere when it happens. We can feel it. I know it sounds stupid, but it's the way it is. For example, last night, I woke up in the middle of the night covered in cold sweat and feeling a sense of dread. Again, I know it sounds unbelievable."

I would have thought it unbelievable when I first arrived at the town, but now, I'm not so sure anymore, Dean wanted to tell the kid.

"Thank you, Jayden," he said instead and reached for the doorknob.

"Mr. Watson?" Jayden called out in a tenuous voice. "If I may be so bold to ask you, if you wouldn't mind it, that is . . . what do you plan on doing?"

Dean looked at him and then at the book on the counter. *It Ends With A Bullet* by Dean Watson. Not one of his better books, in his opinion, but the fans loved it. He had started writing it with a lot of motivation and then ended up half-assing the ending because he had burned out by the end of the three hundred thousand words mark.

"I don't know yet," he said and exited the bookstore.

Chapter 22

"You done fucked up, city boy!" a familiar gruff voice said behind Dean in the alley.

He was on his way to Elliot Wood's place. When he turned around, Lawrence, the mechanic, strode up to him. He was wearing a raincoat and had his hands in his pockets. Dean saw his facial features from the nose down, as the hood covered his eyes and everything else.

Dean froze in place, ready to confront the mechanic if the need arose. Lawrence stopped mere inches from Dean, invading his personal space. Dean refused to budge. Lawrence yanked the hood backward, revealing wet strands of hair that clung to his scalp in various directions. The scowl on his face told Dean that trouble was imminent.

"What do you want?" Dean took the preemptive step as he jutted his head at the mechanic.

"You think you can just go 'round town and cause trouble, do you? Or are you so stupid that you can't follow simple instructions?"

Dean tried to remain calm. If it came to a fight, Dean wasn't going to be the first one to throw hands. If Lawrence attacked him, Dean would act in self-defense. If the word about the fight spread, the town would most likely be on Lawrence's side, but if Dean threw the first punch, then they would *definitely* be on the mechanic's side.

"Look, I'm in a hurry. If you got something to say, say it, so I can move on."

"Oh, I got something to say," Lawrence retorted. "I'm keeping a close eye on you. I've been keeping a close eye on you ever since you arrived. The sheriff might have a soft spot for you, but I don't. If you think you'll be able to get away with breaking the rules, you're sorely mistaken."

"Is there a point to this conversation?"

"Leave the town. You've already caused enough damage. We don't want the likes of you to be here during the festival. Go back to your city. Write your book. Leave us the hell alone."

Dean waited to see if the mechanic would add anything else. He didn't.

"I'm not leaving until I'm done," Dean said. "In case you forgot, a journalist who visited Suicide Town is dead. This is bigger than one fiction book, so unless you have something to hide, I suggest you stay out of my way."

"Oh, you're some kind of police now, eh?" Lawrence said, inching further closer to Dean. The faint stench of booze and something stale wafted into Dean's face when the mechanic spoke. "You should worry about saving your own skin."

"I'm fine. Thanks." Dean grimaced, trying not to breathe in the mechanic's foul breath.

Lawrence's mouth twitched as he pressed his lips together. He then took a step back from Dean. The alcoholic miasma disappeared to Dean's relief, and he could breathe again. The rain drenched Lawrence's head and slid down his temples and forehead.

"This is the only warning I'll be giving you, city boy," Lawrence said as he pulled the hoodie over his head. "Next time, there'll be no talking."

He spun on his heel and left without waiting for Dean to respond. Dean grunted and shook his head, determined not to let the mechanic's threats faze him. Lawrence gave the impression of being a dangerous individual. Unlike the rest of the townsfolk, who were either reserved or didn't speak to Dean because they didn't like him, Lawrence gave the impression of someone who would go out of his way to hurt any outsider who broke the rules. Dean would need to be careful from here on out.

***

Elliot Wood left his house. He was wearing a cap and a thick jacket, just as Dean had seen him in the diner when he bumped into Susan. He had his hands in his pockets, his shoulders were tense, and his head was down as he walked up the driveway toward the sidewalk.

"Mr. Wood," Dean called out.

Elliot took another two steps before registering that someone was calling to him. He stopped and raised his head before looking around. He paused when his eyes fell on Dean. Dean expected a change in his facial expression: raised eyebrows, a frown, a dart of the eyes, a twitch of the cheek—anything that would indicate he was uncomfortable talking to this outsider.

There was nothing of the like. Elliot looked like he was staring through Dean rather than at him. His thick beard made it impossible to discern the expression through his mouth. Just staring at the eyes, Dean could see multiple expressions nesting in there. At first, he saw curiosity. But if he looked longer, he could imagine the eyes conveying irritability, or maybe full-blown anger. Or maybe it was sadness. Either way, the eyes were lethargic and devoid of vigor, Dean noticed.

"You're Elliot Wood, right?" Dean stopped in front of the bearded man.

"I'm not a good interviewee." Elliot shook his head. Dean expected a deep, almost guttural voice to come out of the man's mouth. What came out instead was a modulated, soothing voice that conveyed no hostility or tension.

"I'm not here to talk about the town, Mr. Wood," Dean said. "I want to talk about your wife."

Elliot's face didn't change, and his gander remained fixed on Dean. Dean waited to see what Elliot's response would be. He already had in mind what to say in case Elliot refused to cooperate.

"Why would you want to talk about Rachel?" Elliot asked.

That was one foot in the door. Dean opened his mouth but was at a loss for words. He wanted to say a million things at once, but he had to choose his words carefully if he wanted to receive Elliot's help.

"There was a journalist who came here not long ago. He left the town and then killed himself. I'm trying to get to the bottom of it."

"What does that have to do with my wife?"

Dean's eyes fell on the rake leaning against a house in the distance. A powerful feeling of wanting to stab himself with the tines overcame him. He tried to blink the thoughts away, but that only made things worse because he could imagine the rusted metal going through his eyes and blinding him.

They tricked me. Please, help me.

"Hey, are you okay?" Elliot asked.

Dean looked at his feet, feeling like he was going to pass out from the effort of trying not to think about killing himself. "Yeah, I'm fine," he said.

Elliot looked over Dean's shoulder and then behind himself. The street was empty. The pattering of the rain draped the air. Elliot looked at Dean once more and then gestured with his head toward the house. "Let's talk inside," he calmly said.

***

Elliot Wood's house was the first household Dean had been inside ever since he arrived at Suicide Town. Before he even saw Suicide Town, he imagined a village with ramshackle straw houses, no roads, a tavern, a well, et cetera. Then, upon entering, he imagined poor households with peeling wallpapers, old CTR televisions, and leaking roofs.

He couldn't have been more wrong.

The Wood residence was not a big house, but it was nicely decorated and extremely tidy. Elliot made an excuse about the living room being a mess and led Dean toward the kitchen. Dean happened to glance at the living room on the way to the kitchen, and it looked clean enough, but he didn't want to say anything to Elliot.

"Want something to drink?"

"I'm good. Thanks," Dean said as he pulled out a chair and sat at the kitchen table.

The two chairs tucked under the table shot down any lingering doubts about whether the Woods had any children. He was partly glad that they didn't because those children would have an awfully difficult time understanding what happened to their mother.

"Well, I'll have one, if you don't mind," Elliot said as he opened the cupboard and retrieved a bottle of brown liquor.

"Not at all," Dean said.

Elliot Wood took a glass in the other hand and turned to sit at the table. He placed the bottle and glass on top of the wooden surface and slumped into the chair. The bottle was half-full, and somehow, Dean was willing to bet that more bottles haphazardly laid around the house.

"So, how do you like our happy shithole of a town?" Elliot asked as he poured himself the drink.

"The rain's a real mood killer," Dean replied. "The townsfolk are polite."

Elliot let out a throaty sound that Dean recognized as laughter a moment later. Elliot took a large gulp of the drink like it was water and then added more beverage from the bottle to the glass.

"It sucks," he said. "The whole town needs to be bombed to oblivion."

Dean wasn't sure if he should laugh at that; he found it difficult to figure out if Elliot Wood was joking. He took another sip of the drink and finally averted his gaze from the alcohol and looked at Dean. "You planning on staying during the festival?"

"Not sure yet. I get the feeling that I'm not very welcome here during such a time."

"Ignore those fuckers. Most of the people who live here think they're better than the rest of the world. Not much of a superiority when you can't even leave your own town, huh?"

He guffawed and took another sip.

"So, what did you want to talk about?"

Dean leaned forward. "About your wife. I know it's probably a difficult topic, so I understand if you'd prefer not to speak about it."

"It's fine. I'll tell you everything I know. It might help someone someday. You're familiar with the gist of Suicide Town, I take it?"

"Yeah. Lots of suicides, no one can leave, some important rules to follow."

"Yeah." Elliot nodded. "Well, there are ancient reasons why those rules were invented. It all started with the mass suicide in the seventies."

"Yeah, the ones that happened in Raintown. Jayden Price told me about it. But that still doesn't give me any answers."

"What kind of answers are you looking for, exactly?"

Save me.

Dean ignored the voice and tried to remain composed.

"I broke one of the rules last night," he said.

"So I heard. It's the talk of the town."

"The journalist, Joshua Bauer, did the same. He came to the town, looking for answers. He looked, then something happened to him. Something changed in him before he killed himself. When I first arrived here, I didn't believe in any of the stories. I thought they were just old wives' tales and that there must be some kind of logical explanation for everything you guys have been experiencing here."

Elliot took another sip, but his eyes remained transfixed on Dean. "And now, you believe?" he asked.

"I still don't know *what* to believe. Last night, I saw someone. No, *something*. It saw me as well. And I haven't felt well since then."

Elliot downed the remainder of the drink in his glass and slammed it on the table. Dean thought that he had had enough until Elliot poured another full glass. Either the man was a drunk, or he had insane resilience to alcohol.

"You're familiar with the history of the town, I assume?" Elliot asked.

"Yeah. Mass suicides in the seventies, restriction to Raintown—I know it."

"You don't know half of it." Elliot shook his head. "Do the terms 'Escorter' and 'Protector' mean anything to you?"

"I've heard of Escorters. That guy, Lawrence, works as one, yeah? And their job is, what exactly? Ensuring nobody breaks the rules?"

Elliot leaned back in his chair and sighed deeply as if to tell that the situation was a lot worse than he initially assumed. "When the mass suicide in the seventies occurred, the townsfolk feared that whatever happened in Raintown would spread to the rest of Pineridge. Father Walter, who was still young back then, and a bunch of others, went to Raintown to stop that from happening. Two whole days had passed, and everybody thought they were dead. But then they returned from Raintown, drenched, exhausted, and with wild-eyed looks. One of the men who accompanied them was no longer with them and was assumed dead."

"They actually went to Raintown? Father Walter never told me about it."

"Of course not. Only a few people know about it. My father was one of the men who accompanied Walter. He told me about it four years ago, just before jumping off the roof of the police station to his death."

"I'm sorry."

"Never mind about that. When Father Walter returned, they claimed that their mission was a partial success. They had found the source of the suicides in the town. A parasitic entity of some sort, he said, and they had managed to contain it."

"An entity?" Dean asked.

Elliot nodded. He took a small sip. "My father told me what he saw there many times, but he could never convey properly in words what he saw in Raintown. Whatever it was, it changed him. This entity is the reason for the suicides. What exactly it is or where it came from, I don't know. I don't even know if it's a being or a presence or something entirely different."

"So, what did Father Walter do to stop it?"

"Some kind of ritual. My father couldn't tell me more than that, but apparently, it lasted for days, and they were able to contain the evil but at a price. The entity is too powerful and cannot be banished or destroyed. So, instead, they had to bind it to a person. They called that person the Protector."

Dean sucked in a sharp breath. He looked at the rain-battered window and then back at Elliot.

"How was binding the entity to a person going to help?" he asked.

"Father Walter believes that, by doing so, the entity feeds on the person and leaves the rest of the town alone. Its presence is still strong, and suicides still occur, but the killing spree has stopped."

"And what happens when the Protector dies?"

"A new one is chosen."

"I still don't understand how the whole Protector thing works."

Help me. The voice came to Dean out of nowhere. It still startled him even after hearing it for the dozenth time today, but he ignored it.

"The town's council chooses someone as a Protector," Elliot said. "Based on what they choose, I have no idea. Then the person is bound, Father Walter says a prayer, and the Escorters take the person to Raintown. It usually ends with crying and pleading because, of course, nobody wants to be the Protector."

"Has any Protector returned from Raintown ever before?" Dean asked.

"No. Once they cross the threshold of Raintown, it's the last we ever see of them."

Dean shifted in his seat. He felt restless, and his mind moved too fast. The information he received from Elliot seemed outlandish, yet his brain took it as real.

"How often is a new Protector chosen?"

"There's no designated time limit. Father Walter believes that, when the number of suicides increases, it's time to find a new one."

"Who's the current Protector?"

Elliot looked down at the glass and sighed through his nose. He took the glass and brought it up to his mouth. "It was supposed to be the town's mailman. He ended up killing himself just before the ceremony, so they had to choose a new Protector. Rachel."

"What?!" Dean raised his tone.

Elliot put the glass back on the table without taking a sip. Dean thought he detected slight trembling in his hands.

"Your wife is the current Protector?" Dean asked.

The urge to look around for hidden cameras almost overtook him, but he resisted it.

"Yeah," Elliot said. "I tried to stop them, but I couldn't. It was not supposed to go down like that. She and I came to the ceremony. We planned on going to the arcade later that day. But Father Walter and the Escorters . . ." His pitch rose toward the end, and Dean thought he detected his lip quivering. "The last I saw my Rachel was when the Escorters put the rag over her head and forced her to walk forward. She was calling me, begging me to help her, but I couldn't do anything. I see that scene whenever I close my eyes."

"But that's absurd! There's no way to tell if choosing someone for the Protector role would even work!" Dean protested.

"Father Walter says it does. The people believe him. It gives them the feeling of safety, so they follow his lead, and he follows the council's."

Dean looked at the brown liquid sloshing inside the glass as Elliot picked it up. He suddenly wanted a sip for himself, but he needed to keep a clear head.

"Who are the council members?"

"No one knows," Elliot said after taking a gulp and setting the glass down. "Rumor has it that there are only a few people on the council, but no one knows who they are."

They forced me into this.

Dean suddenly saw everything with clarity. He looked at Elliot with wide eyes.

"What?" Elliot asked.

Just then, a knock came from the door.

Chapter 23

Elliot and Dean froze. For a moment, the only sound that pervaded the air was the muffled rain outside. Three loud knocks resounded, followed by a ring of the doorbell.

"Are you expecting company?" Dean whispered.

"No," Elliot said.

This was bad. Whoever it was was onto them. Dean had learned the entire story, and he knew he was a threat to the town. They would surely not hesitate to eliminate him. He didn't have enough time to think those thoughts through when a familiar, obnoxious, crow-like voice came from the entrance.

"D! I know you're in there! Open up!" Iris shouted and banged on the door again.

Dean groaned, partly from relief, partly from annoyance. "My gosh. It's Iris," he said as he stood.

"Who?" Elliot narrowed his eyes in confusion.

"My old publisher. She's trustworthy," Dean said.

Elliot stood with alacrity and strode out of the kitchen and across the foyer toward the entrance. Dean followed him.

"Come on, D! Don't make me bust this door down! I swear . . . if that bearded hillbilly has done something to y—"

Elliot swung the door open. Iris's look of defiance slackened, and she grinned at Elliot. "Oh, hello. I'm looking for my writer. Is he here?"

"This stalking is getting out of hand, Iris," Dean said.

Elliot stepped aside but said nothing to Iris. The publisher nodded to him and prudently stepped inside the house, keeping a close eye on Elliot. "D, thank

God!" she shouted with spread arms. "I thought these rednecks might have done something to you!" She turned to Elliot. "Eh, no offense to you. Love the beard, by the way. Have you ever thought about posing in commercials for beard-growing products? Hell, maybe even a razor company, like BIC. If they can prove the razor can shave your beard, their stocks are gonna skyrocket!"

"Iris . . ." Dean said.

"Oh, right." Iris coughed. "You can't because of the whole town curse thing . . . well, anyway, still. Great beard!"

Elliot closed the door, walked past Iris and Dean, and stalked back to the kitchen. Dean and Iris spent a moment gazing at each other in the foyer's silence. Of course, it was Iris who broke that silence.

"Nice guy," she said and turned to go into the kitchen. Her voice continued booming from there. "Boy, this weather is crazy! How do you guys ever take walks in parks or play any sports?"

***

"One hundred rule, Iris," Dean said for the fifth time in the last five minutes.

He was annoyed as hell, but Elliot seemed to find the situation amusing based on his occasional chortles. Iris talked about what she'd been up to since she left the motel. Of course, she rambled a lot, and Dean wondered if Iris even had any important info to share.

"Right. Okay, long story short, I found out that Raintown is bad," she said.

"Okay, are you done? Because I have some important info that both you and Elliot need to hear."

"Yeah, I'm done," Iris said, surprising Dean with the brevity of her answer.

All three of them were seated at the kitchen table. The bottle of liquor was still on the table, with two glasses instead of one—the second one being for Iris. The air reeked of alcohol, tantalizing Dean to take just one sip. That one sip would turn into two, two into ten, and so on. It was a rabbit hole that would only promise more the deeper he went. The best thing was to stay away from that rabbit hole entirely.

"Okay, listen," Dean said. "Last night, I broke the rule and looked out the window. At first, there was nothing. But then I saw someone walking on the street."

Elliot's eyes slightly widened. Iris took a sip and remained calm.

"Her hands were bound, and she had a rag over her head. Her clothes were dirty. I'm not sure how, but she saw me. She approached the window and asked me to help her."

Elliot's mouth was slightly agape now, and he was sitting bolt upright in his seat. Dean looked at Iris, who was making a sour face after taking a sip. She noticed him glowering, so she focused on Dean's story instead.

"She asked me to help her, and after some time, she left. And that's where things started to become strange. I'm not losing my mind, and I'm not crazy, so just listen to me. Since waking up this morning, I've been getting these . . . visions."

"About killing yourself, right?" Elliot interjected.

Dean nodded.

"That's how it always is for us," Elliot said.

"It's not just the visions," Dean said as he looked down at the table, pensive. "I've been hearing that woman's voice in my head. She keeps asking me to save her. She says things like 'they tricked me' or 'they forced me,' and I think . . ." He looked up at Elliot. "I think that's Rachel's voice I'm hearing."

"Rachel . . ." Elliot said as if testing the name on his tongue.

"D, come on. You're under stress," Iris said. "You've been in the town for days. The stories are starting to get to you."

"I'm not crazy, Iris," Dean said, offended that she didn't believe him. "I know what I saw and what I'm hearing. I think Rachel is trapped in Raintown and needs our help."

Momentary silence permeated the room. As always, it was Iris who broke that silence.

"D, just think about it. If you saw her last night, then she's not trapped in Raintown. Why would she need your help if she can walk out of it?"

"I don't know."

"Are you sure it was Rachel?" Elliot asked.

"I don't know," Dean repeated. "It was a woman; that's all I know."

"What did she look like?"

"She had a rag over her head—I couldn't see. Are you telling me you seriously didn't look outside for all these years?"

Elliot shook his head. "Never. That's how we've been taught over here. The parents are really strict. Even *thinking* about looking out the window used to get us whooping and a whole week of sweeping the streets. So, we just learned not to look or ask questions."

Dean put one elbow up on the table. Iris took a lady-like sip of the drink and then let out a disgusted sound.

"Haven't you ever been curious?" Dean asked.

"Of course, I have. But you would need to grow up in this town to understand how much they drilled us about it, how they instilled fear in us. That was passed down from generation to generation. But it'll have to end now. I want my wife back. If she's still alive, then I need to get her out of Raintown."

"How?" Iris asked. "The roads are closely watched by those Escorters. We can't so much as peek at the town without one of them giving us a hard time about it. Earlier, I tried striking up a conversation with one of them, you know? The guy wouldn't budge even under my charm."

"What if we sneak in at night?" Dean asked.

"Still too dangerous," Elliot said. "But we could do it during the festival."

"Oh, yeah. Thing's coming up in a few days, right?" Iris raised her glass.

"Yes." Elliot nodded. "The whole town will be on North Street. That's the best time to sneak into Raintown."

"Do I really need to accompany you there?" Iris's voice quivered. "I mean, I'm better at communicating with people rather than sneaking about."

"No, it'll attract too much attention if we all go in. You two should stay behind in case something goes wrong," Dean said. "I'll go to Raintown."

"It should be me," Elliot said.

"No. I'm the one who hears her voice. I need to be the one to do it," Dean objected.

No one disagreed with that. Dean partly hoped that either Iris or Elliot would insist on accompanying him, but it would seem he would be going to Raintown alone. It might be his final trip anywhere—if the rumors about the town were true. Not only would he possibly face something dangerous there, but even if he survived, the townsfolk would execute him for trespassing. He would need to be careful.

"Be careful in there, D. I know you're a writer and all, but this isn't a book, and you're not the main character. You could die there."

"I'm well aware of it. But it has to be done. This isn't just about me writing a book. It's not just about solving the case, either. I looked, and now, I'm tainted. If I don't get to the bottom of this soon, I'll be joining Joshua Bauer."

Iris's face conveyed dismay. She quickly took a bigger gulp of her drink this time.

"The festival is in two days, so we have time to prepare," Elliot said.

"Let's stay in touch," Dean said. "We can go over our plan again before the festival." He looked at Iris, who stared down at her glass with wide eyes. "Iris, you don't have to do this. Leave town and call for help."

"Ah, gee, that's a great idea, D. And what do I tell them? There's a haunted town where a ghost is making people kill themselves?"

"Tell them what you want. But you don't need to do this. It's not your problem."

"Oh, hell no! You're not getting rid of me so easily." She took another sip, emptying her glass.

"Fine, stay, then. Just don't go doing anything stupid or put yourself in danger."

"Heh, you're one to talk," Iris said as she pushed her chair back and stood. "All right, it's settled, then."

Dean stood, too. Elliot had no mobile phone, so they couldn't exchange numbers, but it didn't matter because he told them he would not leave his house during the next few days until the festival starts. Iris and Dean said goodbye to him and exited the house. The torrential rain once again showered Dean's head. He hadn't even realized how comfortably warm Elliot Wood's house was until he stepped outside.

"I swear to God, D. If we survive this, you're so going to publish a book through me," Iris said as she put her hoodie on.

Chapter 24

Dean spoke into his phone's voice recorder. "The visions are becoming more aggressive. I hear her voice in my head. I see myself dying in the most gruesome ways. Is this what happened to Joshua Bauer? I'm convinced that, even if I try to leave Suicide Town now, I will not make it far. The townsfolk warned not to look out the window, but I didn't listen. Whatever ancient horror lay dormant in their town has now taken a liking to me. It won't let me go until I finish it."

Dean looked toward the thick curtains covering the windows. They seemed insufficient, even with the cemented blinds behind them.

"The voice is the key, and Raintown is the door. Rachel Wood has been forced to Raintown and now remains trapped there, but I'm certain she's alive. I need to save her and expose this town for everything it truly is. If I don't manage to get out of—"

His words died in his throat when he turned around, and his eyes gravitated toward the bottom of the bed. A black hand that lay on the floor retreated under the bed ever so slowly. Or did it? Dean blinked hard. Nothing was there. He was sure he saw a charred hand with gray, broken nails just now. Or did he? It could have been a trick of the shadows for all he knew. It was dark in here, after all, but he still had to make sure.

He turned off the recorder, turned on the torch, and illuminated the floor. Nothing but the musty carpet. He got down on his knees and pointed the torch under. Two gleaming orbs stared at him—eyes?!—in the darkness. Dean's scream caught in his throat, but when the cone of his light got in contact with the orbs, they disappeared.

The underside of the bed was home to a thick layer of dust, but nothing more. Dean moved the torch away to see if the orbs would return. They didn't. Feeling unnerved, he retreated to the corner and scrutinized the room from the position in which he could not be attacked from behind.

It was empty, but the walls suddenly felt enclosed and caused him to feel more claustrophobic. He had to get out of the room for some fresh air. He put on his jacket and went outside. He briefly looked at room nine, which Iris had booked for herself. She was in there, but Dean didn't want any company, so he snuck past the rooms.

Baxter was rooted in his seat, still glowering at Dean and refusing to speak more than a word or two. Dean paid no attention to him. It was dark and foggy outside. It was much colder, too. Dean had to tuck his hands into his jacket's pockets because the icy air bit his exposed skin. When Dean looked toward the streetlights, millions of tiny particles fell and swayed in random directions. It was difficult to tell if it was rain or snow.

On his way past the obituaries, his eyes fell on a new one plastered among the others: an old man who had dropped a plugged fan into his bathtub. The town had changed since the last time he was out. Already, posters related to the Survival Festival popped up out of nowhere. Colorful flowers that Dean couldn't identify decorated the windows of some of the households. He thought he saw red-flowering currant and assumed it was a fake since it was a deciduous shrub. Poles for pavilions had been erected on the sides of North Street. People walked out of a nearby shop with festive clothes in their arms.

"They sure take this festival seriously," Dean said to himself as he walked past North Street.

When he first got out of the motel, he had no destination in mind; he just wanted to clear his head. He remembered the sheriff telling him about little Tom, so he went in that direction up North Street.

Dean already felt a little better. The voice, the hallucinations, and the suicidal thoughts would return soon enough, but he tried not to think about it. He thought about Joshua Bauer. He remembered that video of him driving in a hurry out of town. He remembered seeing a black figure crossing the road, forcing Joshua to stop his car. Dean felt compelled to look behind himself.

He just then realized that the road was empty, and the town was behind him. He suddenly felt vulnerable staying outside, surrounded by the trees. The thickets on his left and right were too dark and ominous. Dean imagined eyes watching him from the darkness. Staring at the thick blackness and imagining that same black figure lurking there made Dean feel uneasy and cold.

But he wasn't going to let that fear stop him. He continued walking away from the town, ignoring the trees that poked his peripheral vision. The more he disregarded them, the more they seemed to encroach on him. Dean noticed that he was walking too fast. His stride was almost a jog, and his breathing sounded too loud, yet the air somehow stifled it.

Before he knew it, he had reached the spot where Sheriff Moody had stopped the cruiser. He knew he was in the right spot because of the distinct V-shaped crack in the middle of the road. It was so foggy that Dean could hardly see twenty feet in front of him, but he still refused to stop—he merely slowed down his walk.

With each step he took, the air became heavier, or maybe it was Dean's imagination—he couldn't tell. The stride from before morphed into the polar opposite, and he took each step unsteadily and prudently. It was too silent. His footsteps and breathing accompanied him, and they seemed too loud in the silence that veiled the air.

Dean stopped walking and looked around. Anything could be lurking in the fog, but he dismissed that thought as his imagination—until a rustle came from the trees a moment later. Dean jerked toward the sound and froze. He held his breath as he listened to the rustling growing louder and more intense.

At the back of his mind, he wondered how he managed to get himself in this situation. Not just being in a town where people killed themselves but standing in the middle of the foggy road, wondering what was going to jump out at him. Just two days ago, he would have firmly believed that the stirring in front of him was a human or a stray animal. Now, as it got closer, he envisioned the black figure from his hallucinations stepping in front of him, naked, inky, and smelling of death, with icy hands that would squeeze his throat until it snuffed his life.

"Who's there?" Dean dared to ask, but his voice came out hoarse and tenuous.

In response, the rustling only became more violent. The shrubs in front of him swayed as if the plant itself had come to life. And then it stopped, and a figure on all fours emerged on the road and stared at Dean.

"Fuck me," Dean said as he stared at the stray yellow dog that looked up at him and wagged its tail.

Dean breathed a sigh of relief. His heart was pounding, but the ease of knowing he was not in danger took him over. He squatted down on wobbly legs and motioned for the dog to come over. It didn't look sick or malnourished; only his paws were somewhat dirty.

"Hey, fella. You lost?" Dean asked in an amicable tone.

Skylar would have lost her shit right now. Whenever they were out on a walk and saw a stray animal, Dean would call it over and pet it if it didn't look too mangy. The dogs usually trusted him, the cats not so much. Skylar always warned him that stray dogs were too unpredictable and could end up biting him, but he told her that she was overreacting.

The stray dog took a few timid steps toward Dean and then stopped. It lowered its head and ears, and the tail stopped wagging. *He's scared,* Dean thought. But then the dog snarled, and its nose wrinkled, and Dean knew that it was time to get up and take a step back.

"Easy, boy. Easy," Dean said as he put some distance between him and the dog.

The dog continued growling and then barked viciously. Dean backpedaled, ready to kick the dog if it came after him. He hated the thought of hurting a dog, but he had to defend himself if it came to it.

"Okay, I'm just gonna go," Dean said.

A branch snapped in the woods behind him, and that's when Dean realized that the dog wasn't barking at him at all. Slowly, Dean turned so that he was sideways-facing the sound of the branch. He rotated his head toward the woods, expecting to see someone standing and staring at him, but saw nothing through the darkness and the thick fog. Before he knew it, the dog ran past Dean and jumped into the fog at whoever was in there.

"Dog, wait!" Dean shouted but made no effort to step toward the woods.

The barking resumed, still close by, but then it became distant. Dean heard another snap and something that sounded like the batting of footsteps. The barking became even more belligerent, and then a high-pitched yelp echoed through the woods.

Silence took over.

Dean's breath expelled fumes that dispersed in the cold air. He squinted at the fog and listened intently for any sounds.

Nothing.

"Dog?" Dean called out, his voice barely audible.

He scanned the foggy tree line for any movement, listening intently for any sounds. Footsteps came from a distance, this time calm and slow as if a person was taking a leisurely stroll through the woods. The soft crunching, rustling, and snapping under each step told Dean they were approaching him, and he had no intention of waiting to see who or what it was.

He turned toward the town and booked it, no longer trying to be stealthy about his presence. Whatever abomination was in the woods—and he was sure that it was no human—was aware of Dean's presence. He was going to be just another victim to it, just like Joshua Bauer, just like thousands of people who had fallen prey to it. Killing a dog meant nothing to this entity.

Dean's legs burned, and he was out of breath. The air that he sucked in sharply with each inhale sent icy daggers in his lungs, but he ignored the sensation. He had to return to the town. Once there, he would be safe from that thing in the woods.

Before he knew it, he was at the intersection of North Street and the main avenue. He felt like he was going to collapse from the exertion, so he refused to run any longer. He turned around and stared in the direction he came from. It was much less foggy in the town, much to Dean's relief.

No one followed him. Whatever was in the woods stayed in the woods. Dean leaned on his knees and panted. He lowered his head and stared at the ground while focusing on his breathing. When he felt okay, he straightened his back and looked up North Street again.

He was still alone.

He was sweaty and warm underneath his clothes, but his ears and hands were numb from the cold. Dean turned to leave, and his eyes fell on a hooded figure standing across the street at an entrance to an alley, just out of the streetlight's reach. The person faced Dean, vapor escaping its mouth from time to time. The ember occasionally lighting up around the mouth told Dean that it was smoke. The kyphotic posture helped Dean recognize the figure as Lawrence, the mechanic. The fucker was following Dean.

"Hey, asshole! You following me around?!"

Dean waited for the mechanic to respond. The ember lit up and then smoke escaped his mouth. Dean wanted to cross the street and clock the bastard, not just because of the stalking, but because he hurt that dog.

Lawrence raised a hand to his mouth and then brought it down, dropping the cigarette. He stubbed it with his boot, his gaze unrelenting, even though Dean couldn't see it from the hoodie. Lawrence put his hands in his pocket, turned around, and disappeared into the alley.

Dean suddenly realized that he'd been outside way longer than he had intended. It was almost curfew, and he didn't want to be outside, anyway. He looked toward the road, where he heard the rustling in the woods. It was there, just beyond the fog, no matter how still Suicide Town was at the moment.

Dean put his hands in his pockets and sauntered back to the motel.

Chapter 25

Aggressive nightmares plagued Dean more than before. It was the same dream where he had hit the boy with the car, but more things were happening. He dreamed about hitting the boy with the car and going out to see if he was okay, then finding an empty raincoat on the road instead. He dreamed about hitting the boy in the raincoat, but under the hood was a black figure that slithered out from under the coat and merged with the darkness off the side of the road.

He dreamed about he, himself, being that boy, seeing a pair of headlights approaching him out of nowhere. Although he couldn't see the driver's face, he somehow knew it was Joshua Bauer. Just before getting hit, Dean raised a hand in futile defense and saw that it was black.

He woke up drenched in cold sweat, his heart jack hammering against his chest. He was on his back, staring at the ceiling. A grinning face stared back at him. Dean fumbled for the light switch. It took him a while to find it, but once his trembling fingers managed to flip the switch, the dim light chased the darkness away.

No face formed on the ceiling. It was probably just the way the cracks were shaped. Dean slumped back into the pillow with an exasperated sigh. He was too wide awake, so he looked at his phone. It was a little after four a.m. He wondered if he would see anything outside right now. He couldn't remember what time the restriction of looking outside ended. Everyone just told him not to look after one a.m., but he had no idea when it was safe to actually go outside.

At dawn, perhaps?

Dean looked toward the heavy drapes that shielded the windows. He imagined Rachel Wood wandering the streets, the rag still over her head, her clothes constantly wet from the black rain that poured on her. Dean turned to the side and pulled the covers higher. He left the light on and kept his eyes open.

Eventually, he fell asleep. No other sounds or dreams woke him up until morning.

***

When Iris knocked on his door, he had already been wide awake. Dean opened the door, and a sickly, sweet aroma hit him like a ton of bricks.

"Hungry, writer?" Iris asked as she presented the open box of donuts to Dean.

He hadn't even thought about whether he was hungry until then, but when he smelled the donuts, his stomach rumbled to remind him that he skipped dinner last night. Dean stepped aside and allowed Iris to walk in. She had taken one donut out and took a big bite out of it.

"The selection isn't big," Iris said with her mouth full. "But they look appetizing, at least." She then choked with her mouth closed. Dean had closed the door and got ready to perform the Heimlich maneuver.

Iris pounded herself on the chest, swallowed, then coughed some more. She was red in the face, her eyes full of tears.

"You okay?" Dean asked as he stopped in front of her.

"Oh, man," Iris said. "These things are so damn dry; they're gonna kill me." She coughed some more, swallowed the remaining bits of food in her mouth, and then said, "Oh, geez. That was a close one. Maybe these donuts are the cause of all suicides in the town."

She took another bite. Dean took one out of the box and tested it with a nibble. Iris was right. Even the dry glaze crumbled and fell off the donut.

"So, what do you want to do today?" Iris asked.

"We're supposed to finalize our plan, no?"

"Well, I mean, obviously. We're not on a field trip here. Not that there's anything to see, anyway. I thought a town like this one would have some history to it, you know? A building or a landmark, anything really. But there's nothing. The most historical thing they have is the old woman working at the post office."

"Have you seen Elliot?" Dean asked.

"Yeah, but we couldn't speak too much because there were too many people around," Iris said as she put the rest of the donut in her mouth. "He said he was going to be at the park later. We should meet up with him there."

"I didn't even know this place had a park," Dean said. He had difficulty chewing the dry donut but was determined to down the whole thing. He had no water on him, which would have helped.

"Yeah, I mean, why would you?" Iris said. "Not like you can go and have a picnic there. Not with this kind of weather, y'know? That reminds me: we gotta wrap this whole thing up by Monday tops because I have a business lunch with an audiobook narrator. And he's a talented narrator. He can do all kinds of voices and accents—I mean, wow, you should hear him, D. Really gives life to a book. I was supposed to meet him yesterday, but I put it off for you. You should appreciate how much I value my writers, D."

"I'm not your writer, Iris."

"Well, I mean, technically, you are. The contract for the book we published lasts for another two years."

"Oh, it's still active? I haven't noticed because I rarely get any royalties from that book."

"Very funny, funny-man. I'm telling you, D. The business is growing, and pretty soon, we'll be one of the big names in the industry. You better snatch your spot while it's available because all the big shots are going to want a place with us."

"You know what, let's first try to survive Suicide Town. If that goes well, I'll write a separate story as a recollection of true events that you can publish as nonfiction."

"Deal!" Iris jumped at the offer. She closed the box of donuts and put it on the bed with a disgusted grimace. "I don't think I'm hungry anymore. Here, you can have them. You don't eat enough, anyway."

***

As always, it rained in the town, but that didn't stop the people from preparing for the festival. North Street was so crowded that it felt like taking a tour through Times Square. Dean assumed that the majority of the town was helping with preparations.

They raised pavilions, decorated buildings with colorful flower fixtures, erected a stage in the middle of the road, and rolled empty food stands onto the side of the street. The street boomed with the buoyant voices of the people who shouted commands to their fellow townsfolk workers. They had almost finalized the setup. The only missing thing, Dean noted, was the lack of music.

"No history, huh?" Dean asked Iris as they entered the epicenter of the crowd.

"Well, it's not too horrible—I'll give them that," Iris said.

Being a big city girl her entire life, Dean knew that Iris couldn't stand small towns. The fact that she bit the bullet and came all the way out to a small place like Suicide Town and even stayed for more than a few hours told Dean a lot about her determination to help.

Iris led the way through the crowd, occasionally tossing flattering comments at the townsfolk as she walked past them. Suicide Meat and Lamar Bakery were particularly busy, and tons of people buzzed in and out of the two places. Moody was nowhere in sight, but Dean was sure that the sheriff was close by, obscured by the crowd. He made sure to look around for Lawrence. He couldn't see the mechanic anywhere, so he assumed that even he must have been busy with something.

Or just well-hidden.

As refreshing as it was to walk down a street that had more than two people on it, Dean was glad when Iris turned into an alleyway.

"These guys sure are taking this festival seriously, huh?" she asked. "I wonder if they take Christmas and other holidays as religiously. Hey, isn't suicide regarded as an unforgivable sin in religion?"

"Yeah. I talked to the town's priest about it, and they follow something that resembles Catholicism, but they don't consider suicides to be bad."

"So, they ignore the sins they don't like."

Dean laughed. Given the fact that it was his first thought when he spoke to Father Walter, he appreciated that Iris understood his point of view.

"Well, let's just get to the bottom of this and get out of here before they try to execute us by feeding us those donuts."

They emerged from the alley and crossed the street. The entrance to the park was right there, but Dean hadn't seen it until Iris was already inside. The park looked more like a botanical garden. It consisted of archways covered in nylon, stretching above narrow trails, serving as shelter, with occasional rectangular windows. A gazebo was nearby, and for those who didn't mind the rain, paved outdoor trails lined the park.

The whole place was bleak. Dean could see himself coming to the park on a sunny spring or summer day for a stroll, but with the perpetual rain, that would be impossible. Dean followed Iris through the archways that wound left and right like a maze for a few minutes. That's when Rachel's voice—that had been dormant for the entire time—entered his mind.

Help me.

Dean looked out one of the windows toward the paved trail and saw a lonesome figure standing there facing him. Aloof, he glanced, then looked away before his brain registered that something was wrong. He looked back at the figure, but it was gone.

I'm running out of time, Rachel said.

Whenever Dean blinked, something came into view. Mute images of a crowd gathered in the middle of a road. A priest who he recognized as Father Walter standing in front of the crowd, surrounded by a group of people in raincoats. *The Escorters.* The image of a woman, Rachel, crying and thrashing against the Escorters who held her firmly as Father Walter uttered something in a calm manner and crossed her. The image of a bearded man trying to push his way through to Rachel but getting punched and restrained by a lanky figure that grinned in relish—Lawrence. The image of a rag being put over Rachel's head and her being shoved to walk forward.

Every time Dean blinked, the people in the image would change, but the scene was always the same: a person with a rag over their head forced to walk down the road undoubtedly leading to Raintown as the crowd watched and did nothing to stop it.

Iris was saying something, but the words were imperceptible. He continued following her but focused on his footsteps like a toddler just learning how to walk. A suicidal urge replaced the images in his mind. Nothing in the archways posed a threat to help him injure himself, which was a good thing, because Dean was sure that he would attempt to commit suicide otherwise. The unpleasant sensation was over soon, but Dean's legs were wobbly from it.

Iris was done speaking by then, and he had no idea what it was that she said, but he didn't care. They emerged from the enclosed space and followed a more spacious path until they reached another gazebo. The jacketed figure sitting there didn't catch his eye until they climbed the steps under the wooden structure.

"Hey," Elliot softly said as Dean and Iris approached.

"Of all the places to meet, you had to choose this one?" Iris said. "I know I look like I need to lose a few pounds, but let's leave the cardio for after the mission. Then, again, the food in this town is so bad that I might lose some weight whether I want to or not."

"Iris," Dean scolded.

"I'm just kidding, D. I mean—okay, the donuts taste like shit, but have you tried the food at the diner? Man, oh, man. The burger is—"

"We didn't come here to discuss food."

"Right. Okay, so, Elliot," Iris said as she sat down. "You wanted to discuss the plan."

"Yeah. Let's walk." Elliot stood.

Iris upturned her palms in a questioning manner and gave him an annoyed look. "Seriously?"

Elliot was already on his way, and Dean followed. Iris stood with a groan and went along with them, grumbling under her breath.

"You're suspicious, so the Escorters are keeping a close watch on you," Elliot said.

"I've noticed. That mechanic is always on my ass," Dean replied.

"Then, how are we going to sneak into Raintown, if that's the case?" Iris asked a little too loudly.

Dean shot her a reprimanding glower, and she grimaced, realizing her mistake.

They got back on the archway trail. The path was too narrow for all three of them to walk side by side, so Iris walked behind Dean and Elliot.

"We'll need a diversion," Elliot said. "But I can't be the one to do it because they'll know something's up."

"How so?" Dean asked.

"Because it would be out of my character. Iris will have to do it."

"Me? Do what, exactly?" Iris asked, perturbance in her timbre.

"You'll have to distract the Escorters so that Dean can sneak into Raintown. I'll help you keep watch and stall anyone who goes looking for him."

"Ah, gee," Iris said.

"This is your time to shine, Iris." Dean turned around and flashed her a smile. "You're good at talking, so use that to your advantage."

"I'm good at talking people's ears off and pitching deals, but this? I don't work well under pressure, D."

"You'll do fine," Dean said.

They exited the park through a different exit and found themselves back on the streets of Suicide Town. They stopped and faced each other in a triangle.

"Okay, so it's settled, then," Dean said. "What time does the festival start tomorrow?"

"Wait, it's tomorrow?! I thought it was the day after tomorrow!" Iris interjected.

Dean and Elliot looked at her, confused. She must have realized what their gazes meant because she rolled her eyes and said, "Okay, fine. I'll do it."

"The festival starts early in the morning, but it's best if we do it under the veil of night," Elliot said. "Around five p.m. That's when everyone will be busy with fireworks and drinking."

Dean nodded. Elliot turned around and left without another word, leaving Iris and Dean alone in the street.

"Well, that was awkward," Iris said. "A simple 'goodbye' would have sufficed."

A slim figure stood at the corner of the street and craned his head toward Dean and Iris. When he realized he was spotted, he raised a hand in greeting and scurried out of sight.

"Was that the bookstore guy?" Iris asked.

"Yeah."

"Think he was listening to us?"

Dean sucked in a sharp breath and put his cold hands in the pockets of his jacket.

"Come on. Let's go back," he said.

Chapter 26

Dean could hear the people all the way from North Street to the motel. He opened his laptop and tried to take some notes, but his mind drew a blank. Even writing bullet points for the story was impossible. Whenever something in his mind got close to sprouting into an idea, something else would push it back.

It could have been writer's block, but it was very possible that the stress of being in such a predicament wasn't allowing him to write anything. Speaking into his phone recorder was easy but writing made his hands tremble like he had Parkinson's disease. Eventually, he closed the laptop and got on his phone instead.

"The people here are preparing for the Survival Festival," Dean said into the recorder on as he paced the room. "It will take place tomorrow. I will attempt to sneak into Raintown and rescue Rachel. Once I have saved her, I'm sure I will have all the answers. The people in this town are fanatical. They forcefully push people into Raintown in hopes of protecting the town, but in doing so, they are sacrificing innocent people. While it is true that something unnatural is happening in Suicide Town, the community here is nothing more than a cult brainwashed into believing they are doing something good."

Muffled footsteps came outside his door. Baxter or Iris? He brought the phone closer to his mouth and spoke in a quiet tone. "I'm being watched. I may not make it out alive. There's no telling what the people will do to me when I return from Raintown with Rachel. But I'll record everything and send it to my literary agent. If anything happens to me, I have to be the last person to fall prey to Suicide Town."

He ended the recording and named it that day's date. All the files on his phone and laptop were hidden in case anyone tried to snoop. It was only a little after noon, and Dean was uncomfortable, cooped up in the dark motel room. Staying in the room made it difficult to discern the time of day, which, in turn, made him drowsy at weird times.

While holed up in the motel, Dean also spent extensive time thinking about suicide as a topic in general. He hadn't given it much thought prior to starting this project, but with free time on his hands, the profound thoughts forcibly entered his mind.

He had never been close to anyone who committed suicide, so he didn't need to think about it. Whenever he heard about it on the news, he wondered why someone would do it. He wondered how much a person would need to suffer to even think about going for such a permanent solution.

Whatever made them do it, they believed that life was no longer worth living. Before, Dean secretly considered those people weak. Ever since he arrived at Suicide Town, he developed more of an understanding for suicidal people.

But then there was also the morbid fascination with suicide. He couldn't help but imagine how the person felt in those final seconds of their life. Did they jump and then change their minds while plummeting to their demise? Did they hang themselves but try to get off the noose while their vision darkened? The thought of deciding to commit suicide only to want to go back too late on the decision terrified Dean. He didn't want to think about that anymore.

He would go out for a walk later. This time, he wouldn't be going to the edge of the town. Flashbacks of the events from yesterday gripped him, and he wondered how close he was to actually dying. Dean was convinced that whatever malevolent presence resided in Suicide Town was trying to kill him to stop him from helping Rachel.

He heard her voice in his head, and at the same time, he had bouts of feeling suicidal—it only grew stronger with each passing day. At one point, while Dean was in the bathroom, he imagined breaking the mirror and sticking one of the pointy shards in his throat. He went to the bedroom to retrieve his phone in an attempt to chuck it at the mirror.

As he stared at his reflection in the mirror, admiring the perplexed facial expressions that he didn't even know he could make, he was ready to throw the phone. He raised it above his head like a pitcher, and then his hand vibrated, accompanied by the familiar ringtone of someone calling him.

That made him snap out of it.

He looked at the reflection, but only then did he actually see how pallid his face was and how wide-eyed he was staring at himself. *I was actually going to do it,* he thought. He was seconds away from breaking the mirror. What if the phone hadn't rung?

Dean quickly answered. It was Alex, calling to make sure everything was okay. Dean mumbled an excuse for everything being fine and scuttling out of the bathroom. Alex didn't buy it, but it didn't matter. This would all be over soon, one way or another. The entire motel room suddenly seemed murderous. He had to get out of there, even for five minutes, if possible. Out there, people might stop him from killing himself if they saw him acting strange.

Or would they? They might see him mutilating himself and then go on with their daily lives.

Oh, look. Another suicide, too bad. Wasn't that the writer? Crap, I forgot to buy milk.

On the way out, Dean saw two new obituaries added to the memorial notice: old people who had apparently died from swallowing pills. If the suicides continued at this rate, it would only be a matter of time before the council of Suicide Town decided to pick a new Protector. That's how things worked, according to what he learned—if the number of suicides increased, they would choose a new Protector.

But what if they're right?

It was his own thought, one that had been nagging him at the back of his mind. Dean had ignored it entirely up until now, but he couldn't ignore it anymore. If the townsfolk's rituals were really helping keep the place safe . . .

No, that's stupid. It's a ritual. Rituals don't work. What they're doing is murder.

Just like earlier that day, it was freezing outside. The sudden drop in the temperature irked Dean and only made him more irritable than he usually was. He couldn't stand the cold. Back when he worked as an accountant, the worst thing was working during the winter. Dean didn't miss at all the days of waking up in the early hours for work while it was still dark and having to get out of the warm bed and out into the cold.

After quitting his job as an accountant and becoming a full-time writer, the first thing he did was set a goal about waking up at a specific time each morning. Since he had to wake up at six a.m. for the past few years, as a writer, he decided to wake up at eight and start his work then. With no pressure of having to be anywhere on time, that goal was a miss, and Dean always ended up sleeping in until nine.

Instead of going on North Street, he turned into one of the smaller side streets this time. He knew that there was probably nothing there except naked streets with households, but he was sick of walking down the same places. Giggling erupted from somewhere when he entered one of the alleyways. A young couple frolicked down the street, the boy holding the girl's hand. They gave each other affectionate looks when they disappeared out of view.

It put a smile on Dean's face. He was so enthralled in his investigation that it hadn't even occurred to him how people got married in Suicide Town. A disturbing thought occurred to him that everyone in the town might be related to each other, but he didn't want to think of that cute couple as cousins because it would kill its charm.

Dean had been walking for around ten minutes before he got too cold. It was time to go back to the motel room. An alleyway nearby was his shortcut back, so he decided to cut through it. He stared at the ground as he walked, his mind inadvertently going toward Skylar. He wasn't sure if it was the anxiety or the cold or something else, but he wished that she was here with him. She would know what to do for sure. She probably would have already found enough information for all of them to leave. When Dean first started getting invited to fancy dinners and hangouts, along with other bestselling authors, Skylar was nervous about going. She was self-conscious about being an English teacher and thought it would embarrass Dean. She was a recluse at first and only nodded in silence in front of all the important faces, but then, she learned that most of the writers at the parties either had bimbos as escorts, or they were married to what Skylar would call a "professional parasite," meaning they didn't work and leeched their spouse's money. Skylar later mentioned to Dean that these female escorts were unable to hold the conversation, especially when it came to complex topics.

It wasn't just the women. Dean had met a lot of successful female writers, and their husbands or boyfriends were usually either people running start-ups or young guys in the acting or music industry.

All of that gave Skylar the boost of confidence she needed. Sometimes, she'd end up being the highlight of the news in articles like "Dean Watson's wife shows off amazing body in black dress" or "How to portray confidence like Skylar Watson." It all made Dean proud to have someone like Skylar as his wife.

Voices from the street snapped Dean back to reality. He wouldn't have paid any attention to them had they not sounded so hushed. Dean stopped dead in his tracks, wondering what they were talking about. Maybe a drug deal was taking place right now, and Dean interfering could cause them to panic. He tiptoed closer to the corner. The voices came from the left, but Dean couldn't detect what they were saying. What he could tell was that it was a conversation between a group of people.

"Any orders for tomorrow?" a voice asked.

"No. Just keep a lookout. I'll deal with the rest," another one responded.

Dean recognized that second voice. It was unmistakably Lawrence, the mechanic.

"What about the writer and his annoying friend?" a third voice asked.

Dean thought he recognized that voice as well, but he couldn't put a face to it. The mention of the word writer made him tense up. He pressed his back against the wall, glad to be standing in the darkness of the alley where he could go unnoticed. He tried to tell himself that the people he was eavesdropping on were simply gossiping, but he knew that it was foolish to think so.

"I'll deal with the writer after the festival," Lawrence said. "It'll attract too much attention if something happens to him now."

A more petulant voice spoke up this time. "You're . . . you're going to kill him?"

"I'm going to protect this town at any cost," the mechanic retorted, somewhat louder this time. "I'm the only one competent enough among you useless pricks."

"That's a little harsh."

"Harsh or not, the whole journalist thing could have been avoided if we had done things the way I told you to do them. We're lucky the whole world doesn't know about our town. If they did, we'd be labeled as a satanic cult."

A moment of silence flooded the conversation. Someone sniffled, and someone moved their foot, causing it to shuffle against the concrete.

"You got your hard-thinking face on, Clive. What is it?" Lawrence spoke.

A soft voice broke the silence. "I was just wondering. We obey the council for all the escorting, but . . ."

"But what?"

"The writer, he—he doesn't believe in any of it, obviously. The whole Protector thing, I mean. What if . . . what if he's right, and all of the things we're doing—"

"You shut your mouth, boy!" Lawrence's voice boomed. "You wanna get in trouble?!" A pause interjected before he continued. "Look, what the writer does or doesn't believe is irrelevant. In his eyes, we're monsters. And fuck—maybe we are. But this is our town, and I'm not letting anyone fuck with us."

"But killing him? Are you sure that's the best option?" the familiar voice from before asked.

"He already broke one rule," Lawrence said. "And we're not going to kill him. We'll assist him in committing suicide. No one will ever know we were involved."

Dean's heart was pumping wildly. He knew that the best course of action would be to tiptoe back the way he came and hope nobody notices him. It was either fear or curiosity—he couldn't tell, but he couldn't move.

"We're going against the council's rules here," someone else said.

"You think that makes me happy?" Lawrence snapped. "Look, we're not doing anything wrong. The council would understand that we're just protecting our hometown. If the writer gets out and publishes his book, you know what that means?"

"No, what?"

"People from all over the country will want to visit Suicide Town. The council is having difficulty censoring all the information online as it is. Now, imagine if that dumbass writer puts a book about our town on the shelves of every goddamn bookstore in the country."

"I don't think he's that popular. Why would he be here if that were the case?"

Someone laughed. Lawrence said something, but it overlapped with the laughter and Dean didn't catch it.

"Okay, I guess you know what you're saying," the familiar voice said. "But if we get caught, I ain't taking the blame from the council. No way."

"Relax, it'll all be fine," Lawrence said.

More silence ensued. Dean held his breath during those moments, hoping that he would remain unnoticed. Although Lawrence said he would deal with Dean after the festival, it didn't mean Dean was in the clear. If they knew he was eavesdropping, they would not hesitate to kill him on the spot.

"Okay, let's get back," Lawrence said. "If anyone asks, we patrolled and found nothing suspicious. This conversation never happened. Got it?"

The others agreed. Dean thought he heard four or five other voices. The marching footsteps pulsated. It was too late to move now. A group of figures in raincoats walked past the alley—five of them, from what Dean could count. Any moment now, they were going to turn into the alley and notice Dean plastered to the wall. Two separated from the group and crossed the street, and the others walked past the alley without ever looking in Dean's direction.

Robert, the butcher. That's who the voice belongs to, Dean realized as the footsteps gradually receded. Dean refused to move until the figures were out of sight, when he could no longer hear their footsteps. Only the sound of rain remained and the thoughts that spun in Dean's mind.

He was right all along: the townsfolk were up to no good. The urge to get out of town was almost irresistible. He wanted to sprint back to his car in front of the motel and drive off without even taking his laptop. Then his rationality kicked in, and he realized that he couldn't leave Iris behind. Even Elliot, who was one of them, was not really one of them. Still, there were only three of them against an entire town of lunatics.

Dean peeked out of the alley toward the street where the men had conversed just a minute ago. No one was outside. Dean cautiously stepped outside. Trying to walk as naturally as he could, he crossed the street and made his way back to the motel.

He couldn't shake the feeling that he was being watched the entire time.

Chapter 27

Morning came, and with it, the Survival Festival. Right from the moment Dean woke up, palpable gaiety peppered the air. Music and voices boomed on the street, waking Dean up before his alarm. It was only seven in the morning, but the noises that caused the windows of the motel room to drum and vibrate told Dean that sleep would be impossible.

He put on his clothes and walked out of the room. He knocked on the door of room nine and waited. He couldn't hear anything beyond the door because of the outside noises, so he assumed that Iris was still asleep. He rapped again, louder this time. He was about to do it for the third time as well, but then he heard the lock clicking.

The door opened, and Iris stood in front of Dean. Her hair was disheveled, her eyes half-closed while her head and shoulders drooped. She was wearing a green bathrobe. The gaze that gravitated toward the ground made her look like she didn't even register that Dean in front of her.

"Good morning, Iris," Dean said loud and clear.

She mumbled something and turned around before shuffling back to bed. She slumped into it on her back and groaned. Dean shook his head.

"I guess you can sleep a while longer, not like we gotta hurry." Dean shrugged.

Iris pressed the pillow from both sides against her ears and moaned. "God, what is that racket?" she asked with a raspy voice.

"Survival Festival."

"At this hour? Gee . . ."

"Yeah. I'm going outside. Call me when you're ready to get up."

"Wait. Wait," Iris mumbled just as Dean turned around.

She rolled onto her side with what looked like great effort and then stood. She shuffled toward the bathroom, her eyes slightly more open now.

"I'll be out in a few minutes," she said and closed the door behind her.

Dean sat on the edge of the bed. The music outside stopped every couple of minutes. Dean wondered if it the festival had live music played by a band. Iris came out of the bathroom a few minutes later, fully dressed and looking as fresh as ever. It was as if one person had entered the bathroom and another had come out.

"All right, D. So, what's the plan for today?" Iris asked in her usual joviality. "How about we get something to eat first? I sure could use a cup of coffee. You know, the sheriff says the coffee at the diner is the best, but it tastes like watered-down shit to me. He should try coffee we drink back where I come from, huh?"

Dean was starting to suspect that he liked Iris more when she was sleepy and unable to utter a single sentence. He kept the complaints to himself as they left the motel. The streets were crowded, and even from the motel, the large crowd on North Street occupied the view. Everyone was staring at something out of view around the corner, occasionally applauding and cheering.

"Well, this is kind of nice. Isn't it?" Iris asked. "Been a while since I've been to an event like this one."

"Let's mingle with people. But don't go too far, all right?"

"Why? We might as well have some fun while we're here."

"I'll tell you why in a bit."

Iris put her hoodie over her head, but seeing all the uncovered heads of the townsfolk, Dean remembered that covering your head during the Survival Festival was forbidden, so he reminded Iris to take it off. She conceded with a complaint. As they walked toward North Street, Dean told Iris everything about the conversation on which he eavesdropped yesterday. Her face contorted into that of slight worry, but she didn't panic like Dean expected her to. Instead, when Dean was finished talking, Iris got angry.

"They want to kill you?! They want to kill *my* writer?! Oh, hell no!" Iris shouted.

"Keep it down!" Dean warned her, even though nobody could hear from beneath the deafening music that came from North Street.

Iris leaned closer to Dean and shouted in his ear. "Well, I'll show these hillbillies why they shouldn't mess with someone from New Jersey! Mark my words, D!"

"Don't do anything stupid," Dean replied.

North Street was brimming with people and pushing through the crowd proved to be more difficult than doing so in a night club. Pleasant smells of burning meat coming from the pavilions pervaded the air. People stood in line to buy burgers from Robert, the butcher, and the teenager who worked as his assistant handed out food to customers.

Vendors sold other foods sold as well: hot dogs, donuts, funnel cakes filled with ice cream, etc. Some of the pavilions had tables and benches in them, allowing the people to eat and drink and take shelter from the rain. On the stage were children dressed in rags, dancing something that looked like folklore dance.

With each song that ended, the kids took each other's hands and bowed to the audience, much to the applause and praise of the adults.

Sheriff Moody stood on the side of the road with a cup of coffee. A young police officer was next to him, observing the crowd with intent. Unlike Moody, who was visibly relaxed and enjoying himself, the rookie looked like he was eager for some trouble to start. Father Walter was at a distance, furiously gesturing to the young boys who were carrying heavy-looking draped things on their shoulders into the church.

Dean and Iris stopped to observe the dancers on the stage. Iris tapped Dean on the shoulder and told him she was going to be right back with some food. Dean took the opportunity to look around. Elliot was nowhere in sight. He paid close attention to whether anyone was watching him. Lawrence was nowhere in sight, and the crowd was too focused on the festival to give a darn about some visitor.

That was good. It would give him an ample chance to sneak into Raintown. Iris returned a few minutes later with two hot dogs and a cup of coffee for herself. Of course, the hot dog itself was nothing special. The sausage probably came from a transparent packet of five, and they boiled a bunch of them together, and the bun was most likely a Ball Park rip-off. And yet, there was always something special about eating the overpriced mediocre food at a game or a town fair or an amusement park.

It reminded him of the days when he was a kid, when his parents took him to the amusement park. They always bought him either a burger or a hot dog or cotton candy or roasted chestnuts. After his parents divorced, when Dean was eight years old, things became a little more complicated. It was impossible to go to the amusement park with both parents at the same time, so he had to choose carefully when to go and with which parent. The parents were a lot more affectionate to him after the divorce, and that meant he could have anything he wanted at the parks.

"You see our contact anywhere?" Iris asked before she bit into the hot dog and grimaced. "Ugh, they put mustard on my hot dog! I specifically told them no mustard!"

"You can't eat a hot dog without mustard," Dean said. "And no, I don't see him anywhere."

"Disgusting," Iris said before she took another bite, eyeing the hot dog as if she expected it to come to life.

After the children were done dancing, the music stopped, and a man in a suit stepped up for a speech. He represented himself as the city manager and talked about the history of the Survival Festival and why it's so important to celebrate it. He then spoke about the ones who were no longer among the living and asked the audience for a moment of silence. Everyone hung their heads and remained quiet, leaving the sound of the falling raindrops for a whole minute to fill the silence. Dean followed what the others did. By then, Dean had finished his hot dog. Iris hadn't.

"Gee, what a cheerful bunch. When did the festival transition to a funeral?" Iris mumbled.

Dean elbowed her, and she yelped, attracting the attention of the townsfolk standing next to her. She cleared her throat and remained silent. After the moment of silence, the city manager let Father Walter take over. The priest prayed for the souls of the dead. Once again, everyone unanimously performed one gesture, this time putting their hands together in prayer, saying amen after Father Walter from time to time.

The prayer took a few minutes, and then Father Walter was gone. The city manager introduced a band named Reason to Live and then left. A group of five teenagers, who looked like heavy metal fans dressed in black, climbed on the stage with their instruments. By then, the murmurs of the crowd filled the air with occasional whistling and cheering directed at the band members.

The boys spent ten minutes adjusting their instruments, then test-playing music, and then they finally started playing something that sounded like a mixture of pop and rock. Dean wondered if they had changed their genre to fit the festival's atmosphere or if it was something they normally played in their parents' garage.

The crowd cheered and danced. When Dean looked at Iris, he saw her jiving to the music as well. She looked a little embarrassed when she caught Dean staring, so she shrugged and said, "What?! These guys are not half bad! I'm thinking of giving them an offer to play music for our book trailers!"

The band did a good job uplifting the mood, even though it was already high. Although Dean preferred not going to loud places, this reminded him of the time he went to a Red Hot Chili Peppers concert in LA with Skylar. Skylar was a huge fan and had tried buying the tickets online the moment they went on sale, but they were all sold out. Luckily, Dean already had good connections as a writer back then, so he was able to get two VIP tickets, thanks to Alex. A guy who bought them purely for the purpose of reselling sold them at an inflated price, but Dean ended up not having to pay a dime.

Go on, unwind, and when you're back, I want a good book, Alex had told him. Dean hated the idea of going to a concert, but he wanted to make Skylar happy. He ended up having a great time.

"We should find Elliot," Dean said, wanting to enjoy more of the music, but he knew he had to focus on the task at hand.

"Come on, just one more song!" Iris said as she bounced up and down to the drums. "Man, seriously. These guys could be a hit if only they'd leave the town, huh, D?!"

Dean didn't answer. His perkiness dropped. He envisioned laying on the ground, waiting for the crowd to stampede him, where they would crush his skull to a pulp. He rubbed his eyes to get the vision out of his mind.

I need your help, the voice said, crystal clear above the booming sounds surrounding him. Dean felt his gaze inadvertently pulled toward the intersection of the main avenue that led to Raintown.

Rachel was there.

He thought about sneaking into the forbidden area but then realized that it would be too risky not following the plan. They needed all the help they could get. They had to find Elliot.

The suicidal sensation intensified. He had to get away from the crowd and get some fresh air. The muscles in his throat constricted, and his legs became stiff. He could no longer hear the music. Dean started pushing through the crowd. Some of the townsfolk might have complained, but if that was the case, then Dean didn't notice them.

Gotta get out of here. Gotta get out of here, he thought to himself, feeling like he was having more difficulty breathing. He walked faster and pushed more aggressively. He thought he heard someone yell "hey!"

but he ignored it. If he didn't reach the edge of the crowd, he was going to collapse—he was sure of it.

He broke through the crowd faster than he expected, but the suffocating sensation didn't abate. Dean noticed the passersby staring at him in perplexed manners, so he knew that he must have looked like he wasn't feeling well, but he paid no attention to their gazes as he strode past them. His breaths were shallow, and he got more and more winded with each step he took. He had to stop. He leaned on his knees and inhaled through his nose while exhaling through his mouth to regain his breath.

The corners of his vision were dark, and a prickling sensation swaddled his extremities. *Come on. Go away, darn it,* Dean said in his mind over and over. As if hearing his plea, the darkness in his vision receded, and the strength in his legs returned. He felt nauseous and was sure that he would vomit the undigested pieces of hot dog any minute now, but that, too, retreated. Before Dean knew it, he was feeling like himself again. The music that sounded muffled up until that point resumed at its normal volume, but with the distance he had put to the stage, he could hear the people close to him talking.

"Something wrong?" a voice next to him said.

Dean didn't even need to look to know it was Elliot talking to him. Dean looked up at him. Without the cap, he looked different. He had an unkempt, bushy hair that matched his enormous beard.

"No, I'm fine," Dean said. "We've been looking for you."

"Yeah. Still too early to go," Elliot said as he tucked his hands into the pockets of his jacket. "Too many eyes out there."

"Right. When do you think it's best to go?"

"Around five p.m. That's when the initial fireworks will start, and it's going to be dark, so you'll have a better chance sneaking in."

Dean had almost forgotten that he would be going alone into Raintown. That wasn't a comforting thought, but the fact that he would be saving a human life was.

"D! Where the hell are you?!" Iris's distinct voice came from the crowd.

On cue, something in the middle pushed through the people like a shark skimming the water. Complaints shrouded the air, and seconds later, Iris emerged from the crowd, winded, still holding the hot dog in her hand.

"Geez, D. You could have told me you were here," Iris said as she breathed a sigh of relief and took another bite of the hot dog.

"You were too focused on the band."

"And rightly so! The kids are naturals. I gotta talk to them once they're done playing."

"You're seriously going to give them a business offer?" Dean asked.

"Hey, if there's one thing I specialize in, it's discovering hidden talent. Someone else would look at those boys and think they're nobodies who would never become anything big. But me? I see a diamond in the rough. It's an investment, but the money will return someday."

I'm still waiting for my money to return from the book you published, Dean wanted to say, but he didn't have the strength for witty remarks.

"Oh, and our informant is here. Nice," Iris said. "Any trouble on the way? Do you think the people suspect anything?"

Elliot shook his head.

"Okay, well, tell them about what you encountered, D." Iris pointed a finger at Dean, the corners of her eyebrows arching downward. "Go on. I'm too angry to do it."

Dean opened his mouth, but then Iris interrupted, "He heard people plotting yesterday. They plan to kill him; he heard it. Right, D? Tell him."

"Let's not talk so loud," Dean said, eyeing the crowd that was too close for comfort. Sheriff Moody walked down the sidewalk on the other side of the street with his partner, his lips moving as he spoke something. "And let's mingle with the others. We're a little suspicious like this," Dean added.

They dove into the crowd once more, and Dean hoped he wouldn't get another mental attack. He proceeded to explain to Elliot what he had heard last night when eavesdropping on Lawrence and the others. Elliot's facial expression never changed, and for all Dean knew, he might not have been paying attention in the first place. When Dean was done speaking, however, Elliot inhaled a sharp breath and said, "I expected as much. I heard nothing about it, so whatever they're planning must be extremely secretive."

"Yeah. Lucky you ran into them, D," Iris added.

"Either way, we gotta deal with this today and get out of here before the shit hits the fan," Elliot said.

Dean agreed. He wondered what would happen once Rachel and Elliot tried to leave. Would they die like the stories told, or would they be able to go freely? It was futile mulling over that thought right now. The group went over their plan one final time.

They would go their separate ways, and they would meet at five p.m. at the same spot where Elliot found Dean—in front of Suicide Meat. They would wait for the main attraction to start, and halfway through, once some people saw Dean as present at the event, who could then spread the rumor, he would sneak away. Iris would distract Lawrence—how?—Dean wasn't sure, but Iris assured them she had an ace up her sleeve. Elliot would scout the alleyways ahead for Dean's safe passage. From there, Dean would need to find and rescue Rachel before anyone noticed he was missing.

Elliot told him to stick to the thicket off the side of the main avenue because going via the main road would be suicide. Apparently, an old watch tower stood at Raintown's entrance. Elliot had never seen it, but he heard stories about it.

Once everyone understood the plan, Elliot disappeared into the crowd with a casual "see ya later." Iris and Dean walked back toward the motel. The music had stopped a while ago, and the crowd was somewhat quieter than before.

"This is not what I had in mind when I first arrived here," Dean said, incredulous.

"You always said that it's better to experience something firsthand because it makes for a more immersive book, right?" Iris said with a grin.

"Yeah, but not to this extent."

"Hey, if anything goes South while you're there, give me a call."

"Will do." Dean nodded. "It's gonna be tough, but darn it, we gotta save that woman."

Iris frowned.

"Why do you always say "darn" and "gosh" and "heck" when you're not religious? In fact, I remember hearing you say "goddammit" only once, and that was when you were pissed. So, what's up with that?"

"Habit," Dean said.

"What? Your parents raise you in a strict religious environment?" Iris cackled.

"No. I still have it from when I was with Skylar," Dean said.

"Ah, geez. I'm so sorry, D."

"Don't be."

"To be fair, she doesn't strike me as the religious type."

"She didn't talk about it. But she also wasn't fanatical. I erased those swear words out of my vocabulary because they bothered her."

Iris grew serious. Dean had rarely seen her like that.

"She must have appreciated it," she said.

"She did at first. But toward the end of our marriage, I used to swear when I was irritated just to piss her off."

Iris provided no comment to that.

"Anyway, it doesn't matter," Dean said.

They stopped in front of the motel. Iris had a somber look on her face, one that Dean had never seen before. She looked like she wanted to say something but didn't know how to say it.

"You know, I never thought of you as just a writer publishing for my company, D," she said. "You're also a friend, even if the feeling is not mutual."

Something uncomfortable tickled Dean's heart when he heard Iris's words. Was it guilt?

"You can be annoying, that's for sure," Dean said. "And I wasn't happy to see you here at first, but honestly, I am now. All those friends I had when I was famous disappeared when I hit rock bottom. But not you. You stayed, even though I was no longer a big shot."

Dean wasn't sure what compelled him to become sentimental. Perhaps it was the knowledge that he might die that day—or worse. Deep down, he had a lot of regrets that he would never be able to fix, and they gnawed at him every day and night. He didn't want to add Iris to that list of regrets.

"Oh, come on, D. You're gonna make me blush here." Iris shook her head and waved in dismissal. "I already told you, D, my talent is finding hidden talent. I always knew you had something special in you."

"Let's hope that "something special" helps me survive Raintown today," Dean said as he opened the motel door.

Chapter 28

The closer the start time of their mission approached, the more nervous Dean became. He was already nervous, but that feeling amplified when night fell. The cold that came with it only exacerbated his sense of dismay. The effect seemed to transfer to Iris as well; she wasn't as flippant as she usually was. Elliot looked calm under his beard, but who knew what went on in his head? Dean didn't know anything about the guy except that his wife had been taken from him.

The festivities continued throughout the day. The fact that night had fallen coupled with the rain didn't bother them one bit.

People with nooses around their necks and prop-knives sticking out of various parts of their bodies paraded around the town while carrying balloons shaped as figures hanging from the rope. People playing the drums, trumpets, and other instruments marched along with them. It was morbid in Dean's eyes, but none of the Suicide Town folks had the horrified looks on their faces that he expected to see.

"They do this every year?" Iris asked as the audience gave a round of applause.

"That's what they said." Dean shrugged.

They were standing at the spot where they had met earlier that day and were waiting for Elliot. Although anyone could join the marching of the parade, the spot where Iris and Dean stood was a lot more crowded because the street had been freed for the parade. That worked in Dean's and Iris's favor because they blended in better. It wasn't long before Elliot arrived and took place next to them without greeting them or anything. Dean figured he was trying to remain inconspicuous, as the outsiders noticing could be detrimental to their progress.

"The fireworks will start in a few minutes," Elliot said while staring in front of him. "Be ready to move."

"Ah, geez. So quickly?" Iris asked.

"Yeah, Iris. You need to get ready, too. See that man across the street? The skinny-looking one who's just standing?"

Dean looked for the person Elliot described. Indeed, a long-faced skinny man in a raincoat stood across the street with his hands in his pockets. Dean couldn't be sure, but he thought he saw the man's gaze move away the moment their eyes met.

"He's an Escorter," Elliot said. "He's the only one I've seen close by, so the others must be busy taking care of other things. You need to distract him."

"Like, now?" Iris asked.

"Go, Iris," Dean said.

Iris grumbled something but conceded. "All right. Wish me luck!" she said before she strode into the parade and disappeared among the bevy of people.

"She's . . . unique," Elliot said.

"Unique's one way of putting it, all right."

Dean cast glances at the long-faced man across the street. He was standing with crossed arms, darting at the crowd, even though he didn't look like he was interested in them one bit. Not a minute later, the man suddenly jerked his head to the side when something caught his attention. He dropped his arms to the side, remained stiff for a moment, then bolted in the direction of whatever caught his attention. Iris came into view and flashed Dean a grin and a double thumbs up.

"All right, we're pretty much clear to go. Come on," Elliot said.

Elliot sauntered toward the closest alley, not bothering to look if Dean was even following him. Dean tagged along, and soon, the crowd and the noise were behind them, and their footsteps reverberated through the alley along with the pitter-patter of the rain.

When they were close to the other side, Elliot turned to face Dean. "I'll go check it out first. When I give you the sign, you can follow."

Dean nodded. Elliot walked out onto the street and looked left and right. He casually crossed it as if what they were about to do was the most natural thing ever. When he was on the other side of the street, he stopped under the streetlight and looked in both directions once more. He brusquely nodded in Dean's direction.

Dean walked across the street, trying to maintain an unsuspecting walking pace. The more he did so, the more his behavior seemed plastic. He felt exposed in the middle of the empty street where anyone could be watching him.

Once he reached Elliot, they went into the next alleyway. They repeated the action of safely crossing the town until they finally reached the edge of the woods. By then, the ear-splitting noises from the town were merely white noise. On Dean's left, the main avenue stretched from left to right. He would need to follow it to get to Raintown.

"This is as far as I can go," Elliot said. "It's dark, so watch your step, but don't use your light. I don't know if anyone's patrolling the area. And definitely stay off the road."

"I know. You should go back before anyone notices you're missing," Dean said.

"Yeah." Elliot nodded.

Dean broke toward the undergrowth that marked the start of the woods.

"Hey, Dean?" Elliot called out to him. It was the first time that he called him by his name. It sounded strange coming from the bearded man yet not unpleasant. Dean turned to see what he wanted. "Thanks for doing this," Elliot said.

"Go," Dean urged.

Without further hesitation, he stepped into the darkness of the thicket.

Chapter 29

Elliot was right. The trek through the light-deprived woods was slow and difficult. The forest was filled with the chattering of cicadas that intermittently went from loud to quiet, and the soft tapping of the rain on top of the foliage of the trees. The sound was almost comforting as Dean plodded across the wet ground. His shoes sank into the mud, each step a chore having to pull them out of the mud with a plopping sound. On top of that, it was so dark that he had to feel the ground gently with the soles of his shoes first to then plant his weight on the foot. The last thing he needed was a broken leg.

The road was somewhere to his left, but he couldn't clearly see it from here. The only way he knew he hadn't ventured deeper into the woods was because of the tree line thinning on his left. Dean tried not to look to the right too much. The darkness that stretched there was thicker and more ominous. Anything could hide there, and even if it wasn't a paranormal entity, he would still prefer not to come in contact with it.

Maybe it's the thing that killed the dog.

That thought invaded his mind, and once it did, he could not push it out. The memory of running from the thing in the woods rushed back to Dean, and he had to stop and look over his shoulder just to make sure no one stood behind him. He was compelled to look to the right at the inky darkness more from there on out.

Come on, it can't be that far. Raintown can't be far. Just keep going, he told himself as each step became more cumbersome. His shoes were crusted with mud, and he didn't even want to think about how much of it he got on his pants.

He barely had time to think about that when his foot caught on something, and he stumbled forward. He fell on his hands and knees into the unpleasant, freezing mud. Icy water went through the fabric of his pants and touched his knees, further making him colder.

"Shit," Dean said as he clambered up to his feet.

He shook the excess mud off his hands and then wiped them on his pants. They were ruined anyway, so it didn't matter. He was starting to get so frustrated that, for an instant, he thought about continuing alongside the road.

"I hope Iris is having a better time than I am," Dean said to himself with a chuckle.

Even with the cicadas and the rain, his voice sounded alarmingly loud in the woods. A branch snapped somewhere to his right. Dean jolted his head at the sound, eyes wide, but unable to detect anything through the dark. The hairs on his arms and the nape of his neck prickled, and the icy cold invading his bones made him feel like he was suffering from hypothermia.

Fuck.

Dean slowed down his breathing as he scanned the endless black woods in front of him. He saw nothing, but something else caught his attention. The cicadas had gone quieter. They were still here, but barely as loud as the meager droplets of rain that fell on the soaked ground.

A rustling noise came from the distance, and then Dean unmistakably heard footsteps. He darted across the blackness, trying to pinpoint the sound, but it was futile.

Rustle. Rustle. Snap. Rustle. Rustle.

The footsteps were constant in volume, and it was impossible to tell whether they were approaching him or not. They stopped abruptly, coating the air in a tension that Dean imagined would be visible had there been just an inkling of light.

A person was out there. It wasn't just forest sounds. No, those were human footsteps. That meant that someone was here, and whoever it was, they probably didn't come out here to the inhospitable forest terrain for a relaxing walk or some fresh air. Dean could almost imagine a gaunt figure walking through the woods, its head down as it wandered in a random direction.

A patter of running footsteps came behind Dean. He didn't react in time before he felt something brushing against his back as it ran past him. Dean screamed and shot around. He lost balance and fell into the mud. He fervently scanned the darkness of the woods. Countless lanky figures stood in front of him, and his breath caught in his throat.

Trees—not figures. Trees.

No one was in sight. Silence once again took over.

Then the footsteps came again, slow and deliberate, this time right behind Dean. And they were approaching him, reminding him that he was not alone.

We have people watching the road. You wouldn't be the first one to try and sneak into Raintown, Sheriff Moody's voice entered Dean's mind. *We have someone watching the road.* Was it someone or *something*? That thought caused him to panic.

Dean shot up to his feet and bolted toward the road, not caring that the townsfolk would see him. He had to get away from the woods, even if it took him to hell. He ran as fast as he could, but his sprint through the woods was no more than a jog would be on flat terrain. Dean stumbled and fell on his knees and palms multiple times, but he didn't stop to shake off the mud.

The footsteps were somewhere behind him. He couldn't tell where, but they intermittently went from a stampede to sauntering.

It's the same fucking thing. It killed the dog, and now, it's going to finish you off. You walked right into its trap.

Figures hung from the trees all around the woods, but the adrenaline prevented Dean from stopping. He could see no more than their black silhouettes, but the outline was clear: ropes hung from branches and around the people's necks, their heads drooping forward or lolling to the side, their limbs dangling under the earth's gravity. Some of them swayed lightly in the wind. Dean swore he saw one of the figures flailing its feet and clawing at its neck. He swore he heard the rope straining and tightening under the person's weight. He was sure he saw one person jump off the branch and heard their neck snap as the rope held them in place.

Stop. Fucking stop. Just stop.

The road was supposed to be there, so why wasn't it? Instead, the trees stretched on and on, with more and more figures hanging from the trees all around Dean. He heard gurgling and choking, as well as some distant screams that carried through the woods. Barking had replaced the footsteps at some point, distant but discernible.

No, no, no. This isn't real. Just stop. It's not real.

And then, just like that, it all stopped. Dean's foot caught on something hard again, and he fell forward. Instead of his hands and knees sinking into the mud, they connected with the cold, solid surface of something.

The road!

Dean got up and ran to the middle of the road, hoping to any higher being that existed that he was out of the woods. He turned around and looked at the tree line. Nothing moved there. No sounds except the cicadas and the rain. No rustling. No screaming. No people swaying in the trees and living out the final moments of their lives. Just woods.

"Fuck," Dean said, breathless, his palms and legs and lungs burning.

He stood for a moment, staring at the woods, catching his breath, expecting something to jump out at him any moment. Any louder tap of the rain or whistle of the breeze startled him. Faces stared back at him from the dark, but they disappeared the moment he blinked.

Your imagination. No one's there.

But whose footsteps were those, then? Who touched you when they ran past you? Who were those people in the fucking trees?

It took some time, but Dean had finally managed to calm down and clear his head. He was still shaking, and a distant popping sound averted his attention from the forest. Dean looked to the right toward Pineridge. The sky above the town lit up in crimson from the fireworks, just barely half a mile away. The town seemed like a sanctuary. The road and the forest were a threat and Pineridge a safe haven.

He looked down at the road, admiring how incongruously unkempt it was compared to the one in Pineridge. It had long splits, cracks, and bumps in the concrete but no potholes, Dean noticed. Going through here via vehicle was probably not something that happened often—or ever.

Dean looked at the woods again, only just then noticing a ramshackle structure that might have been a residential house once. Just then, he caught sight of other structures lined up on the left as well. More rundown and derelict buildings with torn roofs and walls, windowless, left for nature to reclaim as their own territory.

When Dean turned to look left down the road, he saw Raintown.

Chapter 30

Dean wasn't sure what he should have expected when he first saw the place. In his mind, Raintown was an abandoned little village whose dilapidated buildings were overgrown with vines. He was right about the buildings being dilapidated, but no vines or grass or anything of the like that came from nature crept anywhere close to the place.

The road had tapered, and Dean noticed that he wasn't in front of Raintown—he was *in* Raintown. Remnants of short structures stretched on his left and right; buildings that might have served as shops just like on North Street stood decadent.

It was too dark for Dean to see how far Raintown stretched, but he figured that it couldn't be bigger than Pineridge. He whipped out his phone and turned on the torch. He felt that it was safe enough for him to do so here. Determined to get this over with, Dean stepped forward.

It felt strange walking between the derelict buildings. He couldn't help but become more interested in the history of the town the deeper he walked in. People used to live here. The streets had probably brimmed with life in the seventies before the mass suicide. Raintown had most likely been as normal-looking as the rest of Suicide Town, and then it disappeared in just one day.

As fascinated as Dean was by Raintown, he had to remind himself that he was here for Rachel—and that he was in danger; both from the townsfolk and from the thing in the woods.

The beam of Dean's torch fell on the road, and he paused. A distinct threshold where the cracked road became black delineated the border. Dean illuminated the road further up and saw that the entire town in Raintown was covered in black. Not just the road. Buildings, too. When a droplet of rain fell on his hand, it left a trickle of black on his skin.

"What the hell?" Dean asked himself, his eyes shifting toward the sky.

From here, the droplets looked like regular rain. But the ones that fell under the light of the phone were as black as a void. Dean took a step deeper into Raintown and black rain started battering him. He pulled the hoodie over his head and moved forward.

He no longer had any doubts. Something messed up was happening in Suicide Town, and trying to explain it using science was only a distant memory to Dean. He knew that everything he had seen up until that point was far too big for one writer to deal with. He would need to ask Alex to pull a lot of strings to start a proper investigation on Suicide Town. This couldn't be left alone.

Not when people's lives were at stake.

The street ended when Dean reached a large five-story building that he assumed used to be a factory. The windows were broken or missing, and the building itself was flayed, revealing the bricks used to build it. It looked fragile enough to crumble under one unsteady touch. The road that he walked on up until that point forked into a T-shape left and right. Dean's instinct told him to go left first.

He was desperate to snap some pictures and record videos to later use for his book, but he had to stay alert. He was on a mission, not a field trip, and the book was on the back burner. Still, despite being focused on finding Rachel, Dean inadvertently slowed down, gawking at the abandoned structures, wondering what they might have been used for. The rusted vehicles with rotted tires had either been parked on the side of the road or left haphazardly in the middle of the street.

Dean imagined the ones who had left the cars parked going to the pharmacy or the grocery store, waiting to go back to their families and have another ordinary day when the mass suicides started taking place.

You're close now, the voice in his mind said. Dean had dreaded hearing it, but at the same time, he knew that it was inevitable for it to visit him the closer he got to Raintown.

"Where are you?" Dean asked. "Where do I find you?"

He waited but got no response. He briefly illuminated himself with the torch and saw that his clothes were entirely covered in the black substance. He ran a hand down his face, and the palm came off watery black. A terrifying thought occurred to him that it might be poisonous.

Too late to worry about it now.

He turned his head in the direction he had come from. The lights from Pineridge were still present but merely specks in the distance. As hostile as Suicide Town was, the light gave him some assurance. That was where the living was. Raintown was the town of the dead.

Dean continued down the path on the left, taking prudent steps alongside the factory. He couldn't help but glance at the black maws that represented the windows on the behemoth of the building. He imagined people standing there and looking down at him. He wondered how many people had worked in that factory, if it was a factory. How many families lived in Raintown before it became known as that? Dean imagined dead women and children splayed among the hundreds of corpses on the day the mass suicide occurred.

The street quickly came to an end and wound to the left around the block. It would probably end up taking him back to the start of Raintown. Dean still decided to check it out. Along the way, shops lined the street. Empty and toppled over shelves stood inside, layered with years and years of dust—but not cobweb, Dean noticed.

Most of the buildings that looked intact had leaking roofs, steady streams of black water dripping from the leaking concave ceilings. Items littered the floor, either meds or packaged foods, exactly as they had been left on the day the suicides occurred.

Human nature dictated that some opportunist would have come to Raintown after its abandonment to pillage all the goods that they could later peddle or use for themselves, but the fact that so many items remained inside the buildings told Dean that either no one from Pineridge had actually tried doing so due to fear of repercussions, or they have, and they never made it out.

These poor people, Dean thought with a shake of his head.

A sound down the street caused him to pause. It sounded like a metallic clink. It was a normal sound, except it wasn't. Nothing in Raintown was normal, and any sound that Dean would have simply ignored or dismissed in the outside world seemed threatening in Raintown.

When he looked down the street, sure enough, he saw someone standing on the sidewalk. His first assumption was that it was Rachel, and that caused Dean's excitement to surge. He took a fervent step forward and then stopped when he realized that the figure in front of him could not possibly be Rachel.

An emaciated man stood facing away from Dean, completely naked, his hands behind his back, his torso hunched forward, and his knees bent, as if unable to carry his weight. A soaked rag covered his head, tied by a rope around the neck. The fabric tautly clung to the skeletal shape of the man's face, clearly showing sunken cheekbones, a crooked nose, and enlarged eye sockets. Dean wondered if there were even eyes in that head.

The man's tightly stretched skin outlined every prominent bone. The man slowly turned, causing the clinking sound again. Between the stick-shaped legs stood shriveled genitals. Shackles around his ankles looked far too big for the man's bony feet.

The moan and gasp that came from Dean's right shifted his attention to the sound. He jerked toward the noise, and that's when his eyes fell on another figure standing under the roof of a building, concealed by the darkness. Rain slid down the roof and fell on the road. The details were indiscernible on this one, but his imaginative mind already conjured up all sorts of abominable images.

Movement on his left caught his attention. A prominently fat figure in the alley took a few steps forward and then stopped, sucking in a loud, high-pitched sound. Dean cast the light on the figure and had to slap a hand over his mouth to stop screaming.

Just like the emaciated one, this one had a rag over his head, but he also wore rags for clothes. They were drenched, stained in black, and muddy. They were torn in places, revealing the big round belly of the person that suffered millions of tiny scars—some of which looked deep and fresh, some old and badly healed to make the abdominal skin look mangled.

The rag on the fat guy's head got sucked in and out at the round shape where the mouth was, as if the person had difficulty breathing in. His hands were not bound, so Dean wasn't sure why he didn't just take the thing off his head. The fat guy shambled across the alley toward Dean and then randomly turned around and walked in the opposite direction.

Dean remained frozen. As he watched the surrounding figures, he couldn't tell if he felt anything or not. They portrayed no fear, that much was for sure. Perhaps his brain could not process what he was seeing in Raintown because it went so much beyond anything he'd encounter in a daily life.

More and more figures appeared, some walking as if on stilted legs, others stopping intermittently as if to rest, and all of them producing raspy moaning, groaning, squealing in what sounded like pain, silent weeping . . .

What the fuck is this place?! Where the fuck am I?!

Dean couldn't move. He was afraid that making one wrong move would cause the figures to lunge at him. He didn't need to guess who or what he was looking at. All the figures had rags, and Dean somehow knew, without a shred of doubt, that the surrounding people had once been Protectors, betrayed and banished by their fellow townsmen, now living a lifetime of agony in a town that constantly rained black rain on them.

But how are they still here? How are they still alive? Are they even alive? Are the townsfolk from Pineridge keeping them imprisoned here? So many questions swirled around Dean's mind that he thought his brain was going to explode.

They won't hurt you. Find me, Rachel said.

Dean's tense body tentatively relaxed. He observed each figure on the street who seemed to be minding their own business. Dean felt a thread safer since Rachel had spoken to him. If she said that they wouldn't hurt him, he believed her.

"Where are you?" Dean asked, this time in a quivering whisper, still prudent about attracting unwanted attention.

Once again, Rachel didn't respond. Perhaps she was unable to. Perhaps some ancient and powerful force was stopping her from leading Dean straight to her.

"Are you close?" Dean asked.

Silence and then, *Yes.*

That was all Dean needed. He took a timid step forward and scrutinized the figures around him for a change in reaction. The emaciated one stood still. The fat one was far on the other side of the alley. The others seemed oblivious to Dean's presence.

Dean took another step and then another until his walk became natural again. He avoided the Protectors in wide arcs just to be on the safe side. They all looked too feeble to take him down anyway, but he then, once again, reminded himself that nothing in Raintown was normal, and that he shouldn't underestimate the figures.

Come on, Rachel. Where are you? Dean thought to himself, looking at every person he came across. He counted eight people, then he reached ten, and after that, he stopped counting. The Protectors looked like they came from all sorts of eras. Some were dressed in modern attire, others wore outdated clothes from the eighties that had begun disintegrating, and some wore no clothes at all.

Dean had turned left, and his gaze fell on a lonesome, feminine being standing in the middle of the road. It was Rachel this time; no doubt about it. He could never forget that figure from the first night. He was too eager to rescue her and get back to town, so he broke into a confident gait toward her.

"Rachel?" he called out.

The figure didn't respond. When Dean got close enough for the torch of his phone to illuminate the person, any minor doubts he had that it wasn't Rachel got washed away. Dean remembered the blouse and the jeans when he first saw them outside the motel window. It was her, no doubt about it.

"Rachel," Dean called out to her as he stopped in front of her.

The black-drenched rag clung to her face. Her mouth was closed, and the rag didn't inflate and deflate with each breath in and breath out Rachel took. Dean saw just how dirty her clothes were. They were completely wet and torn. Persistent mud crusted parts of her jeans and refused to come off, even with the perpetual rain.

"Rachel?" Dean called again, but Rachel gave no indication that she heard him.

She stood still, her head slightly tilted to the side, as if she had fallen asleep in a standing position. Her hands were still bound, and Dean assumed that something must have stopped her from untying herself.

"It's all right," Dean said. "I'll get you out of here."

Dean got closer to her. A stale and musty smell intensified by the black rain came from Rachel. He also smelled a hint of something rotted, and he assumed that she must have had an infected cut. He looked at the rope that tightly squeezed her neck. Dean wondered how she was even able to breathe with that thing on. Upon circling around her, he saw that the rope was actually a clip-on on the backside. If he got that off her, then he would be able to pull the rag off her head.

"Rachel, can you hear me?" Dean asked, but once again, his question was met with silence. "I'm going to take this off, okay?"

He didn't wait for her to respond. He put his phone in his pocket and carefully reached for the clip on the rope.

His hands barely had time to brush it when his skull exploded with pain.

Chapter 31

Dean found himself on the ground, and his head pulsated with sharp pain. His vision spun for a moment, then it stabilized. His eyes fell on the damp, worn-out boots of a person standing in front of him. Dean forced himself to look up at the figure in the raincoat standing in front of Rachel, who was still entrenched in her spot.

"I knew you were up to no good," Lawrence said.

He had a wild look in his eyes, his nose was wrinkled from the anger, and his lips pressed tight into a slit. The irritation Dean had seen in the mechanic in the previous days was nothing compared to this. The person who stood in front of Dean was full of unadulterated hate toward the outsider. Dean had crossed the line for the last time, and Lawrence was going to make him pay dearly.

Dean took one look at Lawrence's hands. A wrench was clutched in one of them. That's what he used to whack Dean over the head, and that's what he was going to use to finish him off. It was a gruesome way to go, worse than hanging on the noose.

"Wait," Dean muttered as he got on his hands and knees.

He didn't know what to say to defuse Lawrence; he was only trying to buy himself time to recover and be able to strike back.

"I'm done waiting. You come into *my* town, and you break the rules on no less than Survival Festival day! You're gonna learn some respect, city boy!"

Lawrence raised the wrench above his head. In this position, Dean's head was perfectly placed for the mechanic to hit with the wrench like a guillotine. Dean pushed himself backward with his palms and got on his feet, but Lawrence made no attempt to strike—yet.

The wrench was still above his head, and he took a menacing step toward Dean. He was quick, and despite his skinny build, Dean knew that he stood no chance against him. At least not without a weapon.

"Let's talk, Lawrence," Dean said.

He hated uttering his name, but he knew that he had a better chance of negotiating that way.

"We're through talking." Lawrence pointed a finger at Dean. "You were going to untie her! You were going to kill us all!"

"Don't be crazy. Freeing her is not gonna change anything," Dean said, ready to backstep or dodge in case Lawrence took a swing at him.

"You don't know what you're talking about!" Lawrence shouted. "She's a Protector! It's her duty to stay in Raintown!"

"You forced an innocent woman into this!" Dean yelled back, causing the pain in his head to flare.

He was done negotiating with Lawrence. He was at a disadvantage, but he was too pissed at the townsfolk like Lawrence to bend under his will. Rachel hadn't moved since the moment it all started. For all Dean knew, she might not even be aware of what was going on.

"And I know you planned on killing me, Lawrence," Dean said. "I heard you yesterday."

Lawrence's reaction remained the same, leading Dean to believe that he didn't understand the severity of the decision he had made—either that, or he didn't care.

"You're a menace," Lawrence said. "You and all the other people think you can just waltz into our town and make stories about it, but you don't understand what we need to deal with over here. You don't understand how difficult we have it. It's not easy for us like it is for you big city folk."

"Yeah, must be difficult sacrificing people for a bullshit belief," Dean said.

That seemed to strike a nerve. Lawrence's lips pulled back, revealing teeth and gums like a rabid dog. He lunged at Dean and swung the wrench at his head. Dean instinctively raised his hands and felt a painful blow on his forearm.

If you survive.

On a whim, Dean swung a fist at his best guess where Lawrence's face would be. He got really lucky because his knuckled connected with something. Lawrence yelped and staggered backward. He lost his footing and fell back but was just as quickly back up on his feet. His upper lip was busted, and when he bared his teeth at Dean again, they were covered in blood.

"You fucker!" Lawrence shrieked and dashed at Dean.

This time, Dean wasn't fast enough. He sidestepped, but the wrench struck his skull, just enough to throw off Dean's balance. Dean would have stayed on his feet had Lawrence not pushed him after swinging the wrench. The shove sent Dean flying toward the ground, and he slammed his cheek against the rough concrete. The blow hurt like hell, but at least he wasn't dizzy.

He saw Lawrence approaching him just as he got on all fours. He had to wait for the right moment. Once Lawrence was a step away, Dean lunged at him and tackled him. A gasp escaped the mechanic's mouth from the collision on his diaphragm, and before Dean knew it, they were both on the ground, Dean on top of him.

A loud clang somewhere behind told Dean that Lawrence had dropped the wrench, and he knew that this was his best chance to get the upper hand. He contemplated between swinging a punch at Lawrence's face or going for the wrench.

That moment of hesitation cost him dearly, and Dean concluded that he was right not to underestimate Lawrence's thin stature.

The mechanic grabbed Dean by the head with both hands and pushed him off. Dean couldn't tell how much force Lawrence needed to get that done, but by the time he realized what had happened, Lawrence was already up on his feet, the wrench dangling in his hand. He was covered in splotches of black rain from head to toe. Standing in front of Dean, he looked like that black figure from his vision in the window.

There was no grand villain speech about what he was going to do after he disposed of Dean. There was no talk about the horrible fate that awaited this outsider for breaking the rules. Instead, the mechanic took a menacing step toward Dean. The wild look in his eyes told Dean that he had no mercy for him.

But he was also smiling. It was the same grin Dean saw in the vision, where they forced Rachel into Raintown. Lawrence didn't care about the town. He only cared about the town's rules so that he could use them to veil the violence on other people. All of it was for his own sadistic pleasure, to take out his frustrations and unhappiness with his own life on other people. The alacrity he displayed when attacking Dean made the writer wonder if he had already killed before, and if so, how many times.

Dean was not out yet. He stood, but another whack on his temple sent him back to the ground. New pain shot through his head again, and he felt dizzy. It was impossible to tell which way was up and which down.

This was it. Dean was going to die in Suicide Town—and not from suicide. In his mind, he laughed at the irony. He looked up at the spinning image of the figure in front of him. Through the blur, he saw Lawrence raising one hand.

He blinked, fully expecting the blow to land on his head. He heard a thump and clang, and when he opened his eyes, the image had changed. In front of Dean stood a smaller figure, the hand no longer raised. *What the hell is he doing?* Dean shook his head to clear his vision, and when it finally came into focus, he learned that his eyes weren't deceiving him.

A smaller figure, indeed, stood in front of Dean, trembling as the black rain battered the hoodie of its raincoat. The person was holding a plank in their hands. At Dean's feet was the unconscious body of Lawrence with the wrench on the ground next to him. Dean forcibly blinked once more and then looked up at the figure who had incapacitated Lawrence.

"I couldn't let him hurt you," Jayden Price said.

Chapter 32

Everything felt like a dream. Dean stared at the young bookstore owner, but his brain couldn't process that he was actually here. For a moment, he believed that he was either dead or unconscious from Lawrence's beating.

"Jayden? Are you really here?" Dean asked, still baffled.

"Yes, sir. I came to help you," Jayden said as he dropped the wooden plank on the ground and offered a hand to Dean.

Dean gladly took it and got up on his feet thanks to Jayden's help. He glanced down at Lawrence's unconscious body and then at the figure standing behind Jayden. Either Rachel had moved while Dean was wrestling with Lawrence, or the two of them had been all over the place during the fight.

"I owe you one," Dean said as he put a hand on Jayden's shoulder.

Even in the dark, the bookstore owner's eyes bulged like ping-pong balls. This must have been a huge deal for him. He had spent his entire life living in Suicide Town, but he never once stepped into Raintown. Now, he was finally here, and he probably needed time to process the scenery—that and the fact that he had just knocked out one of his neighbors.

"But why did you even follow me here?" Dean asked.

"I heard you talking about your plan. Well, not you, but your friend, to be precise. She has a strong voice."

Darn it, Iris.

"I wanted to be a part of it," Jayden said. "I want to get out of Suicide Town. You have to help me, Mr. Watson."

Both Jayden and Rachel were victims of the town. Dean felt a strong obligation to make things right. Maybe it was the guilt from the accident speaking instead of him, but he didn't care.

"I will, I promise. We're going to end this ritualistic nonsense."

Jayden nodded in approval to Dean and then jerked around toward Rachel. "Is that . . . ?"

"Yeah. It's Rachel."

"I saw more people roaming Raintown. Are they all Protectors?"

"I think so."

"How are they all alive? It's been years!"

"I'm as confused as you are, Jayden. For now, let's release Rachel."

With that, Dean strode in front of Rachel. She had, indeed, moved, even if by a little. She stood straight as if she knew what was about to happen. Dean stared at the rain-soaked woman, at the clothes that clung to her body, and at the binds that abraded her wrists.

The sky above Pineridge exploded with red colors of the fireworks. They were almost out of time, and soon, the people would wonder where two of their residents plus one outsider had gone.

Dean approached Rachel from behind and gently touched the clasps with both hands. A groan made his hands twitch, and then he realized that it was actually coming from the direction of Lawrence.

The mechanic stirred and then pushed himself up on his knees with great effort. Lethargic, he turned his head toward Dean and Jayden. The wild look of anger was gone from his eyes now. That changed the instant he saw Dean behind Rachel. His eyes widened in horrific realization, and he outstretched a hand toward them.

"No! Don't do it!" Lawrence said, his timbre pleading rather than proud like it was usually.

Dean froze.

"If you do it, you'll kill us all," the mechanic said.

This was a trick. Lawrence was screwing with Dean, trying to buy some time, perhaps. Or maybe he truly believed that untying Rachel would cause the downfall of Suicide Town.

"Please," Lawrence uttered.

Dean looked at the clasps on the rope. He hesitated. What if Lawrence was right? What if Dean was messing with something he didn't understand?

"Dean?" Jayden called out in a small voice.

One look at Jayden's perplexed face was enough for Dean to make his decision. He pressed the sides of the left clip, holding the rope around Rachel's neck as the clips depressed. He tugged the right side, and the rope effortlessly came loose. Dean let it go, and it fell to the ground.

The rag remained on Rachel's head. Dean could see the imprint of the rope around her neck. He grasped the bottom of the wet fabric, ready to take it off. Lawrence mumbled something in a petulant voice, but Dean ignored him. He looked to the left where Jayden stood. The boy stared at Dean with a breathless gaze, his mouth slightly open in anticipation.

Without further hesitation, Dean yanked the rag off Rachel's head.

***

Too many things happened at once when Dean slipped the rag off. A smoke-like substance billowed in the air from Rachel before dispersing. He would replay it in his mind over and over later on, and he would be sure that the outline of the smoke had formed an elongated figure before it disappeared. It was like an optical illusion where you stare at a random, juxtaposed image for a minute without blinking, and then when you close your eyes you see a certain shape, just for a brief moment before it slips away.

At the same time, as soon as the rag came off, Rachel collapsed to the floor. Dean dropped the rag and got on his knees. She was on her side, and he rolled her on her back.

"Rachel! It's okay, we got you. We're—"

His voice died in his throat when he gazed upon her face. Her glassy eyes stared at the sky. Her blue lips were closed, her face pallid and shriveled.

"Holy God," Jayden exclaimed and clamped a hand over his mouth.

Rachel was dead. Yet, despite that, the voice entered Dean's mind.

Thank you, it said.

"You fool!" Lawrence exclaimed, his timbre hysterical. "You don't know what you've done! You doomed us all!"

Dean looked at Lawrence, then at Rachel's corpse.

Thank you. The voice reverberated in Dean's mind, and he was coming to the slow realization that the voice he'd been hearing this entire time was not Rachel's voice to begin with. An unnatural cold invaded his body all the way to the marrow of his bone. A sense of desperation that he'd never felt before in his life swelled at the pit of his stomach. Not even on that one fateful night.

Thank you. The voice grew less feminine and more shapeless, toneless. Dean focused on it. It was supposed to be Rachel's voice; it had to be. Yet, it wasn't. Dean looked down at Rachel once more. Was she really dead, or was he hallucinating again? It wasn't Rachel's voice; his mind slowly started accepting that fact. And with it came the horrifying realization that he'd been duped.

The rain stopped. The mechanic's crying and the lack of rain was unnatural. Suicide Town without rain was like movies without popcorn.

A dead body lay in front of Dean. A dead body whose voice he had been hearing this entire time for the past few days. *But it wasn't Rachel's voice*, he had to remind himself, no matter how much he wanted to believe that it was.

A metallic dragging sound ensued, and Dean looked toward Lawrence to see him standing with the wrench in his hand. That caused Dean to get up on his feet, ready to defend himself. Lawrence's chest rose and fell as he stared at Dean with a mixture of insurmountable sadness and anger on his face.

"You doomed us all," Lawrence said with a sniffle.

Chapter 33

Sheriff Donovan Moody stood by his cruiser and watched as the crowd released the fireworks into the air. The pyrotechnics whistled and popped toward the sky, where they exploded in their bevy of colors, painting Suicide Town like a canvas. The people cheered, applauded, and whistled with each new explosion in the sky.

Moody's family was somewhere in the crowd, enjoying the festivities. He wished that he could spend time with his family at the Survival Festival just once as a husband and a father, and not a sheriff, but that would be too selfish. The safety of the townsfolk was in his hands, and even though nothing bad ever happened, one could never be too sure. In a few years, he would be able to transfer the duty to his deputy but not right now.

"Any trouble, Sheriff?" Zack Lamar asked him in passing.

"Oh, yeah. Gotta keep watch over all these hardcore criminals," Moody responded.

Moody turned to enter the patrol car when a scream erupted down the street. He jerked his head toward the sound and saw the crowd frozen in their places. The remainder of the fireworks in the sky exploded and then stopped. The colors that illuminated the street were gone. Everyone stood still, staring at each other in confusion.

Sheriff Moody felt it, too: a cold that went through him like a shock wave, leaving him feeling dazed. Moody had never seen a booming crowd stop abruptly. His cop instinct told him to enter the crowd and see what was going on, but his brain and body wouldn't cooperate.

And then the rain stopped. People murmured in confusion and agitation, asking each other if they knew what was going on. They looked to the sky and raised their palms to feel the droplets, but they were gone. Just like that, the rain, which had been a big part of their lives since the moment they were born, was gone. Of course, the first townsfolk's instinct was to assume the worst and not rejoice. That was only something the people from this town would know about.

They knew that worse than rainy weather was no rain at all. No rain meant danger. And the only worse thing than no rain was black rain.

Which was exactly what happened next.

Black droplets showered the town. At first, confusion surfaced, but then the street filled with the terrified and panicked screams of the townsfolk. They dispersed, stampeding each other, realizing the impending danger. Moody's own fear—a fear that surpassed anything he had ever felt in his lifetime of living here replaced the little courage he had to calm the throng of his fellow townsfolk.

The massacre had started.

The sheriff watched, frozen in place as the people started committing suicide right in front of his eyes. They bashed their heads on the walls and the ground until they were smashed into a pulp, and they no longer moved. They cut their wrists and stabbed themselves in the necks with whatever they could find. They jumped off the taller buildings and crushed their own skulls or broke necks and spines.

It looked like a war zone. Screams of anguish and death burst the calm. It couldn't have been more than a minute since it began when hundreds of dead bodies and people who failed at ending their life writhing on the floor in agony littered North Street.

Others ran away, but they wouldn't make it far. It was like running from a remote island toward the ocean. Moody finally willed enough strength to move. His family was somewhere in the crowd, probably already dead. He should have been concerned by it; he knew that much. He should have panicked and rushed in to save them, but the thought of his family in danger was only a blur to him.

"Sheriff! You gotta help us!" Marshall Chandler shouted.

Moody looked at his terrified face. He was covered in black droplets. Moody entered the car and reversed. He drove off in the opposite direction, toward the place where they found little Tom. He turned on the police sirens to warn the people who ran in the middle of the road. He almost hit Desmond Webb but managed to swerve around him in the last moment.

His foot floored the gas pedal as soon as he was past the crowd. The engine of the vehicle roared along with the sirens. Moody looked at the rearview mirror in time to see a figure blowing his brains out with a handgun. Figures buzzed around the street, ignoring the dead bodies of their neighbors.

Moody was approaching the edge of the town, increasing his speed. Buildings on the side of the road were replaced by rows of trees. Before he knew it, he was the furthest he'd ever been from the town in his entire life. Although he'd never seen it personally, his pops once told him that about a sharp turn to the left. Moody didn't worry about that. Not like he intended on taking that turn, anyway.

Never thought I'd die in the same spot as little Tom, Moody thought.

His thought felt foreign. Like someone else was thinking it for him, and it was a powerful thought. He looked in the rearview mirror again, wondering if his family was already dead. He hoped it was quick.

Before he knew it, the car flew off the road. Time froze as Moody watched the thick tree trunks approaching him. The crash was deafening. Moody lurched forward and heard a crunch (it could have been glass, or his own body).

Either way, he couldn't move, and his gaze was stuck on the mangled hood of the car as his vision grew dark.

***

Elliot Wood watched the massacre from the alleyway. Father Walter, who had been on the stage, tried calming the people down, but his voice fell on deaf ears. Even the priest was afraid, which Elliot could detect in his quavering voice. Eventually, Father Walter dropped the microphone and stared at the crowd helplessly as they killed themselves one after another.

His stare went glassy, his life draining out of him. The priest tore the cross hanging around his neck, kissed it, and then put it in his mouth. His Adam's apple bobbed as he swallowed the cross. The priest's face grew red as he fell to his knees. He clawed at his throat, spittle flying from his mouth. Elliot imagined hearing choking, grating sounds coming from the priest, but the booming crowd drowned him out.

Father Walter fell on his back and continued writhing, but his movement grew more sluggish with each passing second. Elliot couldn't stay here. Not only could he not bear to watch his friends die in gruesome ways, but he was running out of time, and soon, he would end up like them. He turned to walk down the alley, wondering what the hell the writer had done to cause this mess.

What about Rachel? Is she okay?

His will to see his wife kept the suicidal thoughts at bay—or so he thought. By the time he had reached the end of the alley, images of himself dead in all kinds of ways flooded his mind. He had intended to go to Raintown, but the weight of his legs rendered it impossible.

The town was stopping him, cementing him from doing anything but the obvious. Elliot's eyes fell on the dead figure splayed halfway through the broken glass display into the shoe-polishing shop. The shards stuck out of the frame. He broke into a gait toward the glass, his eyes fixated on it, with only one intention in his mind.

Don't do it, don't do it, don't do it, his mind screamed at him, but the urge was too strong to ignore. Elliot stood in front of the broken window. The body belonged to a teenager he often saw but never spoke to.

The long and sharp piece of glass that stuck upward from the bottom like a stalagmite, practically begging Elliot to impale himself with it. Resisting that urge felt like resisting a delicious cake while on a diet. Elliot knew that he would regret the consequences later, but right now, he just wanted that cake.

He leaned forward and allowed himself to fall forward. The last thing he saw was the pointy end of the shard approaching his eye.

Chapter 34

Dean stared toward Pineridge. The fireworks were gone, but some sounds boomed from it. He thought he heard something that sounded like a gunshot and faint, distant screams.

"You fucking idiot," Lawrence said. "You killed us all." His tone conveyed defeat. He raised the wrench slightly in a droopy hand and then lowered it while staring at the ground.

"Why? What did I do?" Dean asked.

His throat was dry, and he was freezing. Above that, the feeling of despair that he had felt ever since he yanked the rag off Rachel had only intensified. Dean blinked, and in those split seconds, he saw images of himself dead.

"You released it," Lawrence said.

He inhaled and exhaled long and sharp breaths, white-knuckling the wrench. He was going to kill Dean for sure. The mechanic's body stiffened, and he shot daggers at Dean. But instead of attacking him, he hit himself over the head with the wrench. Still staring at Dean, he hit himself with the tool over and over. The wrench thudded against his skull until it punctured the skin, bloodying his forehead. At first, it was merely a trickle, but with each subsequent hit, the thud turned into a crunch and squelch, and the blood flowed out of Lawrence's head in abundance.

The wrench was covered in blood entirely. Jayden screamed for Lawrence to stop, but the mechanic didn't listen. He fell on his knees, blood pooling on the ground, and continued hitting himself. Each hit came with more difficulty, and the mechanic's hands trembled. Lawrence briefly looked up, and Dean saw just how mangled his face was from the blows.

"We need to go, Jayden," Dean commanded.

He put a hand on Jayden's shoulder. He might as well have been touching a statue with how stiff he was. Jayden stared at Lawrence as he delivered hit after hit after hit, mutilating himself more and more.

"Jayden, snap out of it!" Dean shook the bookstore owner by the shoulders.

Jayden remained transfixed on Lawrence a moment longer before his eyes met with Dean's. His face portrayed horror but also understanding.

"Let's go," Dean said and pulled Jayden in the direction of Pineridge. "Don't stop!"

He looked back to see Jayden following him. He had a zombified stare, but he was following Dean, and that was enough for now. Lawrence's self-bashing faded behind them, and then entirely stopped. Dean hoped that the poor bastard had finally met his end and was no longer suffering.

***

"Wh—what's happening?" Jayden asked, his voice tenuous.

"I don't know," Dean lied.

He refused to look the boy in the eye out of shame. Not just shame but also fear. Jayden Price was a resident of Suicide Town after all, and no matter how much he said he hated living here, the sight in front of them would be more than enough to turn him against Dean.

Dead bodies littered the main avenue, starting from the entrance to Pineridge, and all the way as far as the eye could see. Blood was everywhere. Some of the bodies had visible evidence as to how they killed themselves; others were either facedown or had no visible wounds, which Dean was grateful for.

The town was quiet for the most part. The occasional scream erupted in the distance, the cry of a person who was dying an agonizing death. For a moment, neither Jayden nor Dean could move. Dean was obviously the one in charge between the two of them and should have been the one to tell Jayden to follow him as they zigzagged around the bodies, but he himself couldn't move.

The tools on the ground his eyes were fixed on were tempting. A knife to jab into his throat, a pistol to blow his brains out, a sharp stick to stick into his mouth through the back of his head.

"Did we do this? Is this our fault?" Jayden asked.

The memory of the voice entered Dean's mind. *Thank you.* Why was it thanking him? Rachel was dead, so it wasn't Rachel. Was this the reason it manipulated Dean into getting released so that it could massacre the entire town as it did back in the seventies?

The stories were true. Oh shit. They were right all along. The Protectors somehow held the thing in the town contained and stopped it from killing everybody. And now, I had released it. I killed all these people.

Dean looked at the bodies on the street. A young blonde woman stared to the side with wide eyes, a trickle of dried blood running down her temple. She couldn't have been more than twenty. A man was splayed on his stomach with a gleaming pool of dark blood under him. He was facing a house. Maybe he had been rushing home to save his family before the urge to commit suicide took him.

Only when Dean saw some of the faces of the dead bodies did the realization *really* hit him. It was *his* fault that these people were dead. Dozens of bodies were on the street, and he assumed that North Street probably looked like a mass grave. He wasn't sure if he could stomach seeing that. They had been living their lives peacefully for years, and then one outsider decided that he knew better.

Dean remembered Lawrence's words. *All you outsiders come to the town, and you think you know what's best for us.*

He felt like puking. He felt bile climbing up his throat in small amounts. He swallowed the bitter substance, forcing it back down, ignoring the burning in his throat.

"Mr. Watson? Dean?" Jayden called out. "Is . . . is it our fault?"

Dean put on a straight face as best he could and shook his head at Jayden. "No. Not your fault." *Just mine.* "Let's find the others."

Dean pulled out his cellphone and dialed Iris's number. The line was dead. He tried again, but the result was the same. Dean sucked in a breath through his teeth. He put the phone back in his pocket and jutted his head toward the intersection.

"Stick close to me, okay?"

They stuck close to the sidewalk, the furthest from the dead bodies. Some of the blood still made it over there, and the arm of one elderly woman was splayed over the sidewalk, forcing Jayden and Dean to step over it. The closer they got to North Street, the more noises they could hear. Not just screaming but shouting. People calling out names, most likely their loved ones, pattering of footsteps, thudding, and slamming.

Dean mentally prepared himself for what was on North Street, but no amount of preparation was enough for what lay ahead. The bodies on main avenue were nothing compared to North Street. Hundreds of corpses littered the street, clustered in small groups and piled on top of each other. Innocent men, women, and a few children.

Children.

The face of the child Dean had hit with his car appeared on all the children's faces for a moment, just enough to prod at him and remind him that suicide was still an option. Dead children. His vision spun.

A scream erupted and turned his head just in time to see a woman plummeting from one of the three-story-tall buildings to her demise. The crack when she hit the ground was loud, and her legs contorted at unnatural angles with bones sticking out. The woman had either died from the impact or was unconscious and unable to scream from the pain in her legs.

Some of the bodies were moving, Dean noticed—just barely, probably unable to stand due to their injuries. Failed suicides, Dean assumed.

"Oh, my God. My God. Lord. Sweet Jesus," Jayden said as he crossed himself.

The black rain amplified the pungent odor of blood and death came. Dean felt lightheaded, but they couldn't stop and take in the view. They had to find Iris and Elliot and get out of here. Just then, a loud voice came down one of the streets. It was a feminine voice but too obnoxiously loud to belong to anyone but Iris.

"Hold on now, fellas! Let's talk about this!" Iris said.

She's in danger!

Dean jackknifed down the street and followed Iris's voice to where he thought it came from. It was difficult to pinpoint, thanks to the walls.

"Wait, wait, wait! I got an idea!" Iris shouted again.

"Fuck your idea!" a gruff voice said.

It was coming from the left down the alley. Dean made his way toward the sound just in time to hear Iris let out a petulant yelp.

"Iris!" Dean shouted as he broke into a sprint.

A patter of footsteps resounded, and a figure appeared at the end of the alleyway. The person beelined toward Dean, effectively forcing him to stop dead in his tracks.

"Run, D! Run!" Iris shouted with half a breath as she sprinted down the alley.

Dean turned and ran out of the alley. He waited on the side for Iris to emerge, but she didn't stop running. A group of silhouettes was running after her.

"It's the writer!" one of them shouted.

Oh, shit.

Dean turned around to see where Jayden was. The kid stood arrow-straight and frozen in place, his face pale as a sheet of paper. Dean shoved him in Iris's direction toward the alley across the street. He was afraid that Jayden would remain frozen, but luckily, he broke into a dash. Dean ran after them. Jayden was fast, much faster than both Dean and Iris, and soon, he had surpassed the publisher and turned left when he reached the end of the alley.

Iris's and Dean's panting filled the air, but so did the heavy footsteps of their pursuers. That helped Dean ignore the burning in his lungs. Iris turned left and Dean did the same. Jayden stared back at them from an adjacent alley and motioned for them to follow.

Iris was beginning to slow down, and her breathing became wheezy. "This is . . . not how . . . the book was . . . supposed . . . to go," she exclaimed just as Dean caught up to her and pushed her to move faster.

They followed Jayden into the alley and saw him standing halfway down the place. He was staring at Iris and Dean. "Come on!" he shouted as he stepped to the side and disappeared into the wall.

Dean needed a moment to understand that it wasn't a wall but a backdoor that the bookstore owner had gone through. Iris was the first one who stepped inside, then Dean. Jayden slammed the door shut, and the room was engulfed in darkness. A rusty metallic sound from the inside clicked—a lock on the door, maybe?

Muffled footsteps from outside approached and stopped in front of the door. A loud bang, followed by a series of slams, as well as curse words and threats erupted.

"Shit! They locked themselves in!" one of the pursuers said.

"Leave them," another one said. "There's one of those Escorters on the street. Let's fuck him up. It's their fault this happened, anyway."

The others agreed in unison, and the footsteps receded.

"Yeah! You better run, you losers!" Iris shouted.

"Can it!" Dean reprimanded her.

Shouts came outside, and then someone yelled, "Stop, you cocksucker!"

Someone screamed, and silence followed.

Chapter 35

Silence hung in the air for a protracted moment until shuffling inside the room interrupted it. A click came from somewhere, and light bathed the room. It was so bright that Dean's eyes hurt for a moment. Iris stood close to him while Jayden was across the room in front of the light switch. From what Dean could tell, they were in some sort of a storage unit, perhaps a backroom of a store.

"Man, that was too damn intense," Iris said. "And awesome! The way we gave those guys the slip? That's definitely going in one of the books in the future!" She was out of breath, but her mouth pulled back into a grin.

Dean didn't respond to her trifling remark. He was too focused on regaining his breath, mulling over the fact that he had barely escaped death mere seconds ago. Would the townsfolk really kill him if they caught him? Judging by the scream that came from the street, Dean could count on it.

The Escorter they had assaulted was their neighbor, and they had probably known each other for years, yet they hadn't hesitated to attack him. Dean was an outsider who they only knew by his face.

"Well, D. I have no idea what you did in Raintown, but the situation is officially FUBAR."

"I fucked up big time," Dean said as he leaned against the wall. "Where's Elliot?"

Iris grimaced and shook her head. "Dead. Found him impaled on a piece of glass."

"And the sheriff?"

"I haven't seen him, but I heard someone say that he drove off."

"Then he's probably dead, too. Shit!"

Dean wiped the sweat off his forehead and stared into space as he processed the predicament he had put the town into.

"D, seriously. What is going on here?"

Dean said nothing.

"They were right all along," Jayden spoke in a feeble voice. Iris and Dean looked at him. The bookstore owner was staring at the ground. Dean wondered if guilt ate away at the kid for helping Dean. "We didn't believe them that the Protectors were necessary," Jayden said. "But they were. Now they're all dead because of us. Soon, we'll be, too."

"Come on, kid. Keep your head up. You're young, so no more negative bullshit, all right?" Iris chided Jayden.

"No, you don't understand." Jayden slightly raised his tone. "Whatever is causing this to happen was released when we untied Rachel. It's all our fault." His voice slightly cracked toward the end, but he remained composed.

Thank you, the voice said again.

It wasn't reminiscence of it this time. He had actually heard it in his head again, the voice that belonged to the parasite feeding on the town. It had remained dormant for years, ever since the seventies, and it was free again, and its ravenous hunger knew no bounds. It would stop at nothing.

Almost nothing.

"How come we're not dead yet, kid?" Iris asked.

"There are too many people in the town," Jayden said. "The initial shock wave took out most of them, but now, it's looking for the ones who scattered."

"That doesn't make any sense."

"Imagine it like seeing a <u>school</u> of fish in a pond. They're all bunched up together, and you want to throw a net to catch them. You're going to catch most of them, but some lucky ones will disperse."

"And when they disperse, you'd need to scour the pond to find the remaining ones," Dean said, completing Jayden's thought.

"Right." Jayden nodded. "We're the remaining fish in the pond with nowhere to run. And it's only a matter of time before we're found."

Dean didn't need to question Jayden's logic. Somehow, he knew that every word was correct. Maybe they'd been touched by the same evil presence, and it transferred some of its knowledge onto them, whether it was deliberate or accidental. Dean had no physical proof of anything supernatural happening in the town save for the massacre outside, yet he believed wholly and without a shred of doubt that this town was, indeed, cursed.

"We gotta get out of here, then," Iris said. "We can't wait for the fisherman to find us. I'd make a terrible dish."

"It's not going to be easy," Dean said.

He didn't say why it wouldn't be easy as to not discourage Iris. He assumed that Jayden already knew, but the look on his face conveyed as much confusion as Iris's did. Dean might know more than the two of them because he had interacted with the entity.

He questioned himself to figure out if the information he conveyed was correct, but he couldn't reach a conclusive answer. For all he knew, the thoughts he had were not his own but the entity's. Maybe it was manipulating him, just as it did with Rachel.

"Ah, gee. Coming here was a bad idea, D. We're gonna die here just like everybody else! I can't die just yet! I still have so many books to release, so many authors to recruit!" Iris had her hands on her head. Dean thought she would start ripping her hair out from the panic.

"Relax, Iris. I have a plan," Dean said.

"Whatever it is, I'm willing to listen because if we stay here, we are screwed!"

Dean looked at Iris and then Jayden. The kid was not supposed to be in this mess. Things were not supposed to happen like this. Dean was supposed to return from the town with Rachel—alive—and prove to everyone that their sacrificial rituals were nothing more than superstition.

Instead, he ended up killing the entire town. This wasn't the entity's fault. It was his. The blood of the people who had perished tonight was on his hands, and Dean would need to atone for it one way or another.

"Well, what's the plan, D?" Iris asked, visibly impatient.

Dean scratched his head. He thought things through once more from top to bottom, trying to figure out if the plan would work. It was a very risky plan, and he had no guarantee that any of them would make it out alive, but it was their last desperate attempt at an escape. Dean looked at the ceiling, then down at his fellow survivors. Their gazes were plastered in anticipation and hope. Despite killing the entire town, Iris and Jayden willingly trusted him with their lives. He wasn't sure if it was admirable or foolish of them to do so.

"Okay, listen up," Dean said.

Chapter 36

"Is it clear?" Iris whispered, but she might as well have shouted.

Dean peeked into the alleyway left and right. No one was in sight. "I'm going. Get ready," he said as he opened the door and stepped outside into the cold night air.

Everything was still. No screams, no footsteps, only the tapping of the black rain. Perhaps the entire town was already dead, survived by Dean and his two friends. That meant it was only a matter of time before it was their turn.

"D, are you sure this is going to work?" Iris asked in her loud whisper from the safety of the storage.

"No," Dean answered.

Dean turned to look at Jayden and Iris. Iris had a serious look on her face that told Dean how severe she thought the situation really was because Iris never wore that expression. Jayden was pale and wide-eyed. Living in a peaceful little town all his life, seeing all his friends and family massacred in just one day must have been a shock. He would probably need years and years of therapy after surviving this.

"Remember what I said," Dean warned Iris. "If I'm not back in ten minutes, go."

Iris looked hesitant, but she nodded in agreement before closing the door, leaving Dean alone out in the silent town. He took a deep breath and broke into a confident stride across the alley toward North Street. His footsteps reverberated and bounced off the walls of the enclosed alley, but it didn't matter. In fact, he wanted to attract attention.

When he reached the street, Dean was, once again, greeted by numerous dead bodies. The ones who had been alive earlier and on the ground were either unconscious or dead because nothing was moving. Dean felt like a sitting duck in the middle of the street. He was an easy target, but that's what he aimed for.

"Well, come on!" Dean shouted as he spread his arms. His voice echoed in the street. "What are you waiting for?! You want to kill the entire town, right?! Here I am, the last man standing! So, come on!"

Dean expected to hear voices or footsteps from assailants who would come charging at him, but only silence ensued—at first, at least. Then, an icy breeze blew into the back of Dean's neck. He didn't move—as much as he wanted to. The whole thing felt like a stupid game he used to play as a kid with his friend. They'd stand a couple hundred feet apart, attempting to hit each other with a baseball from that distance. The goal was to earn points from hitting various body parts, the crotch being worth the most. The person who was getting the ball thrown at him would need to remain still; moving rendered point deduction.

Standing in the middle of North Street, Dean felt that same urge as he did more than twenty-five years ago—the urge to move or shield his body part from an impending blow. But he remained still. A crawling sensation prickled his skin, as if fingers were touching him, but he didn't bother to turn around to see if anything was there.

Something terrible had enveloped him; not in a physical sense, something malicious and powerful. An unseen force that has caused the deaths of thousands of people since the nineteen seventies. Something that constantly ate and hungered for more, never able to satiate its ravenous hunger.

Dean's entire body stiffened. The urge to commit suicide was so powerful in him that it was the only thing on his mind. He wanted nothing more than to grab the nearest object and end his life the way Lawrence ended his. The physical pain that he would endure would be nothing compared to the peacefulness that would ensue.

Yet, Dean knew that the peacefulness was a lie. Nothing was gracious or peaceful about suicide—only regret would remain. The entity that controlled this town had found him and was coaxing him into committing suicide. He didn't have much time left.

"But you can't kill everyone, can you?" Dean asked. He tried to maintain a calm and confident timbre while speaking, but uttering that sentence took a lot of strength and effort. "If you kill everyone, you'll be gone, too. Won't you?"

The urge to kill himself slowly receded. Just like that, it was here one moment, and gone in the next. The icy crawling sensation on Dean's neck remained, but it was negligible compared to the urge he felt just a moment ago.

"That's right," he said. "You know that if you kill me, you'll have nothing to feed on anymore. You need me to bring you new victims. You need me."

The icy grip on Dean's neck stiffened. Hard fingers reached toward his throat to choke him. Still, he didn't move.

The fingers retracted, and just like that, the presence enveloping Dean was gone. Dean could no longer keep still. He spun around, expecting to see a black figure grinning at him. Nothing but dead bodies. Dean heaved in a large breath of the stale air. He hadn't realized that he was partially holding his breath until then, his brain yearning for oxygen.

Dean looked around the street once more. Nothing was moving. He looked down at his hands and body. Nothing was different, and he felt no different. He looked toward the alley where Iris and Jayden had hidden and sauntered toward the hideout, expecting the entity to return to finish him off at any moment. But it wouldn't come back because it was already a part of him.

They were one and the same now.

***

"Iris, you in there?" Dean asked as he rapped on the door.

"D, is that you?" Iris's muffled voice came from inside.

"No. It's the fucking Tooth Fairy. Open the door," Dean commanded.

The lock on the inside clicked, and the sturdy door opened. Iris poked her head out and squinted at Dean, as if to make sure that she was staring at the right person.

"Is . . . is it safe?" she asked.

"Yeah, it took the bait. Now, come on before it comes back." Dean gestured for Iris and Jayden to follow.

"Geez, D. Are you feeling okay? I should have come with you. I would have kicked anyone's ass, entity or no entity."

Dean smiled to himself at Iris's display of courage now when the danger was gone. He chose not to say anything to her. He looked back to see if Jayden was following. The kid kept glancing around himself as if expecting danger to emerge at any moment.

The walk on North Street was done on autopilot. Dean no longer paid attention to the dead bodies. They were dead, and dead people couldn't be helped. By the time they reached the intersection, Dean stopped and looked back to see where Iris and Jayden were. Iris was falling behind, even though she walked as fast as she could. Jayden had no trouble keeping up, but he kept his distance from Dean.

When they stood in the streetlight, the boy's expression changed. The look of admiration that he had toward Dean was gone now. Instead, caution—and maybe fear?—had replaced it. He knew. Dean couldn't help but feel like a dog infected with rabies that Jayden was trying to avoid.

"This way," Dean said as he turned on to the main avenue.

"Slow down, D!" Iris said. Her voice became loud again, a testament to her confidence increasing, knowing that they were the only survivors in the town.

The main avenue was swarming with corpses, too. Not nearly as much as North Street, but it was still a mess. The people of Suicide Town had tried to kill themselves in creative ways. The entity was able to drive them to insanity, to the point that they didn't care how they killed themselves but to finish it as soon as they possibly could. Some of the bodies were so badly mutilated that Dean wondered how they were able to do it to themselves. The image of Lawrence bashing his brains out with a wrench was only a distant memory now.

"Those motherfuckers!" Iris exclaimed when they reached her Camry parked in front of the motel.

Dean looked at the car and noticed that one tail light had been busted. Iris rushed past Dean and bent down to look at the car, grabbing her hair with one hand. "Are you kidding me right now?! I just made the first payment on this thing. Goddammit!"

She ran around the car, scrutinizing it for any other scratches or faults. Dean cast a glance at his own car. It looked undamaged, save for the black rain that made it look dirty.

"I cannot believe this!" Iris raised her hands and slapped them by her sides. "A busted light and black rain. How am I even supposed to wash this thing?"

"You can take that to town hall for a complaint if you want them to reimburse you for the damages," Dean said.

"You know what? I think I'm just gonna leave quietly. I mean, we aren't exactly spotless either, huh, D?" She hooked her thumb back toward the street with the dead bodies and then went around to the passenger's side. "You drive, D. I'm too upset."

Dean entered the car from the driver's side. He heard a knock on the passenger's window where Iris stood. "You need to unlock the doors for us, D!" she said in a muffled voice.

Dean looked at Iris, and then at the rearview mirror. Jayden stood behind the car, his eyes fixated on the writer. Dean grabbed the steering wheel with both hands and looked toward the road leading out of the town. It was black from the rain and from the dark. The exit was there, just where the darkness began. He needed to drive out of town.

Leave your friends to me. I'll take good care of them, the voice said.

The key was already in the ignition. Dean turned it, and the engine started, its noise contrasting the silence of the dead town. He gently touched the gas pedal with his foot.

"D, what are you doing?" Iris asked, knocking fervently on the window.

Dean looked at Jayden in the rearview mirror. He was still frozen in place, staring in one spot. It would be so easy to just floor the gas pedal and be out of the town. He could go back to his old life, and no one would ever question him. No one would ever know Suicide Town happened. Dean pressed the button behind the joystick, and the doors unlocked. Both Iris and Jayden got in almost immediately.

"Phew," Iris said. "You had me worried there for a moment, D. I thought you were going to leave without us." She laughed.

Dean smiled, even though he didn't find anything funny.

Chapter 37

Dean swerved past the dead bodies splayed in the middle of the road as much as he could, but there were too many of them. At one point, Dean had to drive over the dead body of an old man. Even if the road was clear, speeding would be impossible because of the black rain that incessantly battered the windshield. It was difficult to see too far ahead with the unnatural darkness that the high beams couldn't penetrate.

Iris spoke, breaking the silence.

"Hell, yeah! Woo! Pen Pals make it out alive!" she exclaimed with raised hands.

Silence.

"What? Not a good name?"

"Well either way, thank God this is finally over, huh? I'd hate to say it, D, but I think your car and other things are gone for good. Maybe the cops will be able to retrieve it, but I assume we'll have a lot of tough questions to answer."

"The cops won't get involved," Dean said, devoid of tonality.

"How do you know that?" Iris asked.

Dean stared at the wipers going left and right, trying to clean the black rain off the windshield but only smearing it over the glass and further muddying the visibility. It all reminded him of the child he had killed.

"You okay, D?" Iris probed.

Iris's confused and focused stare occupied Dean's peripheral vision. He looked in the rearview mirror. Jayden stared at him. When their eyes met, the boy averted his gaze. Dean glanced at the town that became more and more distant with each passing second.

"Ever been this far, kid?" Iris asked as she looked back.

"Never. I never even tried to be honest," Jayden said, with a raspy voice.

"Well, don't you worry. We'll show you what it means to live in a big city. You're gonna love it, kid. Say, I heard you wanna be a writer like Dean, huh? I think I can fix you up with a position in my publishing house. I'll just need to see your writing style. Actually, you know what? It doesn't matter. You survived a mass suicide, and that's gonna sell like crazy. I'm telling you, kid. People love a survivor. We can even give you a guest appearance when we—D, why are we stopping?"

Dean had gradually slowed to a halt. In front of them stretched the ramshackle road that Dean had used to drive into the town. The day the police officer stopped him at the entrance seemed like a million years ago. Dean pulled the handbrake and opened the door.

"This is as far as I can take you," he said as he stepped outside.

"Whoa, whoa! What?!" Iris complained, but Dean was already out of the car.

The rain, once again, tapped on his head. Dean looked at the cones of the high beams. No rain fell there, marking the threshold leading into Suicide Town. Iris and Jayden got out of the car.

"D, what's gotten into you? Come on, let's get outta here!" Iris said.

"I can't." Dean shook his head.

"Why the hell not?"

Dean looked back toward Suicide Town. The lights were close, yet they seemed too distant. Dean felt uncomfortable getting so far away from the town. When he looked in the other direction, dread crept over him.

He knew that death awaited him just past the border where the rain couldn't reach.

"He's the new Protector," Jayden spoke with a quavering voice. Both Iris and Dean looked at him. "He never intended to leave. The plan never was to trick the entity into believing we would bring new victims to it, was it?"

Dean smiled at Jayden's astuteness. "No. It wasn't. Someone has to stay behind."

"D, what the hell?" Iris spread her arms.

"It'll be back soon. It granted you free passage, but it might change its mind. So, you two need to leave before that happens."

"D, this is crazy! Come on, get in the car! We'll talk about it all when we're back in Portland!"

Dean took a step back toward the town. He pointed a finger at Jayden and said with a smile, "I expect a dedication in your book, Jayden."

Jayden didn't reciprocate the smile.

"Stop, D!" Iris shouted as Dean took another step back. "Just wait, goddammit!"

Jayden stepped in front of Iris with palms raised toward her. "Don't. It's not safe to go back to town anymore. This is our only chance to get out." He looked back at Dean. Sadness replaced the caution on Jayden's face, if Dean read it correctly.

"I'll come back for you, D! I swear it! I'm gonna get the police and the FBI and the National fucking Guard, and we're gonna get you out of this place!" Iris's voice boomed in the vastness of the road.

"Drive safe, Iris," Dean said. "And don't talk the kid's ear off."

With that, he spun on his heel, put his hands in his pockets, and sauntered back toward Suicide Town. In the distance behind him, he heard the Camry driving off, its engine fading until only the sound of the rain, and his footsteps remained.

***

He was relieved to be back inside the motel and out of the rain. Hell, any interior would have been fine right about now. He was frozen to the bone and hoped that Baxter wasn't a cheapskate who saved money on heating. Speaking of Baxter, Dean looked at the seat where the motel owner usually was. The chair was empty.

Dean half-expected to see his body splayed in the chair, his head thrown back, his eyes wide open, staring at the ceiling. He was glad that wasn't the case. He assumed that he would have a lot of work cleaning up the entire town. Dean went back to room eleven and turned on the light.

The room was as dim as ever. That would change starting tomorrow. He would remove the curtains and blinds from every room. But not tonight. Tonight, he was too exhausted to do anything. Dean sat on the edge of the bed and groaned. He hadn't realized how tired he was until he sat. His entire body ached, and he felt like he could sleep for twelve hours and still not get enough rest.

Dean pulled the cellphone out of his pocket. He had no notifications, as expected. Dean entered the call history and stared at his list of contacts. He looked for Skylar and tapped the call button. He knew it was a long shot, but he still wanted to try to get in touch with her.

As he put the phone against his ear, he heard ringing. The call actually went through, leaving Dean in awe. It would seem that he had some privileges as the new Protector. After a few rings, Skylar answered.

"Hello? Dean?" she asked with an anxious voice.

"Hey, Sky. How you doing?" Dean asked. His voice sounded downcast in the quietness of the room.

"I'm fine. Is something wrong, Dean?"

It sounded like she wanted to say "What do you need?" but Dean knew her well enough to recognize when she was concerned or scared.

"I wanted to talk to you about something," Dean said. "Do you have a moment?"

"Of course. What's up?"

Dean looked around the room. His eyes fell on the laptop on the floor in the corner. He knew what he wanted to talk to Skylar about. He even rehearsed the dialogue in his head on his way to the motel, yet he could find no words when it came down to it.

"Dean, did something happen?"

"Back that night when we . . . when I hit . . . when I hit Connor, I didn't . . ."

He stopped and sighed at his inability to speak. He never called Connor by his name. He was afraid to utter it, even though he hadn't known why. When he thought about it, he was afraid that mentioning his name would make it too personal. He knew that he killed a child by accident, and he preferred to think of Connor as some random child because if he thought about him as a kid with a name and favorite things and a family and a future, he would go crazy.

I would have committed suicide long before coming to the town, Dean thought to himself with a smirk.

"Back when it happened, I went through the most difficult time of my life," Dean said. "We both did. But not only did I need to worry about my reputation, and mine future, but I also had to live with the fact that I was responsible for the . . . the death of a child."

Skylar listened but didn't say anything to disagree. He wanted to hear that it wasn't his fault, but he didn't expect it, so it was fine.

"I needed you to be there for me, but you left when I needed you the most," Dean said. "I don't blame you. I was more worried about my sales than the fact that I killed someone's kid, and I lashed out at you. I know I said and did a lot of hurtful things that I'll never be able to take back. I'm sorry for making you go through such hell."

Skylar sighed. He couldn't tell if it was a sigh of exasperation or something else. "It's all in the past, Dean," she said. "I already told you. I don't blame only you. It was my fault, too, even if you were the one behind the wheel. It was a terrible accident, but I don't think of you as a monster because of it."

Wait 'til you hear about me triggering the slaughtering of an entire town.

"Yeah," he simply retorted. "Well, I . . ." He felt the need to say something, but his vocal cords wouldn't cooperate.

"How's the investigation for your new book going? Are you still in that town?"

"I am. Actually, I think I'll be staying here for a while." He grinned into the phone, doing his best not to snort in laughter.

"Really? Does that mean you're getting inspiration for writing?" Skylar asked, oblivious to Dean's remark.

"Yes, actually. I think I just needed a change in the environment in order to get my creative juices flowing."

"I'm so happy to hear that, Dean. Hey, if you get stuck at certain points again, feel free to send me the manuscript, and I'll see what I can do to help you."

"Sure. No late royalty charges, I hope," Dean joked.

"Don't worry. I've had enough fame for an entire lifetime." She must have realized what she said, so she quickly added, "I mean, generally, I've had enough of the positive attention and not just because of the negative stuff that happened."

"It's fine."

"But, anyway, listen, Dean. Don't be too hard on yourself. It happened, and you can't change it. What you can change is what happens in the future. There are still so many people who look up to you. You just need to set a good example for them."

"Right." Dean looked at the laptop again. "I'm gonna have to go, Sky. Thanks for the talk. I really needed it."

"Don't hesitate to call if you need anything."

"I won't. You take care of yourself, okay?"

Dean ended the call and tossed his phone on the bed. The conversation with Sky had chased his sleep away, and now, he felt like he could go the entire night without sleeping. More importantly, the urge to put words on paper fastened strong within Dean, and he had to act on that urge.

He picked up his laptop and walked out to the reception. He glanced at Baxter's seat once more, just to make sure he wasn't there. He peeked over the counter, expecting to see his body on the floor. The place was empty. Dean walked behind the reception, placed his laptop on the counter, and sat on Baxter's seat.

"You won't mind if I sit here a bit, will you, Baxter?" Dean said to no one as he opened the laptop.

He opened the writing program and stared at the blank page in front of him. It was no longer daunting—quite the opposite; it beckoned him. The white page begged to be filled with words.

Dean sat upright and typed the first words he had typed in years for a book.

Epilogue

"I'm telling you that this is a waste of time," the FBI agent said, annoyed.

"And I'm telling you to shut up and drive!" Iris shouted. "A person's life is in danger, and I bet all you can think about is where you'll get your next donut and coffee, huh? Well, news flash, buddy! You don't get to sit on your ass all day long and drain money from us taxpayers until you retire! You gotta do some work from time to time!"

The agent—he said his name was Dwayne Malcolm—looked at his partner in the passenger's seat but didn't respond to Iris, and that was enough for her. If there was something she was good at, it was talking; specifically, debating.

The police and the FBI didn't take her seriously for one moment ever since she and Jayden returned to the real world. The detective, who questioned her, even laughed in her face, and it wasn't until Iris threatened to get all kinds of lawyers and lawsuits on their asses that they agreed to bring in the FBI.

Jayden was of no help. On the drive out of Suicide Town, he kept glancing back toward the town, as if expecting something to appear in the dark and come after them. It made Iris jumpy, too. Eventually, she ironically asked Jayden if he wanted her to give him a lift back to the town, and he stopped looking.

At first, neither of them talked. The mood in the car had been gloomy ever since they left Dean back in the town, and as much as Iris wanted to go back after him, she knew that it would be suicide for both her and the kid. Ultimately, her being responsible for Jayden's life made her stay on route to the nearest town.

Iris had tried making conversation with the bookstore owner, but he was unresponsive. Even her witty remarks did nothing to evoke a smile in the young man, so she stopped speaking altogether and turned on the radio.

Upon approaching any signs of civilization, Jayden looked out the window at the buildings like a dog seeing the outside world for the first time. He didn't say a word; just stared at the buildings and the occasional passersby. Iris had forgotten that he had never seen anything outside Suicide Town, and this was all a shock for him.

"Wait 'til you see an actual city. You'll need a heart transplant!" Iris joked, but Jayden ignored her, too mesmerized by the sight passing before the car window.

When they finally reached Medford's police department, Iris told Jayden to stay put in the car while she talked to the cops. As soon as she burst through the precinct's door, the cops grabbed their guns. They didn't draw them, but they were a little too apprehensive for Iris's liking.

She then realized that she was covered in the black rain and probably sounded like a lunatic, but despite that, refused to calm down. Eventually, they cuffed and questioned her. They brought Jayden in, too, and given his catatonic state, they suspected that Iris had kidnapped him. The bigger problem was that Jayden said nothing to refute that. The fact that he had no ID and was a nonexistent person in the dossier didn't help.

Eventually, with Iris's angry babbling and Jayden's meager information, the police were able to deduce that they came from a small town, that thousands of people had just been killed, and that one person's life was in danger.

Naturally, Iris was the prime suspect for that. The cops didn't tell her that, of course, but she could connect the dots. When she finally presented them with all the evidence of Suicide Town, they dismissed her claims as that of a crazy person. They were even about to release her, but she wouldn't have it. There was no way she'd leave Dean in that hellhole with whatever that thing was.

The FBI eventually agreed to go there, but that wasn't enough for Iris. She insisted on going with them. They were visibly annoyed with her incessant jabbering—nothing new there; it was the norm for her—and just wanted to shut her up, so they agreed to take her with them.

"So, how many people did you say died there?" Agent Malcolm asked.

"I don't know. Too many."

"Too many? Didn't you say to the detective that it was about two thousand?" the other agent asked while staring forward.

"Why? Do you have criteria for the number of dead bodies before you decide to do anything about it?"

She saw the side of the agent's cheek stiffening. He didn't appreciate her remark. Iris didn't care what they thought. Right now, they thought of her as a looney case talking nonsense, and she knew the more she talked, the more she put herself in danger of actually getting arrested, but it didn't matter. Dean's life was in danger, and she had to do everything in her power to rescue him. Once the agents see Suicide Town, and the dead bodies, they'd believe her.

"What's gonna happen to Jayden?" she asked.

The FBI agents exchanged glares with each other for a moment before Malcolm responded. "We need to look into him more, find out who he is and where he came from. Right now, we have no information about him. For all we know, he could be a dangerous criminal."

"You're not going to find out any information about him."

"What makes you so sure of that?"

"If you'd been listening to me for the past three hours, you would know. But did you do that? Of course not. All you guys ever do is show up in your rip-off Sam's Tailor suits and try to get confessions out of your suspects. Then sign some paperwork, job's done, you get to be home in time to read a bedtime story to your kids. Fidelity, bravery, integrity, my ass."

"Calm down, Iris," Agent Malcolm said. "We understand that you're under a lot of stress because of what happened. That's why we're going with you—so you can show us where it all happened."

"Don't patronize me," Iris retorted. She was tempted to add more, but Malcolm's lack of reaction gave her no motivation to do so. The other agent seemed more thin-skinned, but as for Malcolm; if any of the insults affected him, he did a good job hiding his feelings.

"We should be there soon, right?" the thin-skinned one asked.

"Yeah," Iris said. "Just follow this road and turn left after the gas station."

Now that they were getting closer to the town, Iris felt more on edge. She sat upright in the backseat and stared out at the road, impatiently waiting for the gas station and the turn toward Suicide Town.

"Here!" Iris pointed, even though Malcolm had already started steering left.

"Interesting. I didn't even know there was a road here," Thin-skin said.

Iris barely heard him because she was so focused on the hole-riddled road; more importantly, on what lay ahead. Agent Malcolm turned on the high beams to further illuminate the road that suddenly seemed to become darker.

They're gonna see the black rain soon, and then they'll believe me.

It wasn't just Iris who was on edge. Both agents went quiet and stiff, Iris noted. Malcolm checked his surroundings more fervently while maintaining the unchanged car's speed. A few minutes went by in silence, and Thin-skin seemed to relax. He turned around and asked, "Are you sure we're on the right road?" The half-smirk on his face made Iris want to pinch him by his pepper-shaped nose and pull hard.

"Yeah. I'm su—"

The sudden lurching forward of all three people in the car stopped her sentence. This was followed by screeching tires for what felt like at least five seconds. Then the car stopped, and silence filled the air for a moment.

"What the hell, Agent Mulder?" Iris asked Malcolm in frustration. "I almost smashed my nose!"

She looked at Malcolm and then Thin-skin. Both were focused on the sight in front. The agents had looked calm the entire night, but now, they had wide-eyed stares. Iris looked at the road and then she saw it, too. Her eyes widened as well.

"What the hell kind of game are you playing?" Thin-skin yelled at Iris, aggression palpable in his voice. Iris ignored him and opened the door to step out of the car. She also ignored his shouts.

Iris walked in front of the car and stared at the impossible sight in front of her. The car doors opened behind her.

"Hey!" Malcolm called out to her. "What are you doing?"

"What are *you* doing?! You took a wrong turn somewhere!"

"I drove exactly where you told us to." A slight pause wedged itself in before he added, "Get in the car. We're going back."

Iris gawked at the sight in front of her but refused to believe what laid ahead. Only when she felt a hand on her shoulder and heard Thin-skin's voice muttering something about going inside the car did she force herself to turn around.

Even as she went back to the car, she kept her gaze fixated on the swamp that stretched infinitely from where the road ended.

THE END

Notes From The Author

If you've made it this far, it means you've read the book to the end. Thank you for that.

I come from a town in Serbia called Subotica. Although the town is not as small as the one in this book, it served as a direct inspiration to Suicide Town.

Subotica used to be known as "the town of suicides" due to the extremely high number of deaths from suicide. In fact, it used to hold the number one spot in all of Europe. I'd even had the bad luck of knowing some people who ended up committing suicide.

The reasons were never completely clear. The people in Subotica generally have a negative outlook, and the townsfolk speculate that it could be because of one of the following things: 1. The area is a flatland with no hill in sight, meaning wherever you turn, you'll see a flat horizon. 2. The weather during fall and winter turns gloomy and most people spend their time indoors. 3. The city was built on a swamp and the more superstitious folk believe that the vapors coming from underground affect the residents' psyche. 4. There's a very old cult titled "The Black Rose" that recruits people and coaxes them into killing themselves in ritualistic fashions (This last one was actually true, but is no longer active in the town).

All of that, coupled with the fact that the city is isolated all the way north near the Hungarian border, might contribute to the high number of suicide cases.

When I first got the idea for Suicide Town, I had no idea which direction it was going to move in. All I knew was I had an idea in my head—there's a town, and if you visit it, you commit suicide.

I took one week off for my investigation. I went around the town interviewing people, but I also went on a road trip through various small towns and villages to talk to the locals.

Many of the things you see in Suicide Town are based on real experiences: for example, how some of the townsfolk lied where they were from, how they had secretive traditions and rules that they hid from outsiders, how they could either be the friendliest bunch or the most unpleasant people you ran into.

The book was in no way intended to capitalize on the unfortunate deaths of my fellow townsfolk. Instead, I wanted to write a story based on the town where I lived more than 25 years.

If you enjoyed reading Suicide Town, I hope you'll think about leaving an honest review on the **Amazon Product Page**. Every review helps me a ton, whether it's good or bad. If you're interested in reading more from me related to horror in small towns, check the next page.

More From The Author

No one ever leaves Woodberry.

AVAILABLE ON AMAZON

It was supposed to be a relaxing vacation. Now, they're on the run from religious fanatics.

AVAILABLE ON AMAZON

No one in Northberry talks about the missing children.

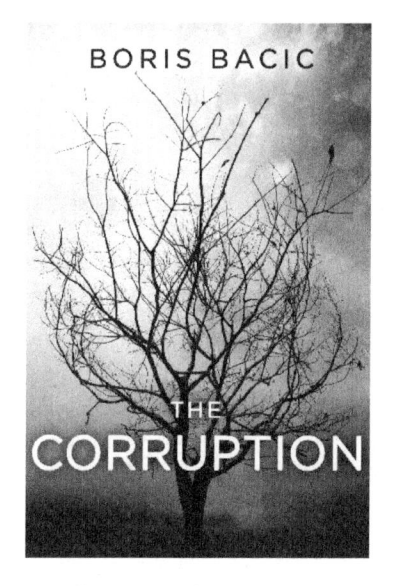

AVAILABLE ON AMAZON

Printed in Great Britain
by Amazon